THE HELLION'S SECRET
ABOUT AN EARL, BOOK 2

JESS MICHAELS

Copyright © 2024 by Jess Michaels

All rights reserved.

No part of this book may be reproduced in any form or by any electronic or mechanical means, including information storage and retrieval systems, without written permission from the author, except for the use of brief quotations in a book review.

For Michael
Always. Everyday. Forever.

CHAPTER 1

Phineas Montague, sixth Earl of Delacourt, did not feel like himself. If he were honest, he hadn't felt himself in a while, even when he was in places he enjoyed, such as the boxing club where he currently stood. He couldn't place the reason for the discomfort. Perhaps it was because he'd recently parted ways with his mistress, though he hadn't been particularly attached to Delia, nor she to him. It had ended well enough—she had even found another protector already.

Perhaps it was the recent death of his sister Marianne's closest friend, Claudia. He hadn't known her very well—she had been a quiet wallflower—but the sudden departure of one even younger than himself did put one's mortality into a new light. And yet he'd never been especially fearful of death. He didn't take wild risks, but he never kept himself from experiencing life for fear of consequences either. So that reason didn't fit.

Perhaps it was turning thirty. *That* had happened a few months earlier. It seemed a momentous year in a man's life. A time when expectations for marriage and the creation of heirs began to truly press on a man's neck. He'd always known that time would come, yet he couldn't seem to picture it now. When he thought of a future it felt so damned…blank. There was no woman in his acquaintance that he felt he could easily settle down with. At least not and be happy with the arrangement. He didn't expect love. Great God, no. Love was the fantasy of children and starry-eyed poets. Finn was too rational to expect such a fleeting, sometimes dangerous emotion. But he didn't want to be miserable with his choice of wife, either, nor make her so.

He sighed and shook all the maudlin thoughts away. He hadn't come to his boxing club to ponder, he'd come to forget all that. He'd come to work out some frustration with a clashing of fists. This was sometimes the only place he felt fully alive.

He moved to the back of the large room and began to strip out of his jacket, hanging it on one of the hooks provided. He was working on his cravat when two other gentlemen he knew stepped up a few feet away to do the same.

"—seems an utterly scandalous thing. It makes me want to quit this club entirely," said one of them, a Mr. Smith.

Finn turned toward them. "What's that?"

"You haven't heard?" the other gentleman, Viscount Greenway, said. "Ripley has a great exhibition planned here for next week. Shocking, that's what it is!"

Finn wrinkled his brow as he unwound his cravat. "We've had plenty of exhibitions here before. It's always entertaining to watch the professionals work. I consider it a benefit of the club. What's the problem?"

"This time it's *ladies* he's invited in to fight," Greenway sneered.

Finn had been about to hang his cravat next to his jacket, but he froze now and turned to face Greenway and Smith full on. "I beg your pardon?"

"Exactly," Smith wheezed in his excitement to condemn such a thing.

"Did you say *ladies* boxing?"

All three men turned to see the fourth who had come to join the conversation and Finn smiled. It was his best friend—closer to a brother, truth be told—Sebastian, Earl of Ramsbury. They'd known each other since they were children and his wild friend was one of the people Finn cared about most.

"He did, indeed," Finn said as he extended a hand to Ramsbury. "You're late."

Ramsbury laughed while they shook in greeting. "By five minutes, Mother, please do forgive." As Finn laughed, Ramsbury turned his attention back to the others. "But this exhibition sounds most intriguing, despite your long faces."

"I understand Ripley has ties to the world of underground boxing," Greenway sputtered, his cheeks growing redder with every word.

"Which we benefit from regularly," Finn said quietly as he cast a glance across the room to where Campbell Ripley stood in the ring. The owner of the establishment was stripped to the waist, shouting moves to two fops he was coaching. He was tall and broad, his nose crooked from his previous life as a champion fighter. Finn had never known the man to be anything but calm and steady, he made no decision lightly.

"Yes, yes," Greenway continued to bluster. "But watching women fight? It's low."

"God forbid you drop down a level," Ramsbury muttered with a side glance for Finn. "Do the women have names?"

"It's Betty Lightly and the Hellion," Smith said with a breathless quality that revealed his excitement at the idea was as great as his judgment. Typical.

"The Hellion," Finn repeated with a low whistle. "Come now, these aren't just alley fighters, stripping down to their skin to fight for their supper. She's a champion, known to be very good."

"She wears a mask, doesn't she?" Ramsbury added with a smile. "It's all very dramatic, I like it."

Greenway let out a huff of frustrated breath. "Well, I suppose *you* would, Ramsbury. You're known as a rake."

"Proudly." Ramsbury gave a cheeky bow. "Does that mean you two won't be attending the exhibition?"

The other two men exchanged a look and Smith blustered for a moment. "Well, I…I mean, we're members of the club and…"

"Ah," Finn said with a grin for Ramsbury. "I see. Well, then we'll all enjoy it together."

The other two men huffed off, leaving Ramsbury alone with Finn. "When is this event that some will pretend to be offended by even as they place their wagers?" Ramsbury asked. "I came in late."

"Next week, I think. We can speak to Ripley about it. He seems to be finished with his lesson."

Together they walked the short distance to the ring and Finn leaned on the ropes to look up at Ripley. "Sounds like you have quite a show coming next week."

Ripley was wiping sweat from his brow with a towel and chuckled. "It's the talk of the club. If you came to complain—" His Yorkshire accent hung in the air between them.

"Quite the opposite," Finn said, holding up his hands in acquiescence. "I'm looking forward to it. I've heard a great deal about the Hellion. I'm interested in seeing if the skill level for the ladies is different than the men you've brought in over the years. And to go to Seven Dials to watch a fight is asking for a picked pocket."

Ripley shrugged and looked around the large room at the gentlemen sparring. "As for the skill level, the Hellion could teach a few of these ones a thing or two."

"I'm sure," Ramsbury said with a smile.

"She's undefeated, yes?" Finn said.

Ripley nodded. "Aye, she is. I know her a little, personally."

Ramsbury leaned up closer. "Do you now? I see."

Ripley rolled his eyes in response. "Get fucked, Ramsbury, that's not what I meant. Go spar, you two. You could use the practice."

Both of them laughed. Ripley wasn't as informal with everyone in the club. Finn actually felt a great deal of pride that he'd been able to earn some respect and friendship with the man. Ripley made those around him earn it.

He and Ramsbury returned to the wall. As they each finished undressing and readying to do as they'd been told, Ramsbury glanced at him. "How is Marianne after last night?"

Finn flinched at the mention of his younger sister. She'd recently lost that best friend of hers and he knew she was hurting. The previous night they had all attended a gathering together, with Ramsbury teasing her a little as he was wont to do.

Finn hung up his shirt and faced his friend. "I'm sure she didn't need you encouraging her in bad behavior with that little drinking game of yours."

A faint smile crossed Ramsbury's expression that Finn didn't entirely like. He'd been clear with his friend that he couldn't turn his rakish charms toward Marianne. Sometimes he wasn't certain that order was recalled.

"I think she can manage herself, Delacourt."

Finn wasn't as certain. He'd spent a lifetime trying to protect his sister. A lifetime where he often failed. She had suffered greatly thanks to the behaviors of their late parents. Sometimes he looked at her and felt so guilty. One more thing in his life that made the weight on his shoulders suddenly heavy.

He cleared his throat. "Why don't we spar as Ripley suggested?"

Ramsbury arched a brow. "Yes. Looks like you could use it."

With that, Finn pushed away all the odd feelings in his chest and followed Ramsbury to a ring. And as they began to exchange punches, he allowed himself to forget everything but the physical exertion. He could pick up all his troubles again later. After all, he knew they would be waiting.

∼

Esme Crawford sat at the bar in the back of the infamous Donville Masquerade, letting the sights and the sounds of the club wash over her. There were few places in the world where she felt comfortable, but here, with a mask fitted over her face, where she could be anonymous, was one of them. She wore many masks, after all. She was most comfortable where she could be observed but not truly seen.

She almost laughed, for two years ago she would have been anything but comfortable at a notorious sex club, with attendees participating in the most shocking of activities all around her. When she'd first come here at the behest of a lover, not quite innocent anymore but certainly not jaded, she had merely stared, shocked that such things could make her feel so tingly all over. When her affiliation with that man had been over, she'd asked him to buy her a lifetime membership as part of his settlement on her and he had obliged. She'd returned after that, and over time she'd allowed herself to participate. To enjoy more and more. Physical pleasure made life so much more bearable.

She smiled as one of the barkeeps stepped up. A handsome man with a plain mask and a flirtatious way. "And what can I get for such a lovely lady?"

"Whisky," she said with a wink. "Rivers' best."

He inclined his head and poured it for her. He looked like he might stay and talk, perhaps she could even convince him to leave his post and come in the back for an anonymous encounter that would slake a physical need, but he was signaled by another patron and he sighed as he slipped away.

Esme turned her attention back to the crowd. This would be her only drink tonight—she was too clever to lose control over herself—so she savored it. She took slow sips as she allowed herself to be aroused by the crowd around her.

At one of the gaming tables to her left, a woman was passionately kissing a man as they played cards, her arm moving under the table like she was fondling him. Straight ahead of her on the dancefloor, a gentleman cupped a lady hard against him, massaging her backside as they staggered to the music, oblivious to those around them. She turned her attention to her right where other tables for drinks and conversation…or other activities were spread in a small area near the bar. Many were taken up by couples or more, talking or touching or even fucking in the case of one group.

But in the center of it all was a man, seated alone, wearing a black mask adorned with a few scattered diamonds across the bottom edge. So rich, probably. A gentleman. He was well-favored, with an angled jaw and full lips. And he was watching her, his dark eyes sweeping over her from afar. She smiled and he stood, a slow unfolding of a tall, broad-shouldered body that looked very fine even with all those pesky layers of clothing covering it.

Oh yes, if he wanted to play, it looked like a very good time to be had. He stepped closer and she leaned an elbow on the bar behind her, casual even as she devoured every step he took.

When he reached her, he tilted his head. "Good evening."

She froze, all erotic thoughts and fantasies fading in the moment she heard his voice. She knew it. It came from a different life, one she had fled. One she continued to flee. And if he realized who she was, everything she'd built could come crashing down around her in an instant.

CHAPTER 2

Finn hadn't planned to spend an evening alone at the Donville Masquerade. After they sparred, Ramsbury had promised to join him, but Finn had been there nearly half an hour with no sign of his friend. He'd been frustrated by that, but all had faded the moment he'd looked across the crowded, writhing mass of lovers, and found the woman at the bar.

It wasn't just that she was beautiful. Even from a distance and with the mask half-covering her face, she was the kind of person that drew the eye. With thick, auburn hair that was done in a half-up, half-down fashion made to make a man think of tangled nights in sweaty bedsheets, she was a beauty. She had a wide smile, like she laughed often and loudly. He didn't know the color of her eyes, but he'd wanted to the instant he saw her.

He hadn't approached at first. He'd simply observed. Watched her flirt with the barkeep, who seemed equally charmed by her. Watched her laugh with a confidence that Finn had always been drawn to in a lover. She was sure of herself and that was exactly what he wanted. No mincing, no pretending, no playing games.

When she'd looked at him at last, her expression transforming into something heated, something inviting, he'd felt his cock start to harden. And as he got closer, as he realized those eyes of hers were a startling shade of dark green, he'd been even more drawn. Oh yes, this night was going to be memorable.

He reached her at last and smiled. "Good evening."

Her smile, which had been inviting, faded a fraction. Not much, but he felt the shift. "Good evening," she repeated, her tone a little flat. Her posture had changed, as well, gone stiffer.

Was she playing a game? Did she invite him over with her smile and then expect him to beg a little for more? Earn a moment perched between those probably spectacular legs?

Perhaps he didn't hate games quite so much as he had told himself earlier.

"May I join you?" he asked, motioning to the empty seat beside her.

She hesitated a moment and then nodded. "Of course."

He took his place and motioned to the barkeep, pointing to her glass. The man met his eyes and inclined his head, the message received that Finn would like one of the same.

"It's Rivers' best," she said softly.

A warning, he supposed, that the drink would be expensive. Kind of her, honestly, since those who came here were of varying classes and financial abilities. He inclined his head. "Then I'll be sure to pay for yours, as well, if you'll allow it."

"I never turn down a free drink," she said.

She turned her face a little and Finn stiffened. Now that they were so close, he could see a dark mark that peeked out just below the edge of the mask beneath her right eye. A bruise, and a rather bad one, he thought. Someone had hit her and a protectiveness rose up in him. He had always despised men who took advantage of women, who hurt them.

"And what is the name of the man who offers me a free drink?" she asked, her tone light. Was it falsely so?

He chose to ignore her injury for the moment. If the chance

came later to bring it up, he would. "We're anonymous, yes?" he said. "Unless you want to give me *your* real name."

"Miss X," she said evenly, and he could feel her judging how he would respond.

"Ah, how perfect, as I am Mr. Y." He extended a hand. "And I would very much like to dance with you."

Her breath caught slightly and she stared at the offered hand. Her hesitance made him wonder. He'd assumed she must be a lightskirt or a high-class courtesan. Often they had the confident attitude she exuded. But when she drew away, it made him question that supposition. Perhaps she wasn't. So who was she? Had she changed her attitude toward him because she wasn't actually ready to play a game here? Or because someone was forcing her to do so? Even the same man who had blackened her eye.

"I'd be happy to dance with you," she said at last, and took his hand in her gloved one. When they touched, he found himself catching his breath.

He guided her to the dancefloor and set a hand on her hip. He drew her close, far closer than he would have in a proper ballroom, and she caught her breath. Her green eyes lifted to his as she wrapped one arm around his neck and placed the other in his hand. They began to move, a slow sway in the writhing crowd.

"So, Miss X," he said, playfully accentuating her pseudonym. "What brings you to the Donville Masquerade?"

She laughed. "Is it your first time, sir? Are you an innocent amongst the wolves here?"

He couldn't help but smile at her teasing. "And what if I were? What if I lied and told you it was my first time here? What would you say?"

"Well," she said, her fingers brushing the back of his neck. Even though the wound layers of his cravat he felt a tingle at the touch. "Let me see. First, I'd tell you to look around you."

He did so, watching the surging crowd for a moment and all its erotic games. "It's stimulating."

"Indeed. The club is meant for pleasure. It's unlike any other hell in London. Any other hell anywhere, I'd wager. So if you want something...*need* something...this is the place to come. If you're brave enough."

He gazed down at her, away from the crowd. It was odd how easy it was to make everything else fade away and only see her. He didn't think he'd ever experienced that with any other lover at Donville.

"You seem *very* brave," he said softly.

Her eyes moved away from his. "And you guessed that after only a moment's acquaintance."

"Yes," he said, and the swiftness of the answer brought her gaze back to his with surprise. "Come now. From the few moments I observed you before we spoke, from the short time we've been speaking, I think I can read certain things about you, just as I'm sure you can do the same for me. And even if I couldn't, it seems you've been through something and you're still so confident. So attractively certain."

She wrinkled her brow. "Been through something?"

He lifted his hand and brushed it against her cheek, up to the edge of her mask and traced the shadow of the bruise that was almost hidden there. "Haven't you?"

She stiffened in his arms and reached up to adjust the mask, covering the mark fully so he could no longer see it. "It isn't your concern."

"I suppose not," he said, and dropped his hand back to her hip. "But if you're in danger—"

"It's not your concern," she repeated, but her tone had gentled.

He frowned. That eased none of his worries about her safety, but what could he do? He didn't know this woman, he wasn't responsible for her. They stared at each other a long, charged moment before he nodded. "Very well, it's not my concern."

"Thank you."

He let his fingers bunch in the small of her back and felt her shiver in response. Her pupils dilated slightly and the ache he'd felt for her when she smiled at him across the room returned.

"You're very beautiful," he said softly. "I wonder if you might join me in one of the back rooms."

She swallowed hard and her fingers tightened in his hand. He could see that she wanted to say yes. It was in her eyes, it was in the way her body leaned into his for a moment.

But then she pulled away, her fingers dropping from his. She shook her head. "I-I don't think that's a good idea, my lord. Good evening."

He stared as she turned away and darted into the crowd without further explanation or even a look over her shoulder at him. And then her words sank in.

She had addressed him as "my lord". Now, perhaps it was because he put off the air of someone titled. But it didn't feel like a guess. It felt like the mystery woman had *known* him. Which left him wondering just who the hell she was and what had just happened.

It left him wondering if he would see her again to figure it all out.

∽

Esme stepped into the small home she had been living in for over a year, and for the first time all night, she was able to breathe. She locked the door, checked the window and pulled the shades a little tighter before she went into the parlor off the foyer, placed her mask on the table and threw a few logs on the coals left from the fire earlier in the day. As she waited for the flames to raise up, she sat down in an overstuffed chair and tugged off her slippers, rubbing her sore feet with a sigh.

She willed her mind not to go to the same place it had been going all the way home from the Donville Masquerade, but she couldn't seem to make it stop. All she could think of was *him*. The man who had approached her. The Earl of Delacourt.

She'd recognized his voice the moment he spoke to her and it was like being bodily yanked into another world. Another life. How often had she heard the man speak over the years, murmuring to her father in a parlor late at night while she sat in the hallway listening? Or at supper when she would sit on the other end of the table, watching the two men deep in conversation, entirely forgetting she was there. They'd been friends, despite their disparate ages, but Esme had always known the truth: her father had seen Delacourt as the son he never had.

Her eyes stung with the thought and she was about to get up to find something to distract her when the front door closed in the distance.

"Jane?" Esme called out, willing her fear not to rise up.

"It's me and yes, I locked the door," Jane called back.

Relief washed over Esme. She'd shared this home with Jane since Esme found it last year. Her friend entered the room, pale blonde hair a little mussed and her expression tired.

"You look like you had a night," Esme said. "Did you eat?"

"I did." Jane flopped herself onto the settee across from Esme and opened her reticule. "And I took some of the food with me, for us to share. The cake is particularly good, so I brought you a slice."

She set out several items wrapped in napkins and Esme couldn't help but laugh as she helped her open the sloppy packets. Unlike herself, Jane had grown up in the streets and had no compunction about taking what she needed. They couldn't have been more different when they met, but somehow Jane had taken Esme under her wing. Helped her run from her past and the wolves that rushed at her back.

Helped her make a life.

"How was it then?" Esme asked as she tucked her feet up under herself and used her fingers to eat the cake Jane had so kindly brought for her.

Jane sighed and chewed thoughtfully on what looked to be a few cold slices of chicken. "The usual. A few of them were handsome and one was rich, so that's where I got the food. The handsome ones do make it easier."

Esme shrugged. She and Jane both made their livings from their bodies, though in very different ways. Her friend's life as a lightskirt wasn't one Esme had ever taken to in the short time she'd participated, but Jane didn't seem to hate it.

"What about you?" Jane asked. "That eye looks nasty."

Esme lifted her hand to the bruise and thought of Delacourt's concern earlier in the night. His expression had appeared truly troubled though he'd stopped pushing after she refused to share.

"I caught a right from the new chit Biggs is training," Esme explained. "There's nothing to worry about, it will heal up soon enough." She stared at the half-eaten cake a moment and then back up at Jane. "I went to Donville tonight."

Jane set her empty napkin away and arched a brow. "Did you now? And did you have any fun?"

"No. Well, not that kind, anyway," Esme said, and then shifted. "I…I saw a man I knew in passing from…from before."

That made Jane sit up straighter, her eyes widening. "What?"

"I had my mask on," Esme said swiftly. "He didn't recognize me. Even if he'd seen me, I doubt he would have. I wasn't that important to him back in those days."

Jane got up and paced the room, her anxiety on the subject plain. "This is exactly why I'm so opposed to you doing that exhibition at Ripley's next week, Esme! Those exact kinds of men will be there. Men you'll surely know from your time as Lady Charlotte Esmerelda, daughter of a duke."

"He was a marquess," Esme said her softly, and tried not to think of her father's face, his smile.

Jane sighed. "It's all the same to us, love. I promise you that."

Esme shrugged. She corrected out of habit, even two years after she fled her previous life, her title, her money…and the horrors that went along with it since the death of her father.

She took a deep breath, calmed herself, at least outwardly.

"Ripley owns the club and he'll pay me and Betty a good sum for the time. Enough to pay for the house for almost three months and put aside some after. Plus, I get a cut of any wagers and who knows how much that will be. You know those fops love to bet on anything and don't care how much they lose."

She could see she was making headway with Jane with those arguments, even if her worry was still plain.

"You'll still be in my corner that day, won't you?" Esme asked.

Jane rolled her eyes. "Of course. I've been the corner woman for the Hellion since she made her stunning debut. I wouldn't abandon her now, would I?"

Relief flowed through Esme. "Good. If you're there you can keep any of them from trying to talk to me afterward. And I'll be masked anyway, so they won't have a clue. They only see what I want them to see, don't they?"

"They do at that," Jane agreed. "If there's one thing about those fops, it's that they could never imagine someone like them falling so low as us."

Esme bent her head. "That's definitely true. Anyway, I'm sure they've all forgotten the old me. Or believe her to be dead. All that's left of me now is the Hellion, London's Bruising Lady Champion."

"I hated that board," Jane said with a laugh. "And the drawing they had of you was awful."

"I looked a little like a fiend, I agree," Esme said, and now she was laughing too, despite the emotions any talk of her old life brought up. "Come on, let's take the rest of your treats to the kitchen and eat them there and then I just want to collapse in my bed and sleep off this day."

Jane smiled at her and motioned for the door. "Agreed."

Esme followed her friend from the room with her smile falling. She feared that her encounter with the Earl of Delacourt wouldn't be so easy to forget, but she had to do just that. Her life was here now, completely separated from his. And if she was lucky, she'd never see him ever again.

15

CHAPTER 3

It had been a week since Finn's encounter with the mystery woman at the Donville Masquerade and he'd been trying to forget her ever since. The encounter had been brief, after all. It hadn't led to any pleasure. There was no reason for thoughts of her to enter his head. For questions about her injury to make him pace the floor at night.

And yet he'd found himself thinking of her more than once, pondering why she'd called him *my lord* and wondering if he would ever see her again.

"Finn, are you going to drink your tea? It's getting cold," his sister, Marianne, said, reaching across to cover his hand gently.

They were seated in her parlor at her home and he forced himself to stop thinking about inappropriate things and focus. "I'm sorry. I've just a lot of my mind."

Her expression softened. "I understand that."

He leaned closer, examining her face carefully. She looked tired, her brown eyes that were so like his were sad. "I know it's been difficult for you lately," he said gently. "With the loss of Claudia."

She stiffened slightly at the mention of her late friend and nodded. "It has. It's difficult for such a thing not to make you examine your own life. To make you question…I don't know, question everything."

He pursed his lips. She wasn't wrong. How could one not ponder one's place in the world under such circumstances?

"You have such a long face," Marianne said with a frown. "Are *you* well, Finn?"

He forced a smile. Thanks to unreliable and often cruel parents, the two of them had never had anyone but each other. The old habits of defending each other, worrying over each other, died hard. Perhaps it was good that they never did.

"I'm fine," he said, and didn't quite believe it. "I've been thinking about our upcoming trip to the country and also about upgrades to the estate in Delacourt."

He'd also been obsessed with a certain young woman from a sex club, but there was no way to bring that up to an innocent spinster of a younger sister. And what would he say at any rate?

But she knew nothing of those thoughts and instead leaned closer as they began to discuss both their trip and the estate. And he found his mind was eased, at least for a while, though the discomfort that had haunted him recently still sat in the background, waiting. It would find him again soon enough.

∽

He entered the boxing club an hour after he'd left his sister, trying to shake off continuing troubled thoughts and found it was crowded. Of course it would be—the exhibition match between the Hellion and Betty Lightly was that day. Despite the complaints of some members, it seemed they'd all come to watch the show.

He edged his way into the crowd, moving toward the front and the large ring now set up in the middle of the room. Ripley stood in the middle, talking to two young women.

"Look a little small to be champions," one of the men around him said.

"Naw, that's their corners," someone else answered. "Look at that blonde one. I'd love to go a round or two with her."

The two laughed and Finn turned his nose up in disgust as he moved away to find some more pleasant company. He found it when he saw the Duke of Northfield closer to the front.

He moved toward the man. He'd gone to school with him and they'd always been friendly. Plus, the man knew how to throw a punch. He had to be respected either in or out of the ring.

"Northfield," Finn said as he reached him.

"Ah, Delacourt, good to see you," Northfield said as he shook his hand. "It's quite a crush. Looks to be an excellent match."

"Indeed," Finn agreed. "Have you seen Ramsbury?"

"No. I don't think he's here."

Finn wrinkled his brow. Sebastian had said he'd be coming today. He hadn't thought his wild friend would miss this kind of exhibit, but he'd been so strange lately. Breaking appointments, acting odd when they spoke. He'd been closed off, distracted, sometimes it felt like he refused to meet Finn's eyes. It seemed everyone in his world was out of sorts and Finn didn't like it.

Ripley came to one unoccupied corner of the ring and posted up on one of the ropes. "Gentleman, let's quiet down. Today you get a real treat, so I hope you appreciate it. We get to observe two of the greatest women in the business doing what they do best."

"Are you sure it's what they do best?" came a lewd voice from the crowd.

Ripley's mouth thinned and he stared out into the chuckling group with steel in his stare. He said nothing and the laughter faded. Once it had, he said, "Are you finished?"

Silence greeted him and he nodded. "Good." His tone shifted to something a little different, rather like a barker at a fair, trying to draw the crowd in. "First, let me introduce Betty Lightly. She's a bruiser from Cornwall, one of the finest in her class."

From the back of the room behind a curtain, a woman came. She was dressed in a long, simple blue gown that was sleeveless with leather corset tied tight at her waist. Her dark hair was bound back in a severe style and her crooked nose spoke to the fact that she'd taken more than few blows.

There was polite applause from the men before Ripley continued, "And our second fighter is new to the game, but oh so impressive. She's undefeated and mysterious as hell. Welcome the Hellion."

The applause was louder now as the men craned their necks to see the second woman come out from behind a different curtain. She pushed it back and exited. Unlike Betty, the Hellion's face was covered with a red leather mask that matched her red sleeveless gown. She, too, wore a leather corset at her middle, which only served to accentuate lush curves.

Finn stared, not because she was beautiful, which she was. Not because she had confidence and power as she entered the ring and turned, arms outstretched, to show herself to the crowing men.

He stared because he instantly recognized her. She was the woman from Donville the week before. His captivating Miss X who had walked away from him without even a backward glance. It explained her black eye, but he remained astonished by this information.

"Your mouth is open," Northfield said with a chuckle. "She is a beauty, one can hardly blame you. Though I vastly prefer my lovely wife."

Finn shook his head, brought back to reality by the friendly ribbing. "Indeed," he muttered.

In the ring, Ripley held up a pound mark in each hand. "The rules are simple. Each woman will hold a coin in her fist. The first to drop their coin twice loses the battle. Has everyone placed their bets with Brentwood?"

He motioned to the assistant at the club, who nodded toward Ripley.

"Excellent. Then…" He handed each lady her coin and the two shook hands before they gripped the coins. "Fight!"

Finn leaned forward, holding his breath as the two women began to circle, their hands raised, fists clenched. As his shock faded, he truly took in the Hellion. She was more relaxed than her opponent, at ease with the ring. When Betty Lightly swung on her, she stepped back, blocking the blow with one hand while she threw her own with the other and connected with the other woman's midsection.

The crowd around him let out a little cheer and he jolted. He kept forgetting that he was in the middle of a room full of practically drooling men. Even the ones who had complained about bringing women to exhibit were leaning forward, eyes wide as they ogled. He frowned and then put his attention back to the women.

The Hellion threw another punch and connected, this time with Betty's chin. It sent her spiraling back a step and she sneered before she lunged and the two grappled for a moment. But the Hellion seemed unbothered and threw her off to bounce off the ropes around the ring before they reset in the middle of the space to circle again.

The men were settling as the fight continued, becoming more interested in the battle than the women. When the Hellion landed another punch square on Betty's jaw, a cheer went up and when Betty regained her footing and lunged forward to land her own punch on the Hellion's midsection an impressed *ohhhhh* went through the crowd.

All through it, Finn kept his gaze firmly on the Hellion. She was powerful and elegant in her moves, almost like she was dancing rather than plodding forward like her opponent did. But when she punched, it wasn't playful or light. That was borne out when she hit Betty again and this time the other woman stumbled to the mat on her backside and the coin she clutched in her fist came bouncing out onto the surface.

Finn joined the crowd in a roar as Ripley rushed in and picked up the coin. "The Hellion takes the first point!" he declared.

Betty was cursing up a storm as she and the Hellion went to their respective corners. The Hellion had a slender blonde woman on her side who gave her a sip of water and wiped her brow. They talked for a moment, strategizing, it seemed and then Finley rang the bell and returned the coin to Betty.

The Hellion rolled her neck and shoulders as she approached the center of the ring. Betty came forward with more malice this time, clearly annoyed that she had been bested for the first coin drop. But her anger was not her friend. Finn found himself twisting along with the Hellion, using his body to will her to dodge as Betty threw her weight into the first punch. The Hellion stepped out of the way with ease and managed to land a punch in her opponent's side.

They grappled again and he could see the annoyance in the Hellion's expression at the stall tactic. An annoyance that only increased when Betty shot out a leg and kicked her hard in the shin.

"Oy, we don't do that here," Ripley called from the side. "This ain't the street, Betty."

It seemed the Hellion didn't need the intervention, though. She shoved Betty back and then landed a hard shot to her cheek, then another to the other side. It was evident Betty was stunned by the blows, for she staggered, though she didn't drop the coin. The Hellion threw another punch, snapping Betty's head back and she fell, hitting the mat. She was stiff and still, but her fist was still clenched on the coin.

"Get her!" someone from the crowd shouted. "The fight's not over."

The Hellion shot an annoyed glare toward the person who had said it and motioned to her still opponent. "She's out," she said to Ripley.

"She didn't drop the coin!" another man from the group yelled.

Northfield's body tensed beside Finn. "The woman is clearly unconscious. I hope she won't pummel her more."

So did Finn, but the Hellion was coming toward Betty. He waited for her to rain down another punch, but instead she leaned in, unclenched Betty's hand and let the coin slide from it to the mat.

Ripley jumped in and raised her hand. "Our winner!"

If the crowd had wanted more violence, they still seemed appeased by the fight. They cheered wildly as Betty's corner came in and got her sat up. She was awake again, shaking off the cobwebs. The Hellion leaned in and offered her a hand up and Betty took it. They shook before the Hellion made for her corner.

"Hellion! Hellion!" the men were chanting and Finn joined in, impressed by his mystery woman's talent, as well as her sense of right and wrong at the end of the fight.

She smiled toward the crowd and waved before she ducked out of the ring and headed toward one of the small rooms in the back of the club. Finn nodded toward Northfield.

"It was a good fight," he said.

"Indeed," Northfield agreed. "They're both impressive, but the Hellion is very talented."

"Very." Finn glanced toward the room where she'd gone. He very much wanted to speak to her, to see what she would do if she saw him again, this time without a mask. Would she acknowledge she knew him from the club?

Would she explain why she'd addressed him as *my lord* like she knew him. Would the heat between them be the same when they weren't at a notorious sex club?

"Excuse me, will you?" Finn asked.

When Northfield nodded, he slipped away, moving through the surging, excited crowd around the ring. It was quieter in the direction where she'd gone and no one seemed to notice as he ducked behind the curtain Ripley had set up for the introductions and started down a short hallway toward the rooms in the back.

∼

Esme drank deeply of the draught of cold tea that Jane had set before her and grunted as her friend rubbed her shoulder muscles roughly to keep them from locking up after the fight. The mask she had removed from her face bounced on her leg as Jane did so.

"That bitch kicked you," Jane said with a laugh.

Esme laughed too. "She did. I'm going to have a hell of a bruise on my shin, I wager. But she got the worst of it. She was up when I went back, though, so I'm sure she'll be fine."

"Such a soft one," Jane grunted. "Always worried about the opponent."

Esme shrugged. "Betty isn't so bad. She's talented, too. Why should I hate her for trying to make her life? I'm no different."

Jane smiled at her softly before she said, "Ripley said there were a great many wagers before the fight and that I could collect your percentage from Brentwood after. Will you be well back here if I go do that?"

"I think so," Esme said. "I couldn't see my friend from Donville in the crowd, and I think most of the toffs in the crowd are more interested in talking to each other than lowering themselves to me. Go get the money."

Jane patted her shoulder and then ducked from the room. Esme heard the door behind her close and sighed before she drank more of her tea. It had been a good fight, but perhaps she should have tried to drag it out more, put on a bigger show. Perhaps she even would have allowed Betty to make her drop her coin to give the fight more drama. But the moment she'd been kicked, she'd just wanted it to be over. To protect herself.

She sighed. "Letting emotion reign. Foolish girl." The door behind her opened again and she laughed without looking. "That was quick, Jane. How much was it?"

"It's not Jane."

She froze at Delacourt's voice behind her, just as recognizable as

23

it had been that night at the Donville Masquerade. She grabbed for her mask and tied it before she got up and pivoted on him.

"You shouldn't be back here," she said as she looked at him.

The night at the masquerade he'd been masked like she was, so this was her first time seeing his full face in years. And he was stunningly beautiful. He was built like a fighter, in truth, with broad shoulders and narrow hips. He was all hard angles and dangerous lines, but with the most beautiful brown eyes.

Eyes that were now flitting up and down her just like they had at the masquerade.

"I only wished to congratulate you," Delacourt said. "You were most entertaining."

She drew in a breath. Most men would have said that with a lewd double meaning, but even though it was clear Delacourt was looking at her with interest, he wasn't disgusting about it. He seemed to truly respect her.

"Thank you," she said softly. "My lord."

A slight smirk quirked the corner of his mouth. "That is the second time you have referred to me by title. I'm beginning to feel at a disadvantage."

She straightened. "I don't know what you mean."

He tilted his head. "Do you not? Are you going to deny that you met me days ago at the Donville Masquerade, Miss…X. Or do you prefer Hellion?"

She let her breath out in a long sigh and folded her arms, widening her stance just as she did in a fight. "I suppose it would only be a waste of time to pretend as though it wasn't me at the masquerade that night. And that it wasn't you."

"It would be," Delacourt agreed. "Though if you want to spar and pretend, I'm happy to play the game."

"I'm sure you are." She said it quietly but it seemed to hit its mark for he straightened and the smirk fell.

"How do you know me?" he asked.

"Who says I do?"

"The *my lording* does imply it since I never said who I truly was. Nor have I said it now."

She arched a brow. "You have a *my lord* way about you. Most toffs do."

She waited for him to get annoyed, to scowl at her, perhaps even to demand an apology. But instead he flashed a grin that made him even more handsome somehow. "I see. Well, if you don't want to tell me the truth, that's your prerogative. I'll play along. The Earl of Delacourt at your service, Miss…"

"X," she said. "You already know that."

"Very well." There was still no animosity in his tone. "I do have to say that realizing your blackened eye likely came from sparring or a sanctioned fight, rather than some bastard beating you, is a relief."

She stared at him. That sounded truthful. He, who didn't even know he knew her, who thought her nothing more than a gnat beneath his shoe, had actually been concerned about her.

"I told you that night there was nothing to be alarmed by," she said. "And it's healing either way."

"Good." He stepped closer and she realized in that moment how small the room was. It hadn't seemed so small before, but he filled it with not just his body, but his presence.

She had no idea what he might do or say and she found herself leaning in, just as she had in Donville. She found herself wanting him like she had that night when she'd convinced herself it was just the location and the moment. It wasn't. It was him, it turned out.

But before things could progress, there was a knock at the door and then it opened, revealing Campbell Ripley, the owner of the boxing club and one of Esme's dearest friends.

"Ah," he said, glancing at Delacourt with his brow wrinkling. "I didn't realize you had a guest, Hellion."

Delacourt's gaze flitted to him and there was a sudden tightness to his mouth before he said, "I was just congratulating the champion. But that done, I'll leave you two. Good day, I do hope we'll see each other again."

She inclined her head and he strode out past Ripley with another quick side glance. When he was gone, Ripley fully entered and shut the door behind him. "Was he bothering you?"

She shook her head. "No. Is he the type to worry about?"

"Delacourt? No. I just didn't expect to find him here."

She paced off and removed her mask again, turning it over and over in her hands. "Men like that go wherever they please. I know that better than most."

Ripley was watching her. She could feel it, but he merely said, "I'm sure that's true, Esme. Jane has your blunt. I think you'll be most pleased. You were wonderful, by the way. All they can talk about is your skill."

She faced him with a smile, pushing away thoughts of Delacourt. "And Betty? She's well after the knockout?"

He nodded. "She is. More sore from the loss than the punch. She already took her blunt and left. If you want to follow, I can take you out the back so none of them out there will bother you."

She slid the mask back on once more. "Lead the way."

She followed him, making small talk as they weaved out into the back alley where her carriage and Jane were already waiting. But even as she spoke to her old friend, she couldn't help but think about Delacourt. He said he hoped he'd see her again. And she found herself hoping for the same, no matter how dangerous that reality could be.

No matter how much his very presence threatened the delicate world she had built for herself since she ran away from her old life.

CHAPTER 4

When Ramsbury had sent a message apologizing for missing the fight and suggested meeting at the Donville Masquerade, Finn had told himself he could go there without thinking about his mysterious Hellion. That he could find someone else to warm his cock and forget about her. It turned out he was wrong.

The whole time they'd been there he'd been looking for her. Watching the games around him hadn't taken off the edge of wanting to find her, nor had several drinks.

It was bloody frustrating.

He glanced over and found Ramsbury staring off into the crowd with much the same distracted look on his face that he, himself, felt. Normally he could depend on Ramsbury to drag him from a mood, but that wasn't going to happen tonight, clearly.

"Are you brooding to attract the attention of the ladies, or is something truly on your mind?" Finn asked as he sipped his drink.

Ramsbury jolted as if he'd forgotten Finn was there at all and looked at him, but he didn't answer. It was as if he immediately got lost in thought. Finn stared at him, waiting for what felt like forever, then threw up his hands.

"Ramsbury." No answer. "Ramsbury," he repeated, sharper. Finally he shook his head. "*Sebastian!*"

At that rare use of his first name, his friend shook his head. "My apologies. Woolgathering, I suppose."

Finn almost laughed. Weren't they the pair, both unable to focus. His problem was a woman, but he couldn't imagine that was true with Ramsbury. He'd never allowed himself to be connected to a lady in his life. He seduced and played and carefully extracted himself.

And here Finn was daydreaming about a woman he hadn't even touched. "About what?" he forced himself to ask.

Ramsbury's cheek twitched ever so slightly. "Nothing of consequence. How is your sister?"

Finn wrinkled his brow at the change of subject. One he very much didn't want to discuss when there was a woman moaning in pleasure just a few feet behind him.

"Marianne? She's fine, I suppose." Once he said it, he hesitated, for he wasn't certain that was true after their tea earlier in the day. "Still mourning her old friend, I think, but otherwise well."

To his surprise, Ramsbury pressed and for a few moments they talked about his sister.

"Why ask me about Marianne?" Delacourt asked at last. He adored Ramsbury, but he'd always warned him about playing his games with Marianne.

"She's my friend, just as you have been, so I'm always curious about her welfare," Ramsbury said with a dismissive shrug.

"Hmmm. Just don't take advantage."

"Yes, I know your rule about that," Ramsbury said, his tone tinged with annoyance. "About her. I assure you I would never go too far."

Finn looked out into the crowd before he responded and as he scanned over the tables close to them, his heart thudded. There was the Hellion, his Miss X, sitting not ten feet from him. And she was watching him, tracing the edge of her wineglass with one fingertip in a way that made his entire body heat.

Their eyes locked, held for what felt like an eternity, and the hunger Finn had felt from the first moment he encountered this woman came to life.

He glanced at Ramsbury, who looked irritated, and forced himself back to the subject at hand. "Excellent. But I don't wish to talk about Marianne anymore, not here." He looked again at Miss X and she worried her lip in the most appealing fashion that drew him like a moth to a flame. "We came here to get our cocks wet. I intend to do so and I suggest you do the same."

He didn't wait for his friend's response. God knew Ramsbury could take care of himself when it came to the ladies. He just patted his arm and then moved off into the crowd toward her. Toward what he hoped would finally be a slaking of the odd, intense need she seemed to create in him.

~

When Esme had seen Delacourt standing across the room from her, what she should have done was depart the Donville Masquerade before he noticed her. In fact, she never should have come here at all. She'd told herself it was for fun, a reward after a hard fight earlier in the day.

But that wasn't true. She knew it was because she wanted to see the very man who was now striding across the room toward her, all powerful elegance and repressed strength. The man who looked at her like he would devour her whole.

He stopped at her table, standing over her with a long look that almost melted her from the inside, and then motioned to a chair. "May I join you?"

She swallowed hard. This was a dangerous game and yet she kept playing. Foolishly, inexplicably. "Yes."

He sat and smiled at her. "A new mask."

She lifted a hand and touched the blue leather, stitched with tiny paste pearls. "I have a great many of them."

"I imagine so," he drawled.

She shifted, for he had no idea, in truth. "Is there something I can do for you, my lord?"

His gaze lit up at the double entendre she hadn't meant to make. Or perhaps she had. Nothing seemed in her control anymore. "I thought we could finish the conversation we began earlier today. The one that was interrupted at the boxing club."

Her heart was beating so hard she feared he could hear it even from across the table. "Was there more to say?"

"I think so." He held her gaze steadily.

Lord, but his eyes were beautiful. Soulful, even, betraying a deeper truth beneath the bored, rakish aristocrat he seemed to be. Perhaps she wasn't the only one who wore masks.

She stiffened. It wasn't her place to know that, to care about that. And the deeper she went into this, the more danger she placed herself in.

"I don't know what you could mean," she said. "Like you, I come here to relieve the tension of the realities of my life. That you know I'm truly the Hellion isn't so shocking a thing, is it?"

"But who is the Hellion?" he asked, and leaned closer. He smelled good. Like sandalwood soap. She felt a strange longing to rub her nose along the angle of his jaw and breathe him into her body.

"I thought the purpose of this place was anonymity," she said, and was pleased her voice didn't shake.

"You're still anonymous. You wear a mask, you have no name."

She laughed at that idea. It wasn't so far from the truth. "I have a name."

He leaned even closer. "And may I guess it?"

That should have made her tense, but there was a sparkle in his eyes that made her laugh even more at his teasing. "Why do you need it so desperately?"

"Because I want to know what to call the woman who has somehow haunted my dreams since I first met her."

Her smile fell at the seductive tone of his voice and the way he reached out to take her hand. His fingers stroked across hers and she shivered without meaning to. "How often does a line like that work, my lord?"

He shook his head. "It isn't something I say to manipulate ladies into opening their legs. There *is* something about you that has captivated me."

Her breath was nonexistent now. She no longer inhabited a world where someone would be captivated by her. She survived and when she needed to feel something she either fought or fucked. But she never sought more. Never sought the intensity of the man who was tracing her palm so lightly and making her body tingle in response.

She swallowed and tried to recall how to formulate words. "I suppose you wouldn't like to be unmasked any more than I do."

His gaze held hers, a flutter of sadness in the brown of his eyes. "You've already unmasked me. You know my name, you've seen my face. And I could remove my mask right now in the middle of this room and it would likely be meaningless."

"Yes, because it's different for men," she said, unable to control the bitterness in her tone.

His expression softened. "That's true." He sighed and released her hand. "I'll continue to call you Miss X or Hellion, whichever you prefer. And if I ever earn your true name, then I'll be pleased with it."

She drew back. He was retreating from his request, not turning it into a demand? How many men would do so? She could name few.

"Now, why don't we speak of more pleasant things?" he suggested as he waved to a server. "I'll have an ale. And for the lady?"

"The same," she said, knowing she could keep her wits with

something so light. She clearly needed them. As the man left them to fetch their drinks she leaned on the table with her elbow. "So, are you a regular member of Campbell's club or did you just attend to watch the exhibition."

He straightened up a little. "*Campbell.* I hardly ever hear Ripley called by his first name. Are you two close?"

She tilted her head. "Are you asking if I've fucked the man?"

He shut his eyes briefly. "It wouldn't be fair of me to do so, I suppose. It's none of my business."

"No, it's not. But I haven't." She almost laughed at the thought. "He's more like a brother to me, in truth. When I first…" She trailed off. Was she about to tell this man her story? What was wrong with her?

He smiled as they were brought their ales. "When you first?"

"I shouldn't get into it," she said with a sigh.

"Why not? We don't know each other, I have no one to whom I'm interested in telling your tale. And I'm fascinated by how a woman finds herself participating in a combat sport."

She sighed. If she kept her wits, she could give just enough to quell his interest and never enough to identify herself. "I-I didn't start out in the place I am now," she said carefully. "But I wasn't safe where I was. I ran away and found myself in Seven Dials, totally out of my depth."

"It's a dangerous place," he said, concern in his tone that was very much like when he'd first noticed her black eye. As if he had some right or even duty to protect her.

"It is, especially for someone who had no idea how to defend herself." She shook her head as her mind took her back to that terrifying time in her life. The fear was muted now but she could still access a version of it. "This older woman approached and saw I only had the clothes on my back. She offered to help me and she seemed so kind. I was going to go with her when this petite blonde came screeching out of an alehouse across the street. She chased the woman off and scolded me."

"Why would she do that?" Delacourt asked.

"Because the old woman was a bawd. It's an old trick, to put a young woman who knows little into her debt by providing her with clothing and shelter. Then the price comes, you see. The interest on a loan you never even knew you took. Once a person like that has someone in their clutches, they can force them to work the trade to repay it so she doesn't get carted off to gaol."

He flinched. "The sex trade."

She nodded. "Yes. So the young woman rescued me. She got me something to eat, yelling at me the whole time about being more careful and wise to the ways of the street. But eventually she realized I was as stuck as I was hopeless and offered to help. Luckily my trusting nature didn't get me into trouble twice."

"That sounds like a good friend," he said softly.

"Yes. My dearest friend. She was the one working my corner this afternoon."

"Does she also fight?"

"No. She works the trade, but not under a bawd," Esme explained.

He nodded. "So how did you eventually come into boxing?"

She shrugged. "I..."

She hesitated. She'd never been ashamed of what she'd done to protect herself. Who she'd become. But this man was from her old world, even if he didn't know that she'd once belonged in the same glittering halls that he did. Telling him the facts was harder somehow.

But perhaps it would put him off her in the end and that would be good for them both.

She let out a shaky breath. "I followed her into her work," she said slowly, watching for horror to cross his face. "I sold my innocence to a man willing to pay for it. And then I worked for a little while that same way. Mostly the men were fine. Merchants on the whole. A few wanted to keep me, but I didn't want to be kept. Occasionally there was one who was...cruel."

33

He bent his head. "They hurt you?"

She nodded. "I think one would have gone further than hurting. He was being rough with me at a hell. Not the Donville Masquerade, of course. Rivers would never allow for that here. But you know how it is in some of the others. This bastard backhanded me and suddenly Campbell...*Ripley* was there. He yanked the man off and helped get me home. He knew Jane."

She came to a halt in her story. She hadn't meant to say Jane's name, didn't want to give this man too much. He seemed to sense it for he arched a brow. "You said it earlier at Ripley's and it's a common name. I'll pretend you've given it as a pseudonym."

"You have no idea if it *is* a pseudonym, after all," she said.

He smiled broadly and her heart did another little flutter at how absolutely stunning he was. Like a statue in some garden where only the rich were allowed to go and see the beauty.

"Where was I? Oh yes, Campbell. He offered to teach me to defend myself. I was resistant, but you cannot deny Campbell and Jane when they are working together on something, and she kept encouraging me to listen to him. Once I gave in, it turned out I was a natural. So I gave up the trade and the rest is history, as they say."

If she expected him to recoil at her story of opening her legs for money or turning to fighting to defend herself from men who would take what they couldn't earn, she was surprised. He looked no less interested as he stared at her now than he had before.

She blushed under his regard. "I fear my story is not so romantic as you wished it to be."

"It's real," he said. "And I appreciate that you were willing to share it. It sounds as though you are even tougher than you appear in the ring. And that's saying something."

She smiled at the compliment. "Thank you. But what about you? You're a member of Ripley's club, but that doesn't mean much. Half those toffs couldn't block a punch from their own mothers."

He laughed. "A harsh but valid criticism. Are you assuming I'm one of the bad half or the better?"

She looked at him closely. "You've a pretty face and that might make you want to protect it."

He smiled. "A pretty face. I don't think anyone has called it that before."

"Not in front of you," she mused as she examined that face even closer. Even half masked he couldn't hide what he was. "But I promise that women say it's pretty behind your back because it is. But…but there's something else about you. Hard angles, fierce lines. The way you hold yourself says you're a fighter. So I doubt you do anything by half, including spar. If pressed, I'd wager you're of the part of Ripley's boxing club that could actually hold his own."

He had grown silent with every word she said about him, his smile fading as she went along. But now he swallowed. "I don't think anyone has ever broken me down like that. But I appreciate that I came out on the right side."

"So far," she teased, and was pleased that it made him smile.

"I'll try not to let you down."

Her body tensed at that promise. It was a throwaway one, she knew that. A part of their flirtatious exchange that was meaningless and yet it somehow moved her.

"Will you dance with me again?" he asked softly.

She glanced toward the swaying couples, thinking of when he'd held her there just a few days before. She should have said no, but instead she nodded without speaking. He got up and held out his hand, his lean fingers offering her temptation that could burn her world to the ground.

She took them and tried not to suck in her breath at the feel of his warmth and strength. He guided her to the floor and put his arms around her, tucking her too close as they began to sway in time to the music. She could feel the entire length of his body from chest to thigh, feel the coiled strength there, feel the way he wanted her without trying to take what she hadn't offered.

She was dizzy with it, dizzy with his warm scent, dizzy with the way his fingers splayed across her back, tracing her spine gently just as he would if he were removing her gown. Oh, how she longed to have him do just that. To rest back on a bed with him and forget everything but his taste, his touch. To pretend she was still Charlotte Esmerelda, who belonged with a man like this.

To know that a man like this still wanted her when she was just Esme, even if it was just a passing fancy meant only for a night of pleasure.

"You are so beautiful," he murmured, his gaze locked on hers. "I truly cannot look away."

With any other man, that would have felt like a manipulation. But it didn't hit her that way when he said it. It felt...real. It felt like he hadn't even meant to say it out loud, like he was reminding himself, not her.

She felt herself being tugged into the warm fantasy of something she shouldn't risk and some distant part of her rang alarm bells. She needed to pull away. Walk away. Never dance this close to the edge again.

"Delacourt," she said softly.

He shook his head like he already knew what she would say. "I'm leaving London very shortly," he said. "I'll be gone a fortnight, to the country with my sister and some friends. I won't see you for a while because of that. Please, please...will you come in the back with me? Will you let me touch you the way I ache to touch you?"

Her breath was nonexistent now as she stared up into those brown eyes that pulled her in, drowned her, reminded her of who she'd once been before life had destroyed any hope she had of a future as a lady. If she went with him, she would surrender. She knew that. She would give over and she might not be able to stop. He would strip her clothing away, her barriers, she feared her masks would go too. Not just the one she wore on her face but the ones that protected her soul, her body, her life.

And yet she still longed to do just that. To give herself in every way to this man who seemed so driven to protect her even when he didn't know her.

She blinked. He couldn't know her. She couldn't let him any closer.

She stared up at him. He was patiently awaiting her response. Not pushing, not asking, not demanding. He was just waiting, almost like he understood that this was complicated and she needed a moment to consider.

God, but she wanted him. And she couldn't deny herself just a taste of what could have been.

She lifted up on her tiptoes and cupped his cheeks, her fingertips playing along the edge of his mask. She drew him down, tilted her head and took his lips.

He tasted of ale, of desire, and she opened to him, tracing his lips, swallowing his moan when he drove to meet her tongue. The desperation, the need that had coursed between them since their first meeting was evident in the ever-increasing passion of the kiss. His arms came tighter around her, his body grew harder against her stomach. She lifted against him, fingers clutching at his jacket as she tried to find some way to mold herself even closer.

Her head was spinning, her body was trembling, between her legs she throbbed with desire more powerful than any she'd felt in a very long time and she never wanted this to end.

But she had to end it regardless. At last she pulled back. He released her, both their breath short as they stared at each other. He seemed as stunned by the power of that passion as she felt.

She swallowed hard. "I can't, my lord. It wouldn't be wise. Good—good night."

She said nothing else, but slipped away from him, just as she had the first night they met here. And just like the first night, he let her go without demand or anger or frustration.

Only this time she knew it would *be* the end. He said he was leaving London for a while. His ardor would cool, helped along by her rejection, and the likelihood that they would see each other again was miniscule.

A fact that made her heart ache, even though she should have felt nothing about it, nothing about him, nothing about any of this except for relief that she hadn't revealed herself and ended the life she'd spent so long building.

CHAPTER 5

Normally when Finn went to his country estate just outside of London for his annual gathering of friends, he was carefree. He forgot whatever troubles were going on in his life and just enjoyed himself. But he'd been at the estate for days now and all he could think about was his last few moments with the Hellion. God, he wished he knew her name. He knew her taste, he knew the feel of her hands moving against him, he knew the way she sounded when she let out a quiet sigh of pleasure.

But he still knew nothing at all and he couldn't stop tormenting himself. He dreamed of her. He was distracted from all events at the estate. He even found himself trying to talk about fighting with friends, not because it was a shared pastime, but because he wanted to know if any of them had information about the woman beyond what he knew, himself.

He tried to refocus on the present for the tenth time in an hour and glanced across the parlor where the party were talking and laughing. He found his sister in the group, standing with Ramsbury. Standing very close to Ramsbury, staring up at him as they seemed to speak quite seriously.

He frowned. When Ramsbury glanced down at her, there was

something in his expression. A longing as hard as his own that hit Finn in the chest. What was going on there? Had he missed something just beneath his own nose?

Marianne executed a brief curtsey and left Ramsbury's side. As the earl watched her go, his mouth a thin line, Finn made his way across the room to him.

"That's a hangdog expression," Finn said carefully as he reached him. "Is there anything you wish to discuss with me?"

Ramsbury's scowl deepened. "You're one to talk," he snapped. "You've been moping about since our arrival. Is there anything *you* wish to discuss with *me*?"

Finn stiffened. In truth, he did wish he could bring up the subject of the Hellion with Ramsbury. He needed to tell someone that he longed for a woman whose face he'd never fully seen and whose name he didn't know. That he was drowning and had no idea where to swim to find safety again.

But what a fool that would make him. He had no future with the woman, she didn't want him, if her continued rejections were any indication.

He cleared his throat. "I'd be more interested in talking to you about my sister."

Ramsbury looked at him and to Finn's surprise his friend's expression was suddenly desperate and filled with pain. "I cannot. Excuse me."

He pivoted and stalked away, Finn staring after him in shock. He'd known Ramsbury for a lifetime, but never seen him like this. He turned and found Marianne next. She was standing at the fireplace, absently worrying a little figurine that normally rested there. He moved to her and forced a smile.

"Have I thanked you yet for organizing another successful gathering for my friends?" he asked.

She glanced up at him with a wobbly smile of her own. "I'm glad you're enjoying yourself. You've seemed off lately. Is there anything you wish to discuss?"

He blinked. He'd been about to ask her the same thing, press about whatever was going on with Sebastian. Make sure it wasn't something that could threaten the well-being of his beloved sister.

"It seems there's something off in the air lately," he said with a sigh. "Perhaps everyone is feeling it."

"Hmm." She was noncommittal in that response and turned the figurine in her hand.

He slipped it from her grasp gently and placed it back on the mantel. She glanced up at him a second time and this time she held his gaze. "If you need me, you know I'm here, don't you?" he asked and meant it.

Her lips parted and she seemed to struggle with something for a moment. But then she reached up and patted his cheek. "I know. The same goes for you."

The conversation should have assuaged his worry. Marianne was distracted, but she'd just recently lost a friend. Perhaps that was what she and Ramsbury had been discussing. He was seeing something else because he was so tangled up in his own romantic issues. There was no use looking for trouble. He had enough already.

"Why don't we dance?" he suggested, and motioned to where a few of the others were mangling a country jig while someone played piano for them.

She took his arm and her worries seemed to evaporate, so he forced his own to do the same. "I'd like that."

∽

"What do you think about a match on Tuesday?"

Esme blinked and forced herself to pay attention to Ripley as he looked over a schedule on his desk in the back of his boxing club. "I'm sorry?"

His brow wrinkled. "I know you came to the club to spar, but usually you want to discuss fights to be made. You had the exhibition recently, but you haven't had a real match since you won that night against Hilde Parson down at Seven Dials. I'd think you'd want to get out there and there's a space available in a round of matches coming to the Dog and Pony Hell."

She shook away her distractions and nodded. "Who would be the opponent?"

He flipped through the pages. "Viall is trying to build up Murder Mary."

She rolled her eyes. "Murder Mary. I fought her back at the beginning, if you recall."

"I do. You put her on her arse after five minutes." He laughed. "I knew I'd picked the right woman to train after that night."

"She hardly has a left hook at all." Esme sighed. "But yes, I'll take the fight. The blunt will be nice."

Ripley leaned back in his chair. "You're miles away."

She pursed her lips. She was, even though she'd never admit to him or to Jane or to anyone else where her mind took her. But since Finn's departure from London a week before, she hadn't stopped thinking about him. It was ridiculous, for surely he'd erased her from his memory. After she'd rejected his request for a fuck twice? A man like that had certainly written her off and moved on to someone willing.

"Esme."

She looked up at Ripley. "Do you ever think of getting out of it all?"

He held her gaze for a moment. "I did get out of it all. Took my blunt and started the boxing club so I'd stopped getting punched in the head."

"You just teach others how to take that punch." She said with a laugh.

He smiled a little. "You've been doing this a while, Es. Most women don't last more than a few years in the circuit. And you've set aside a lot of blunt doing it and living as simply as you and Jane do. So if you're starting to think about moving on, letting go, it makes sense. You've nothing to prove."

She bent her head. "Sometimes I try to picture what would come next, but it's always blank. I had the idea I'd be some fop's wife for so long back when I was someone else. I could imagine that life forever. And then I started doing this and it saved me. But when I look to the next thing it just seems…"

"I know." Ripley drew in a long breath. "I know what it seems like. So think on it. What would you like to be next? You don't have to know today or tomorrow, but preparing for the future is never a waste of time."

She smiled and then got up. "I'll go punch the bags a bit. Will you write up that information on the fight so I can give it to Jane when I get home?"

He shifted slightly. "I will. I'll write her a little note, too."

Her smile widened as she exited his office to go into the half-empty fighting area where a few other ladies were sparring and practicing for their own bouts down the line. "She always loves that," she called back to him.

If he answered, she didn't hear it. She focused instead on the heavy bag hanging from a beam on the ceiling. She slung a half-hearted punch at it and felt it shiver in response. She thought of Ripley's question. What *did* she want in the future?

A brief image of Finn kissing her jumped to her mind. Finn holding her down on a bed as she rose beneath him in writhing pleasure. She blinked the unwanted image away. That wasn't possible. There was no future there, no matter how many times she dreamed of the man.

She had to move on. That was all there was to it.

∽

The ball was in full swing but Finn was hardly attending. He looked around the room for what felt like the fifth time and then shook his head at his butler, Bentley. "I don't see her. Where could Marianne be?"

They had been looking for his sister for almost ten minutes, since there had been a question about the location of an extra case of wine she'd had set aside for the gathering. She never shared these little details with Finn and no one else on staff seemed to know what arrangements she'd made.

"You're looking for your sister?" one of the partygoers asked from his elbow.

He turned and found it was an old school chum, Inglewood. "You've seen her?"

"I think she followed Ramsbury onto the terrace a bit ago. He was acting very strangely."

Finn pursed his lips at that statement, but didn't respond. Instead he weaved his way through the ballroom, Bentley on his heels, and peeked out onto the terrace. He didn't see Marianne or Ramsbury anywhere.

"Perhaps she went into one of the parlors off the other side of the terrace, my lord," Bentley suggested.

"Yes." Finn shook his head, for he was beginning to get a very odd feeling. "Let's go down the hall and check them."

They left the ballroom together and moved up the hallway together. Finn opened each door as they did so, but found them all empty until the fourth chamber. There he stepped inside and froze.

Ramsbury lay across the settee before the fire, a lady pinned beneath him. But it wasn't some widow from the shire who had come to the ball, it wasn't a stranger he'd smuggled into the house for an assignation. It was Marianne. They were kissing passionately, her clothing half down, his trousers unfastened and so low on his waist that it was obvious what was happening.

They noticed him then and both gasped. Marianne turned her face into his shoulder, Ramsbury blocked her as if he could protect her. Protect her when he was ruining her.

"Marianne?" Finn watched as her fingers gripped harder against Ramsbury's arm even if she refused to lift her face.

"Delacourt, please…" Ramsbury began.

But Finn didn't let him continue. Incandescent rage washed over him as he crossed the room to the man he'd called friend. The man he'd only ever asked one thing of, and that was not to trifle with his sister. He'd always known Marianne had tender feelings for his friend, he hadn't wanted her to be hurt. But now she would be. He cocked his fist back and swung, landing the punch across his friend's cheek and knocking him off the settee onto his arse on the floor.

Marianne let out a screech as she lifted her gown up to cover her chemise and held it there.

Ramsbury stared up at him as he worked his jaw back and forth. "That was the best punch you've thrown in years."

Finn shook his head. "Don't try to joke your way out of this." Without looking over his shoulder he said, "Bentley, get out. Say nothing of this, do you understand?"

"Yes, my lord," Bentley said, his voice shaking as he exited the room and shut it behind him. At least Finn trusted his servants wouldn't betray him.

"Finn," Marianne began, her pale lips trembling.

Finn shook his head. There were tears in her eyes. Pain he hadn't prevented and it would surely only get worse now. "Don't say a word until you've fully dressed." He wanted to make his tone gentle for her, but he couldn't in his shock and horror. So he turned toward Ramsbury, who was still on the floor. "Get up, you foul fuck, and turn your back so my sister may have some privacy."

Slowly, Ramsbury did as he'd been told and then reached down to fix his trousers. Finn growled out his anger and then turned his back on them both. He tried to draw breath, tried to calm his racing heart and mind.

"I need help buttoning," Marianne said softly. "Sebastian, will you?"

Finn pivoted and stepped toward her. "There is no way in hell that Ramsbury is going to button your dress, Marianne."

If he expected his sister to crumble, she surprised him. She met his gaze without hesitation and lifted her chin with a strength he hadn't fully given her credit for. "Then we're at an impasse. You have ordered me to dress. I cannot do it by myself. I doubt you want to go calling for servants to come in and have even more of them see what you've witnessed. And I have no interest in *you* buttoning my clothing, Phineas. I assume you don't either. It seems a bit too intimate for siblings, does it not?"

He flinched at the idea. She had him there. And since he had no argument, he threw up his hands. "Fine, bloody hell, let him button you." He pivoted on Ramsbury. "But I swear on everything that is holy, Ramsbury, if you go too far—"

"I think we can all agree it's a bit late for that. I have no intention of doing anything untoward to Marianne with you glaring daggers into my soul."

Finn turned his back again because watching his friend dress his sister seemed like something he shouldn't see.

"Do everyone a favor, Delacourt, and light some lamps or set the fire," Ramsbury said softly. "I doubt you want to have whatever conversation is coming next in the dark."

"No, we only soil things in the dark, don't we?" Finn snapped. "You only sneak around in the dark ruining my sister."

"Finn, light the fire, for heaven's sake," Marianne said, and now her voice *was* trembling.

Finn drew another long breath and moved to the low fire. He threw in a log and stirred the flames with the poker. Behind him he heard Marianne and Ramsbury talking in low tones. He pursed his lips in frustration. "Stop whispering, you two."

When Finn turned back to light a few lamps, he found Marianne had already returned to the settee. She was seated with her back straight and hands folded in her lap. Waiting for judgment, he supposed. He had no idea how to meter it at this point and he was suddenly exhausted by this, by everything.

"I'm doing my best not to shout and draw the attention of over fifty people gathered in our ballroom," he said at last when he found words. "So I will ask that you two do not trifle with me, do not lie to me. What the hell is going on that I would find you two in such a situation?"

"I tricked him," Marianne began. "He thought I was someone else."

Finn stared at her, at the idea that she would be so duplicitous. That she would force herself into such a situation when she had always been so shy, so locked to the wall where she hid. He supposed they had both done quite a bit of hiding after their mother's death. He winced at the thought.

"That's *not* true," Ramsbury said softly, drawing Finn's attention. He was staring at Marianne and in that moment Finn saw something in his eyes. He saw that his friend, the consummate rake, *cared* about her.

"Sebastian." Marianne rose and stepped toward him. "Don't. Don't."

He shook his head. "You are too good, Marianne. Too good for me, certainly. I won't let you do this."

Now all Finn could do was stare from one to the other as what was truly happening here became increasingly clear. "So she lied."

"To protect me," Ramsbury said. "Yes. What you walked in on is exactly what you think it was. I engaged in ungentlemanly behavior with your sister. I knew the consequences to our friendship if you were to find out. I did it anyway because my attraction toward her was irresistible."

Finn swallowed hard. "He took advantage."

Marianne shook her head. "*Never.* Never once. I know it's hard for you to see me as a woman with feelings and needs and a heart," she said. "But I *am* those things, Finn. I didn't want to have so many regrets and missed opportunities when I'm at the end and looking back. Sebastian has been my friend for so long. And I've…I've cared for him as more than a friend for nearly as long."

And there it was. The thing he'd always known was true, the thing he'd always tried to protect her from. And yet, as he looked at

Ramsbury, it was apparent he'd misunderstood a great deal in this situation. But he still needed to manage this. To distance them, to give himself time to process what to do next. How to handle this. How to handle everything, because in that moment his entire life felt out of control.

"Go up to your chamber, Marianne," he said softly. "I'll explain to those at the party that you were stricken with a headache. The result of all your hard work to make this ball so successful, no doubt."

"You're banishing me," she whispered.

"No." Finn met her gaze. "I'm allowing you a chance not to have spying eyes on you when your hair is half down thanks to him. Not to be forced to pretend that this untenable situation hasn't happened. And giving myself an opportunity to calm down before we speak about this again." He moved forward. "Please, Mari. Just go."

She looked toward Ramsbury, a world of unspoken communication moving between them. Then she lifted her chin and strode from the room as she'd been asked. He noted she didn't shut the door behind herself.

"Still protecting you, it seems," Finn said as he moved to do what she hadn't. When he turned back, he leaned against the barrier and shook his head. "You betrayed me. Betrayed my singular request of you."

"I did."

Finn waited for more, but Ramsbury remained quiet now. "That's all you have to say?"

A long silence hung between them and Ramsbury shifted. "Is there anything I could say?"

"I don't know." Finn threw up his hands as frustration overcame him. "For years and years, I've stood by you. I never judged your worst impulses. Hell, I sometimes indulged in them. I knew who you were, or at least I thought I did. And I asked you this one thing, out of respect for me and our friendship."

"I know," Ramsbury said.

"So tell me you regret doing this, tell me you're sorry you did something that will change our friendship irrevocably."

The silence stretched out even longer this time. A lifetime. Then Ramsbury's expression collapsed a fraction and he said, "I'm—I'm not sorry that I touched Marianne."

And there it was. What he now suspected put into words, at least as close as he thought he would get given the circumstances. There had been an affair between his innocent sister and the biggest rake in England. But it was more than that. On both sides. Now what would come of that...remained to be seen. He sighed. "In the morning, you'll leave at dawn. I don't care where you go, but you won't be here. I'll make some excuse about an emergency that called you away."

"I understand."

Finn shook his head. He had a thousand reasons to be angry at this situation and yet one feeling overwhelmed the others. He was envious. His sister and his best friend seemed to have dived headfirst into something they were willing to risk their worlds for. And Finn couldn't help but think of the Hellion and how she wouldn't even risk her name.

He pivoted and moved to the door.

"Don't be hard on her," Ramsbury called out. "She doesn't deserve that."

Finn stopped moving. Marianne had tried to protect Ramsbury. Now he returned the favor. "No," he agreed softly. "She doesn't."

Then he left the room and shut the door firmly behind him. He staggered as he made his way back toward the ballroom. He had no doubt Ramsbury would follow his order and leave in the morning. And Finn would talk to Marianne and they would come to some understanding. But nothing would ever be the same. The only thing that would remain as before was that he would spend his days pretending. Pretending everything was well, all while he tried to find some way to resolve the damage that had been done.

And that was nothing new at all.

CHAPTER 6

Esme stared at the crumpled page of London's notorious *Scandal Sheet* gossip rag. Every week Jane stole a copy for Esme to enjoy, and normally she did. There was some fun to peeking back into the life she'd once led. But today she had read the main item three times and felt no pleasure at the voyeuristic experience. Only worry.

> *A certain wallflower who just spent time at her brother's estate has come home and within days become engaged to a once-wicked earl! Who knows what wiles were employed to land such a catch, and if the stunning development will damage the lifelong friendship between the groom and his equally powerful now future brother-in-law? Earls will be earls, it seems.*

The blind items of the sheet were never meant to be difficult to decipher, just easy to deny if someone wanted to make claims of damage against the paper. It was obvious this was referring to the Earl of Delacourt and his best friend, the Earl of Ramsbury.

"Oh, Delacourt," she said softly as she pushed the paper aside.

She could only imagine his feelings on the subject. He'd always been protective of his sister, she'd known that even when he was little more than a phantom her father adored. To have her marrying someone well known as a scoundrel and under what sounded like potentially scandalous circumstances…

Well, it would weigh on him.

"You look like you will cry," Jane said as she entered the parlor and flopped herself into the chair across from her at their small table. "What could possibly be in that paper to make you look so?"

She shook her head. "I'm being ridiculous, I know."

Jane folded her arms. "Is this about that marquess again?"

"He's an earl," Esme corrected softly.

Jane pursed her lips and dragged the paper to herself, reading the blind item swiftly. "I see. And is he the one marrying the sister or the one who lost her to his friend?"

"He's the one who is seeing his sister marry a friend," Esme admitted with only a brief glance toward Jane.

Her friend snatched the paper up and crossed to the fire, where she tossed the page in. When she looked back, her expression was lined with worry. "Esme, you've worked hard to build some safety for yourself. To break free of a world that would have likely killed you had you stayed. Why would you endanger all you've created over some *man*?"

It was a valid question and Esme put her head down on her arms because she couldn't face Jane when she answered. "I don't know! I've known plenty of handsome men, been attracted to men over the years, but I wouldn't risk myself for any of them. I suppose that the fact that my…my father cared for him might have something to do with it."

Jane's mouth dropped open. "He knew your father? Why didn't you tell me that before?"

Esme looked up at her. "Because you'd give me the very look you are now. I knew you would scold."

"Why shouldn't I? That is even more reason to stay away from this man! Far away. He is actually from your old life—if he ever found out who you were..."

"I know." Esme shook her head. "I know you're right. I'm being the worst kind of fool and I despise myself for it."

Jane sighed. "I'm sure I can't imagine what it must be like to walk away from everything you ever cared about. Everything you ever knew."

Esme looked at her, saw her friend's strength and steel. "Of course you do."

Jane softened a little and took her hand. She gave a little squeeze. "I'm spending an evening with a very fine merchant tonight. He's taking me to the theatre."

Esme was grateful for the change of subject and nodded. "How exciting. What will you wear?"

"The blue silk, I think. As long as you weren't going to wear it tonight."

She and Jane often shared gowns, with Jane stuffing the bust to fill out the space Esme needed more of. What was the point of spending twice the money on clothing when they could economize and save even more just in case? In their world, there were so often unexpected issues. Like one's foolish obsession with an earl, for example.

"No, I didn't intend to wear it," she said when she realized Jane was waiting for the response.

"Excellent. And what will you do tonight?"

Esme glanced toward the fireplace. The paper was long gone now, nothing more than ash, but she knew what it said. If his sister was back in Town, Delacourt was, too. So she might run into him at the Donville Masquerade.

"I think I'll just stay in," she lied. "Read a book, go to bed early."

"Well, I might not be back at all tonight, so you should enjoy your time," Jane said. "Now come and help me, will you?"

Esme followed her to her chamber to help her dress and fix her hair, but all along she could only think of seeing Delacourt again.

Even if she shouldn't.

∼

Finn felt sour as he stood along the wall at the Donville Masquerade. He felt no pleasure in watching the games around him. His mind was too twisted up in knots to do so. He could only think of Marianne and Ramsbury, he could only think of a woman he would never see again.

God, he needed to get drunk beyond reason and just forget everything for a while. He turned to order another drink and start that very process, only to find the Hellion standing just behind him. His breath caught at her sudden arrival, like some apparition he'd conjured with inappropriate thoughts.

"Good evening," she said softly.

He let his gaze flit over her. Tonight she wore a silky red gown that left little to the imagination, it was cut so low. Her mask matched and had black stitching. She looked like a fantasy, yanked from his very addled mind.

"You know," he said, trying to rein himself in. "For a woman who isn't interested in my company, we certainly keep seeing each other often enough."

Her lips parted at his peppery tone, but she didn't back away as some ladies might have. "Some moths go to the flame even when they know they'll be burned."

He barked out a humorless laugh at that assessment and his thoughts returned to his sister once more. Things were resolved now. Marianne and Ramsbury were engaged and deeply happy, but he still hated himself for not seeing what had been right before his eyes. "Oh yes, that seems to be entirely true."

Her expression softened and for a moment she almost seemed to understand. How she could, he didn't know. She extended a hand toward him, a lovely hand despite the faint bruise on one knuckle that reminded him of who she was. Or who she pretended to be in public, at any rate.

He should have turned away from it. He wasn't in a pleasant mood and the idea of being rejected once more by this woman did not rank as something he wished to experience at present. But he was as much a moth to her flame as anyone else. And he found himself reaching out to take her hand.

She said nothing, but guided him to the dancefloor. He sighed as he put his arms around her and they began to move in time. She was quiet for what felt like a very long time, just staring up at him. Her dark green eyes were somehow a comfort as they held his, like a cool walk in the woods.

"I never said I wasn't interested in your company," she said softly.

He drew in a shallow breath. "You've refused me two times, Miss X. Forgive me if I'm confused."

She swallowed and for a long moment she was silent, her gaze never leaving his. Then she said, "I won't make you ask again, my lord. Will you come to the back with me? Please."

His heart began to pound as he stared at her. Was this happening? After the days apart when he'd been obsessed with her? After all the heated dreams that woke him hard and aching in his twisted sheets?

If it was another of those dreams, he didn't want to wake up. He released her from his arms and motioned toward the back. "Lead the way."

She took his hand and did so, weaving them through the writhing crowd, guiding them toward the secret rooms in the back where couples played out their fantasies with more privacy. She motioned to the servant guarding the space and he nodded his head, putting up four fingers to tell her which room was open. It was obvious she had done this before. Briefly Finn wondered if she'd ever cared about anyone she brought here, but he pushed the thought from his head. It didn't matter. This was a night of pleasure, nothing more.

They moved down the dimly lit hall and she pushed open the correct door. He followed her inside and watched as she locked the door and then crossed to a panel on the wall opposite a big bed. It was meant to allow for voyeurism for those in the passageway behind the rooms, but she slid it shut and then faced him.

"This is just for us," she said softly.

He nodded, unable to form words when she was coming across the chamber to him, her hips twitching and her pupils dilated with as much desire as coursed through his own veins. All other thoughts and worries and pains slipped from his mind as she lifted up on her tiptoes and tugged him down to kiss her.

Whatever would happen next, he wanted to savor this night. He wanted to drown in it, and in that moment he didn't really care if he ever surfaced again.

∼

Esme hadn't intended to find herself in the backroom of the Donville Masquerade, her tongue tangling with Delacourt's while his strong arms came around her. Or perhaps she had, and had only been lying to herself when she'd told herself she only wanted to see him, only wanted to talk with him, only wanted to dance with him.

All she knew was that when she saw the brokenness, the lostness of his expression in the hall, she had needed to touch him. Needed to be with him. She knew that look all too well and sometimes pleasure was the only way to quell the harder emotions.

He drew back from the kiss, looking down at her, his breath short. She said nothing, but unfastened the buttons of his jacket and slid her hands beneath, where his body heat was trapped. She hissed in a breath at the hard strength of his chest, at the way her short nails raked the brocaded fabric of his waistcoat.

"I want to know your name," he whispered as he bent to take her lips again. She moaned as his tongue tangled with hers, making her body tingle with anticipation.

"Why?" she muttered against his mouth, the word ending on a gasp as he guided his hand to her shoulder, down her arm, cupped her hip and molded her even closer.

"I want to say it while I take you, I want to moan it."

She squeezed her eyes shut, her hands stilling on his lapels, even as he continued to massage and stroke and awaken her with desire. He began to unfasten her dress, one button at a time. It hooked in the front, made it easier for her to maneuver and take care of herself. He bent to press his lips to her collarbones, her chest, the very tops of her breasts as he slid the fabric open wider with each button.

"Esme," she whispered.

He lifted his gaze, held hers a long moment, and then he smiled. "Esme. Beautiful, delicious Esme. You've always had me at a disadvantage when it comes to our names, but Finn. You must call me Finn when we do what we're about to do."

Her heart throbbed. She'd always thought of him as Delacourt. Sometimes she'd heard her father call him Phineas. But this nickname, it felt intimate. Something only his closest friends or family would use. And he gifted it to her.

"Finn," she repeated softly, and he gripped her hip harder, like it pleased him.

"Again," he said, and drew the fabric of her gown away, baring her from the waist up.

"Finn," she gasped when he brought his mouth back to her flesh and slid it over her nipple.

She dug her hands into his hair, holding him there as he began to suck her, gently at first, then ever harder as she arched against him, gasping for breath and purchase. He backed her toward the bed and laid her back, continuing to lick and suck from one nipple to the other.

His hands crept lower, thumbs catching in the folded fabric at her hips. She lifted them, grinding against him even as he shoved the fabric down and she kicked it away so that she was naked with him save her stockings and slippers.

He pulled back, got to his feet and stared at her. She knew what he saw. Her days training made her body more muscled than the typical lady and she had bruises here and there from her fights. Sometimes when men saw her they acted like they didn't like those things. They wanted everything to be soft and gentle. She had been forced to leave soft and gentle behind years ago.

"You are gorgeous," he whispered as he unwound his cravat, shed his waistcoat, then tugged his shirt over his head.

She sat up as he did so and smiled at the toned body she'd known was lurking beneath all that propriety. "And so are you."

She got up and now it was her turn to touch. He stood still as she flattened a palm to his chest and dragged it lower, feeling the warmth of him, the firmness, the wiry hair that peppered the muscle. He was a fine specimen and oh, she relished the idea that she would claim him, even just for a little while.

Her hand glided over his stomach and his breath hitched as she played her fingers at the waist of his trousers. She met his gaze, held there and then cupped his cock. He was hard, pressing against the straining fabric and her palm as she rubbed him.

"Very nice, Finn," she whispered.

He laughed. "I aim to please."

"As do I." It was true. In this moment, all she wanted to do was please him, make him lose control. Make his legs shake while she tasted him. She flicked open the buttons of his fall front. The placket of his trousers dropped away she lowered to her knees, looking at his cock as she stroked him. He was as beautiful here as anywhere. He was thick, the flesh a shade darker than the rest of him. She smiled at him, darted out her tongue and licked.

"Esme," he gasped.

"Yes," she whispered between continued teasing licks. "Keep saying it."

He dug his fingers into her hair, his fingers briefly touching the cord that held her mask in place. She froze, but he didn't try to reveal her. He simply adjusted his hands with a moan when she took him into her mouth fully. She squirmed as his fingers gripped the back of her head, urging her to take more as she sucked him. She did, reveling in the feel of his hardness every time it touched her throat. Reveling in his increasingly incoherent sounds of pleasure as she eased him to the edge. She rocked with her strokes, aroused by pleasing him, by the command of his touch, by the edgy need of his moans and cries.

She would have finished him that way. She would have finished him and licked her lips like a cat and then demanded he play with her until he was hard again and they could start over. But he seemed to have other ideas.

He caught her armpits and lifted her, tugging her off of him and pressing her back so she fell into the bed. His dark eyes were glittering as he caught her thighs, massaging them before he tugged her to the edge of the mattress. He lowered his mouth and she widened her legs, aching for what she could see he would do.

"Yes," she cried out as his mouth covered her sex. He peeled her open, massaging her as she began to grind up to meet him. His tongue traced her, teased her, tasted every inch of her. When she twisted against the pleasure, he pressed a hand to her hip and held her steady.

And then he began to swirl his tongue against her clitoris. She gasped, gripping the coverlet with both hands, rocking against his tongue as he expertly brought her up to the edge with just a few swipes. She had never felt so close to coming so soon with a lover. Normally she had to work for it, but this was like floating, flying, as if it was something she had been built to do with him.

He started to suck her and her back bowed off the bed as waves of electric pleasure roared through her. "Finn!" she cried out, loving how he moaned against her, the vibration only making the pleasure better, higher, deeper.

He gave her no quarter, continuing to suck and lick until at last her body collapsed, her legs still shaking and her body weak with pleasure.

Only then did he rise up over her, wrap her legs around his hips. He pressed his mouth to her, letting her taste her pleasure as he speared her in one long thrust.

She jolted as she stretched to accommodate his thick length. He drew back and took her again, his fingers digging into her thighs as he moaned, "Esme…"

She lifted to him, holding his stare as he claimed her over and over, grinding his hips against her already sensitive clitoris, bringing her pleasure back to a peak that she couldn't resist. He smiled as she gasped and groaned beneath him, feeling the edge of that pleasure so sharp between her legs.

"Again," he murmured, just like before, but he meant for her to come.

She let herself fall, twisting and arching against him. He moaned at her body's grip, at the waves of her pleasure, and she reveled in how the tendons in his neck tightened, showing her that she had dragged this man to the fine edge of his control. She wanted to break him. She wanted to feel the cracks as he shattered above her.

She rocked harder, her pleasure gripping him, and he cursed. His face grew red, his breath sharp and unsteady. Then he shouted her name, withdrew, and the heat of him splashed against her stomach as he came.

He collapsed over her, dragging her back onto the bed so they were no longer half off the sheets. She adjusted her mask to be certain it was still secure and then rested her head on his chest, their breath slowly matching as they both came down from the high of pleasure. She found herself tracing the lines of his chest, memorizing the ridges and valleys of him.

"Was it worth the wait, my lord?" she asked, glancing up at him.

He smiled. "Very much so. I needed that."

She tilted her head. She ought not to push, but somehow she couldn't stop herself. "Why?"

He drew a long breath. "I've been...out of sorts the last few weeks. It's partially your fault, you know."

"My fault?" she repeated.

He nodded. "All I could think about was you since we last parted."

Her heart fluttered at that. "Compliments, compliments. But you said only partially. What was the other reason?"

He shook his head and the teasing light went out of his eyes. "My sister and my friend are...they're marrying. He's a rake. A rogue. I always warned him off her, for fear he would seduce her. And he... he did."

She sat up a little. "Oh. Was he forced her marry her?"

"No." His lips pursed briefly. "He—he claims he loves her. I sent him away, but they reunited upon our return to London. She is ecstatic and every time I catch him watching her, it's with true regard."

"But isn't that good?" she asked carefully. "Would you not wish your sister to marry for love? Or is the man not of your world?"

His answer meant everything to her. Would he dismiss someone below him, as he thought her to be? As she was in truth now, after the years lived where and how she had.

"He is. He's an earl like me," he said. "And yes, I've only ever wanted her to marry someone she actually wanted. I never would have forced her to do otherwise."

Esme smiled a little. Not many brothers or fathers or cousins could have the same said of the women in their care. For most ladies of distinction, their only value was seen in trading them for marriage. They only existed through their relationship to some man, either the one who sired them or the one who tried to breed the next heir with them.

Finn sighed. "I just...I missed the signs. I wasn't a good brother.

What if I'm missing them now? What if she will be hurt because I'm distracted by my own problems?"

She saw the true worry in his expression, the pain. Once again he looked lost and she wanted to help him. Needed to, it seemed. She cupped his cheek gently.

"Finn," she whispered. "You can only do so much. If they seem to be in love, then you must simply be pleased by that and hope for the best."

"Perhaps," he said softly. "I only want to protect her."

She smoothed her fingers over his cheek again and thought of the sister he so adored. She had come out after Esme, and they had been in different circles. But she'd always liked her. Always thought highly of her intelligence and gentle kindness to those around her.

"Perhaps you needn't. I think Marianne has always had a good head on her shoulders and—"

His brow wrinkled and he sat up suddenly to stare at her. "Marianne? How do you know her name? How do you know anything about her?"

She froze. How in the world had she made such a mistake to not only use his sister's name, but also to imply she knew her? The answer came up swiftly, though, slapping her in the face. She'd wanted to comfort him so much, and she was so easy with his company, that she had forgotten herself for a moment. The mask, at least figuratively, had slipped and now she had to put it back before he revealed her completely.

"I-I don't know anything," she said, scooting back from him a fraction. "You said her name earlier."

His nostrils flared slightly. "No, I didn't. I know I didn't. I never said her name was Marianne. And that wouldn't explain how you'd speak of her with such familiarity."

She folded her arms, faking indignation when what she truly felt was terror, tingling down her to her fingertips, throbbing in her pounding heart, making the room tilt ever so slightly. "I didn't. I don't know what you mean."

Frustration lined his face. "Stop lying, Esme. You said my sister has a good head on her shoulders."

She threw up her hands. "I misspoke, I meant to say I was certain she did considering what you've said about her and who you are. You're making something out of nothing."

"I wish I were," he said, and leaned closer. "Who are you?"

"I'm—"

"Who are you?" he repeated, slowly and succinctly.

She swallowed. He was too clever to lie to, too clever to believe whatever she said to put him off. Oh, she had failed herself, drawn in too much by a man who put her off-kilter. Jane had warned her and she hadn't listened.

Why hadn't she listened?

"Who are you?" he said again, this time more gently as he reached out and drew his fingers along the bottom of her mask.

"Leave it alone, Finn," she whispered, but it was a plea, not an order. There was no stopping this now and she knew it.

He pinched the mask edge between his thumb and forefinger and gently lifted it, pulling it over her head and tossing it away. She prayed he wouldn't recognize her, but she knew those prayers couldn't be answered as he stared, mouth slightly agape, eyes wide.

His voice trembled as he cupped her cheek and said, "Charlotte?"

CHAPTER 7

There had not been many people in Finn's youth who had given him support and friendship. There was Ramsbury, of course, and his sister. But his father had been abysmal and his mother constantly troubled by her relationship with the late earl, rather than present with the one she might have with her children.

It had left him looking for a mentor and he had found that in the Marquess of Chilton. The man had taken Finn under his wing, indulged him in philosophical conversation and practical knowledge about taking a title and holding it with honor. He'd been kind, gentle. And Finn had loved him like the father he'd never truly had.

He hadn't known the man's daughter, Charlotte, well. He and Chilton often met at the marquess's club and if they returned to his home, it was long after the young woman had gone to sleep. Out of respect for his friend, Finn hadn't sought her out at balls or parties, even though he *had* noticed her. It was impossible not to notice her, as she was a beauty.

When Chilton had died, suddenly and unexpectedly, Finn's heart had been broken. And not long after Lady Charlotte had vanished. It was one of Society's great mysteries, explained away by the new marquess—her cousin, who wasn't half the man as her father had been—that she had taken her saved pin money and fled to the continent to go wild.

But she *wasn't* on the continent. She was sitting on a bed next to Finn, her green eyes bright with unshed tears as her hands trembled in her lap.

"I don't go by Charlotte," she said at last, turning her face away from his hand, which still pressed to her cheek. "It's Esme, just as I told you."

He blinked, still trying to process this utter shock. "Why?"

There was a long pause and she drew a few long breaths, as if speaking the truth were a challenge. "My middle name is Esmerelda," she explained at last. "I hated the name Charlotte anyway, so I chose that instead."

"No," he said, shaking his head. "Not why Esme. Why…why this? Why run away from your life? Why come to places like this?"

She folded her arms. "You didn't mind it so much when you thought I was just some girl from the slums. Now that you know I was raised a lady it's not good enough?"

He let out his breath in frustration and pushed from the bed. This conversation could not be held when he was naked with her body still brushing his. It was entirely too distracting and he needed to not be distracted so he could understand the unfathomable.

"It's not about good enough or not good enough, Char—" She glared at him and he inclined his head as he shoved into his trousers and fastened them. "*Esme*. You've been missing for two years."

"You think I don't know that? You think I don't know the exact day, hour, moment since I last saw the home I grew up in or the friends I once adored?" she snapped, her eyes flashing now as she, too, exited the bed. Naked. Gloriously naked before she grabbed her dress and struggled to put it on.

"I only want to understand," he said.

She stopped fighting with her buttons and sighed heavily. "Why? Why does it matter, Finn? I'm Esme, the Hellion, Miss X. Nothing has changed just because you once knew me by yet another name.

This was a lark, a brief moment of pleasure. Why do you need to dig into anything else?"

"Because I loved your father," he said. "Like he was my own. And since he isn't here to protect you, I feel I...I must try."

"You mean because you feel guilty over your sister, you somehow need to transfer that attempt at control to me," she said.

He flinched at the charge. Perhaps she wasn't so wrong that he wanted to solve a problem and now he would take on hers. But he still said, "No."

She rolled her eyes like she didn't believe him, like she could see into his soul. "I don't need your protection, Finn. I think you saw in the ring that I'm more than capable of taking care of myself. And whatever happened to me in the past, it's...it's none of your business. I'm Esme, I'm the Hellion. Forget you know anything different."

She had managed to get her dress buttoned and she smoothed her hair before she caught up the mask he had removed. When she settled it over her gorgeous face, he could almost do as she demanded and pretend he didn't know who she truly was.

Almost.

"What we shared tonight was wonderful," she said, and her eyes softened a little with those words. "I don't want to regret it. So please don't make me. Goodbye."

She pivoted then and exited the room, leaving him staring after her. He grabbed for his forgotten boots and shoved them on, swearing at how long it took to button them. By the time he was able to chase after her, she was long gone into the main hall, into the crush of grinding bodies and the loud laughter of the masked participants.

"Fuck," he muttered, running a hand through his hair before he put his own mask back on.

He should do as she asked. He should back away and just let their night together be an experience he cherished. Whatever else was going on, Esme didn't seem miserable in her life.

And yet he couldn't stop thinking of the tears in her eyes, those ones she hadn't allowed herself to shed, when he spoke of her father. When he spoke of her past life.

And he knew he couldn't let her go so easily, not without understanding more about what made her so haunted.

~

He wouldn't let her go. As Esme rattled home in the hackney she'd managed to hail after she fled from the Donville Masquerade, that was the thing she knew above all else. Finn…Lord Delacourt…whatever she called him, he wouldn't stop. He would be as relentless in trying to uncover all her secrets as he had been in drawing pleasure from her shaking body.

She covered her face. How could one night be so shattering in two such different ways. And why did it all have to be ruined by the meshing of deep pleasure with the stark terror that now gripped her?

What if he went to her cousin? What if in his deepest desire to help her, he actually steered to her doorstep a man who would destroy her?

"Fuck!" she burst out, slamming her hands on the worn carriage seat. Her palms stung, but she had solved no problems with that outburst.

Eventually the carriage slowed and stopped at her small townhouse and she got out. To her surprise, the candle was burning in the window. That meant Jane was home. She shook her head as she handed over a few coins to the leering driver.

Jane. She would never be able to hide the truth from Jane. Her friend would scold and shout and she would be perfectly right in every single thing she said.

With a sigh, Esme trudged through the door and locked it, checked the window and then moved toward the front parlor. Jane was seated by the fire, reading a book Esme had purchased for them to share. She couldn't help but smile at the image. She'd taught Jane to read and now her friend was a great fan of novels.

"There you are," Jane said, tossing the book to the side and getting to her feet. "I thought you were staying in tonight, enjoying some time alone."

"And I thought *you* were going to be out all night enjoying some merchant's hospitality and his huge cock," Esme returned as she tossed her mask on the table.

Jane stared at the mask and then slowly back at her. "His cock isn't huge. How big was the one you landed at the Donville Masquerade?"

"There's no hiding from you, is there?" Esme sighed and came to stand before the fire, warming her suddenly cold hands by the glow. Images of Finn's mouth on her flashed into her mind and she turned her head.

"You went looking for *him*."

It was a statement, not a question. Esme nodded without looking at Jane.

"You found him," her friend continued, stepping closer.

"I did." She did look at Jane now. She'd expected frustration, even anger on the other woman's face, but there was only concern. "I did find him. And he...he found *me* out, just as you predicted, so you ought to crow about that."

Jane staggered back and fell into the chair she had departed upon Esme's entry into the room. "I wouldn't crow about you being in danger, I hope you know me better than that. Sit down and tell me everything so that I know what we're facing."

"We?" Esme repeated as she took the chair across from Jane.

"Of course *we*, you dolt," Jane said. "I didn't save you just to sacrifice you at the first hint of some toff's wrath."

Esme's eyes filled with tears at the support from her friend. "Oh, I adore you."

"Of course you do," Jane said with a smile. "Now tell me."

So Esme did. She unburdened herself of everything that had

happened from the moment she entered the Donville Masquerade to when she'd taken Finn to the back room. She told her about giving him her name and her body and her pleasure. And then she told her the rest. The pain. The unmasking and his driving need to find out each and every secret she'd attempted to keep for two years.

When it was over, Jane was curiously quiet as she strummed her fingers together. "He sounds an interesting fop, at least."

"He is." Esme gave a humorless laugh. "Far too intelligent for his own good."

"And driven," Jane added. "He sounds like a driven one. Rather like you, I suppose."

"I wasn't driven enough if I couldn't even protect myself from being unmasked." Esme got up and paced the room. "I folded under his questions like I was just arrived in the hells."

"Which makes me wonder if you…"

"If I what?" Esme asked, facing her when her friend trailed off.

"If you…if you *wanted* him to know," Jane said softly.

"What?" Esme took a long step toward her. "No! Why would I want him to know? Why would I risk everything like that?"

"Because this life is hard. We pretend it's fine, and it often is. But it's not easy. And he gave you a glimpse at the comfortable life you once had. Perhaps part of you wanted him to know because he might be able to save you. To bring you back to what you once had."

"After what I've done the last two years?" Esme said. "There's no going back. Not ever. Those at the top wouldn't allow that kind of pollution." She scrubbed a hand over her face.

Jane pursed her lips. "Yes. There's a reason the French built guillotines, isn't there?"

That made Esme smile a little, for it was a statement they often made when they encountered the entitled. But the smile fell as she thought again at Finn's focused concern. "He won't stop. He cared for my father, so he won't stop."

"Then what's the worst-case scenario? What do you need to protect yourself from?"

She sighed. "He'll go to my cousin."

Jane flinched. "A very worst-case scenario, indeed, since that bastard is a true threat. What do you do about that?"

Esme thought of that. In the backroom, with their clothes still akimbo from passion and Finn's dark eyes boring into hers with shock and horror and desire all mixed, she hadn't been able to think straight. She'd run because that was her nature now. But with distance, with Finn no longer in the room making everything upside down with his presence and his heat and his focus, she could truly analyze the situation.

"I-I suppose the best thing to do is to find Finn before he finds me, or goes to my cousin," she reasoned slowly. "I need to make sure he understands that Francis is *not* my savior." She shivered. "Even though that will require further confession. Further revelation of my soul."

The very idea was terrifying. But what other choice did she have now?

Jane took a long, deep breath. "Under any other circumstances I'd tell you to stay far away from this man."

"You already did," Esme muttered.

"Yes, I'll say I told you so some other time. But in this case, I think what you've suggested in the best option. Do you want me to come with you?"

There was something comforting about the idea that Jane would be there, an angel on her shoulder keeping her from making further mistakes. But then again, being alone with Finn again did have its advantages. And if she couldn't convince him to her side in one way, perhaps she could use another. She certainly knew he wasn't immune to her physical charms. Nor she to his.

"No," she said softly. "I'll handle it."

Jane reached out and covered her hand gently. "Whatever happens next, I'm here."

"I don't deserve you," Esme whispered.

"Of course you don't, no one does!" Jane said playfully. "Now, do you want to know about the next chapter in our book?"

Esme smiled. Jane was trying to make things well for her and she appreciated it so deeply. She settled back and closed her eyes. "Tell me everything."

She just hoped she wouldn't have to tell Finn everything when she went to him. That she could protect some slender part of herself so he wouldn't have seen all of her and make her entirely vulnerable.

CHAPTER 8

Finn clenched his jaw as he scribbled a letter. He hadn't slept since last night when he'd departed the Donville Masquerade, his mind still reeling from all he knew, and all he didn't know, about Esme.

The name really did fit her better than Charlotte. Rolled off the tongue just like her pleasure when he tasted her.

"Bollocks," he muttered as he gripped the quill tighter and tried to focus on the words swimming before him. This was important, it had to do with his sister's upcoming nuptials, and he owed it to her to give it his full attention.

There was a light rap at his door and he looked up, uncertain whether to be relieved by the interruption or irritated by it.

"What is it, Bentley?" he said as his butler opened the door just wide enough to peer in.

"You have a caller, my lord."

Finn wrinkled his brow. It was after supper—he expected no guests. But perhaps it had to do with Marianne's engagement. Now that word was spreading, there had been much to do, as well as much to discuss with both well-wishers and the gossips looking for a reason that Ramsbury would marry a wallflower like Marianne.

He pursed his lips at the thought that he would have to defend his sister again. "Who is it?"

"A Miss Esme Crawford, my lord."

Finn stared at him a moment, trying to digest those words. Trying to come to terms with the fact that a woman he'd made love to, then watched walk away and assumed it would be forever, was now awaiting the answer to whether or not he would receive her.

"Show her here," he said, and noted how his voice cracked. "And do not worry yourself about anything else tonight."

Bentley inclined his head slightly and then disappeared out of the room. Finn set his quill aside and stood, smoothing his waistcoat. He'd removed his jacket long ago and rolled up his sleeves as he worked, and now he wondered if he should put himself back together, replace his armor so he wouldn't be quite so undone when he encountered Esme again.

But there was no time. Bentley reappeared and said, "Miss Crawford, my lord."

He stepped away and Esme took just one step into the chamber. Finn caught his breath. He'd never seen her without her mask save for the previous night, when he'd discovered her identity. They had both been naked then, vulnerable in a variety of ways.

Today, though, he could truly soak in her beauty. She had a slender face with high cheekbones and fine brows. She had pulled her dark red hair up in a loose coil of sleek ringlets and waves. Her lips were full and he couldn't help but recall how they had felt pressed to his own or latched around his cock. Her eyes were a dark green and were still rimmed with the faintest remnants of the bruise he had first seen under her mask the night they'd first encountered each other.

"You may close the door, Bentley," he said softly, without taking his eyes off of her.

The butler did so and they were alone in the room that suddenly felt small and close. She swallowed hard and then there was a coolness that entered her stare. The walls this woman put up to protect herself.

"I've never been to your home," she said softly.

He cocked his head. "No, I suppose not. Though your father was here several times over the years."

She flinched ever so slightly. "Your relationship with him was entirely separate from mine."

"Why Crawford?" he asked.

"What do you mean?"

"Your father's family surname was Portsmith."

She arched one of those finely shaped brows. "I wouldn't be hiding very well if I were to use his surname, would I? My grandmother's maiden name on my mother's side was Crawford. Far enough back not to be immediately recognized. Close enough that I could recall it if someone referred to me thus when I began."

He nodded. "Clever. But I'd expect nothing less."

She drew a little breath and pink entered her cheeks. She'd blushed the same way when he made her come.

"Would you like a drink?" he asked, and moved around the desk to the sideboard. He felt her watching him as he did so, felt her tracking his every step, and he couldn't help but be as aroused as he was confused by that.

"No," she said softly. "I'll keep my head, I think."

He glanced back at her. "Very well." He poured himself a whisky and then faced her, leaning back on the sideboard with what he hoped was perceived as bored indifference. "I'm surprised you're here, after the way you stormed out of the Donville Masquerade last night and told me not to pry into your life."

For a moment, there was a flash of emotion she couldn't wipe away from her eyes. It was fear. Finn saw it and recognized it and it troubled him. But then she lowered her lashes and said, "My lord—"

"Finn," he corrected softly.

She drew a shallow breath and forced her gaze back up. "*Finn*, I hadn't intended to see you again, if I'm honest."

He fought not to react even though his chest tightened painfully with that thought. He took a slow sip of his drink and then said, "What changed your mind?"

She worried her hands before her. "Self-preservation, I suppose." He frowned at the idea that she thought she had to protect herself from him, even as she continued, "I-I never would have revealed my true identity to you on purpose. I shouldn't have danced so close to the flame when I was aware it could unmask me. I should have stayed away from you, I knew better."

He pressed his lips together at the idea that she would have rather avoided him than share the dance they'd been dancing since their first encounter at the Donville Masquerade. Rather kept away than experienced the night of passion that had been haunting him for nearly twenty-four hours.

"Then why did you?" he asked.

She didn't answer that, but kept on speaking as if he hadn't said anything. "I fear that you are the kind of man who is driven to try to help, even when he is actually hurting."

He wrinkled his brow. "And what does that mean?"

Only he knew what it meant. He had tried to manage his sister over the years and sometimes had done more harm than good. Same thing with his friends. How could she see that character flaw so easily?

"Are you going to try to go to my family and involve them in some kind of attempt to save me?" She met his eyes unsteadily and the fear she had controlled was back again. Stronger.

He blinked. "I-I must be honest that I hadn't thought that far ahead. I'm still trying to come to terms with who you are and what I now know. But it isn't the worst idea, is it? Your family must be beside themselves with worry after your absence these last two years. Whatever separated you, couldn't you overcome it and return to the safety of their embrace, rather than stay on the street where you must endure some suffering?"

Her nostrils flared slightly and her fingers clenched into trembling fists at her sides. "You know nothing of suffering, my lord. Nothing of the truth."

Her voice quavered as she said it and he took a long step toward her in the face of her distress. "You owe me nothing," he began. "But I wish you would tell me. Make me understand how all this came to be and why you are so adamant about your position."

She let out a long sigh and a weariness came over her expression, like the weight of the world had settled onto her shoulders. "Fine," she said, her voice very soft. "If cutting myself open is the only way to get what I need, then I shall."

She paced toward him with long, sure steps and he straightened up as she came to a stop before him. She slipped the whisky from his fingers and took a long sip. The intimacy of her lips being pressed where his had been a moment before wasn't lost on him.

She set the drink aside and looked up into him, those green eyes unreadable beyond their exquisite beauty. "Do you know how my father died?"

He flinched at the pain that question created. "It was...it was a sudden illness, wasn't it?"

"That is what they say, but I don't believe them." She struggled for a moment before she continued, "I believe he was murdered."

~

There, it was out. The words Esme tried not to repeat any more often than she must hung in the air between them and from Finn's expression, he was as shocked and horrified by what she'd said as she was to know it.

And now she would take a true measure of him. Would he call her silly? Deny the possibility? Dismiss her? Or would he be more? She found herself wishing for the latter.

"Why do you believe that?" he said at last, his voice thick with emotion.

She stepped away from him. It was impossible to say these

things when he was so close. "You knew my father—in some ways I think you knew him even better than I did. Because of that, you know as well as I do that he was healthy. He hadn't been ill, but suddenly he was stricken and then almost immediately dead."

Finn nodded. "Shocking, yes. But not unheard of. He was in his sixties, after all."

She pursed her lips. "I'm not a fool. I know that someone can be taken without warning. But it was such a violent illness. So…" She trailed off as she tried not to think of the horror of her father's last days. He'd vomited blood, he'd writhed in pain. It had been horrific.

"I'm sorry," Finn said softly, and his hand came out to catch hers. She watched as their fingers intertwined and was shocked at the warmth that spread through her with the touch. The peace.

She tugged her hand away. This man could not be her peace. No man could be, it was simply too dangerous.

"My cousin inherited. Francis and I had never had a close relationship, but once he moved into the estate just a few days after my father's death, it was like he became a different person. Whatever veneer of civility he'd shown to me came off without my father around to protect me."

Finn frowned. "What did he do?"

"He was incredibly abusive to the staff, he made demands that all remnants of my father be immediately destroyed or packed away. He removed my pin money and held over my head the fact that he would be in charge of my inheritance until I married. And if he drank he would…he would say things about my father."

She could see Finn digesting all this, increasing concern lining his handsome face. She had hoped she'd never have to tell him any of it, but she found it was actually a relief to do so. To say these words out loud to a person who was from the world she had grown up in. A person who understood its ins and outs in a way Jane or Campbell Ripley couldn't, even though they were her saviors and dearest friends.

"I met your cousin several times over the years," Finn said at last.

"I admit I never liked him. But you're implying that he killed your father, yes?"

She nodded. "I believe it with all my heart."

"But I don't understand why," he said gently.

She threw up her hands. "He would say my father's death was not worthy of grief. He would laugh when people referenced his illness. And once, deep in his cups, he held up a bottle of brandy in my father's study and told me it was my father's favorite, but that he would never drink of it. He smiled with such cruelty, such violence that I wondered then if he had...he had..."

"Poisoned it," Finn whispered. "That is troubling, but—"

"Please don't say but," she interrupted. "I'm not asking you to believe me. I explain all this to you without any thought that you would do anything about it, except understand why I cannot and will not ever go back to my family. To my cousin."

Finn let out his breath in a long exhale. "I understand, Esme. I hear you. If you believe this, if it very well might be true, there is no way you *could* go back. And I understand why you would leave everything behind." He hesitated. "Was the...was the story you told me before I knew your identity the truth?"

She flinched and stepped away. "Yes. I left and I became a lightskirt for a time, then a pugilist. Does that trouble you more now that you know I was born a lady? Because I'm not ashamed of what I did to survive."

His brow wrinkled and he stepped toward her. He touched her cheek, his fingers splaying out with the most exquisite gentleness as he stared down into her eyes. "Nor should you be. I admire you just as much now as I did when you first told me. And I grieve just as much that you were forced into such a difficult position in the first place."

Her breath hitched as she stared into the brown depths of his gaze. His kindness was like a balm on her battered soul and that was so utterly bewitching, but it was also dangerous. And yet she still couldn't step away from him. Not when he was so damned handsome, not when she wanted him as much as she had the night before. And he wanted her—she could see it in his eyes. Truly her, not some masked temptress that he enjoyed chasing.

"So you won't tell him?" she asked.

He shook his head. "No. Never."

There was such a firmness to the way he said those words. A solid truth that she found faith in when her world had contained little of it for the last two years.

He was still stroking her cheek and she leaned into his fingers and smiled at him. Then she lifted up on her tiptoes, wound her arms around his neck and drew him to her. He took a short breath before their lips met. It was gentle at first, almost exploratory despite the pleasures they had shared the night before. But when she parted her lips, when she sighed into him, his arms came more tightly around her, he made a low groan from deep in his throat and he claimed her.

She lifted into him, tasting him, drowning in him, trying to get closer to him even when all the layers of clothing and propriety separated them. When one of his hands came into her hair, his fingers bunching against her scalp, she tilted her head and the kiss deepened further. Everything else spiraled away, leaving only desire, leaving only need and want and the tingling of pleasure through every nerve ending.

He pulled away slightly, staring down at her with wide eyes that almost looked like they were filled with disbelief. "Esme," he whispered.

She nodded, answering a question he hadn't asked but she saw nonetheless. "Yes, Finn. Yes, yes, yes. Take me upstairs, please just take me upstairs and let's forget everything but pleasure."

CHAPTER 9

Finn's head was spinning as he stared down into Esme's gorgeous face. She wanted him. And God knew he wanted her, even if some gentlemanly part of him was telling him this was now wrong because of where she'd started in life. Unfair, he realized. She had no less value no matter where she had begun, nor deserved any less from him.

"Please," she repeated, her voice shaky.

He swallowed hard and then bent his head to kiss her again. God, she was sweet and he wasn't strong enough to resist her. So he wouldn't. He would give them both what they craved and decide what to do next afterward.

He somehow managed to pull back a second time and caught her hand. Her fingers laced through his, almost like they were made to fit, and she smiled at him. He drew her through the chamber, through the door, up the stairs. His thumb stroked the top of her hand relentlessly even as they moved through his dim hall and toward the set of double doors at the end. He couldn't stop touching her, he needed it just as he needed breath in that charged moment.

When they reached the door to his chamber, he paused, trying to find some control again. He faced her and said, "You owe me nothing. I want this to be for your pleasure, not out of fear or repayment or anything else."

She pressed her hand to his chest and he knew she could feel his heart pounding there through his waistcoat and linen shirt. "I do this because I want to, Finn. Just as I did last night. I do this because whatever this heat is between us is irresistible."

He nodded and pushed the door open, revealing the antechamber within. He heard her soft intake of breath as she entered the room, bright from lamps and the glowing fire. It was a fine chamber he and Marianne had worked hard on over the years since he inherited. They had slowly transformed it from the austere coldness of their father's taste to the warmer, more inviting one of his own.

Esme glanced at him. "It's lovely. But I want a bed, my lord. Is it that door?"

She pointed to the door by the fire and he nodded. She walked away without another word and he was shocked that as she did so, she shed her gown, leaving her naked beneath just as she had been at the Donville Masquerade.

"Don't make me wait," she tossed back over her shoulder without looking as she disappeared into his bedroom.

He didn't have to be asked twice. He rushed after her, unbuttoning his waistcoat as he did so. He entered his bedroom and stopped to stare at her climbing up onto his bed, settling back on his pillows. She looked like she belonged there and he wanted to keep her just where she was for days, weeks, months, doing what he was about to do over and over until neither of them could recall a life outside these walls.

"Are you going to stare all night, or join me, my lord?" she asked. "Because I can start without you if you need a moment."

She snaked a hand down her body and settled it between her legs, opening them wider so he could see her stroke her sex.

"Bloody hell, Esme," he grunted, and crossed the room in a few long steps. He covered her with his body, loving how her naked curves rose up beneath him, and claimed her lips, this time with more force and passion.

She made a little cry of pleasure and wrapped her arms around him, meeting his tongue stroke for stroke, her nails raking against his shoulders through the fine linen of his shirt. He rocked against her, his body out of control in the pleasure any touch created. Even through his clothes, she made him ache, made him throb for her.

She leaned away and smiled up at him, wicked and knowing. "I think you need to be less clothed."

He nodded. "Very much so, yes. Why don't you start again while I do that?"

He caught her hand and pushed it back down between her legs, letting his own fingers sweep against her and feel her wet heat. She shivered and arched just a little, then parted her folds while he stepped away.

He didn't know how long it took to undress. It felt like far too long as he watched her grind her hand against herself, lifting to her teasing touch while all the while she held his gaze. He only broke that stare when he tugged his shirt over his head. She sat up a little then, her fingers working faster and her breath coming quicker.

Good, at least they were both half mad with this physical connection. He wasn't alone with it.

"You are beautiful," she whimpered.

He smiled. "Beautiful? I thought you said I was pretty before."

She nodded and her fingers increased their speed against her body. Her breath was short as she said, "Pretty is too diminutive. You're built like a god. Like a statue." She arched her back then and moaned, her body shaking as she came.

He swore and all but tore his trousers off. He moved to her in a few long steps and pushed her hands aside, sliding his cock deep in her clenching body, feeling her pulse with release around him as he began to stroke slow and steady.

She dug her nails into his shoulders, her cries of pleasure becoming louder until he caught them with his lips and devoured them like the sweetest dessert. She was unmanning him almost immediately, making his balls tighten with pleasure, his body ache with a driving need to release. He had to control that, control this. Make it last.

So he withdrew as her flutters faded and she relaxed against the pillows with a shuddering sigh. He slid down between her legs, cupping her hips as he buried his mouth against her slick sex. He lapped at the salty-sweet evidence of her pleasure, swirling his tongue across every inch of her slit and loving how she gasped and moaned and twisted beneath him.

He held her steady, building the pressure, the focus of his tongue until she stiffened again and the rush of pleasure coated his lips and chin. He lifted her more firmly to his lips, sucking her clitoris as she dug her fingers into his hair, pulling him closer, pushing him away, releasing a torrent of mindless, senseless moans and cries.

"Please," she gasped at last. "Mercy."

He lifted his eyes to hers with a smile, licked her one last time and then said, "Giving up the fight already, Esme?"

She nodded and curled her finger to bring him to her. "Sometimes one must know when they're bested."

He felt intensely smug as he came to her, covering her, kissing her so she tasted herself on his lips. They kissed for what felt like a lifetime and he relaxed against her to enjoy every moment.

So he wasn't prepared when she hooked a leg over his, threw her body weight and flipped him onto his back so she could straddle him.

"And sometimes," she whispered, her expression wicked as she aligned his hard cock to her body, "One needs to know how to take their opponent off guard and obtain the upper hand in the battle. Like this."

And then she took him inside in one long, slick stroke.

The feel of Finn's body stretching and filling her own was just as powerful this time as it had been before. More so, perhaps because she was in charge now. He was hers, pinned beneath her clenched thighs. The fact that he could easily take back control didn't really matter. He didn't seem to be in any rush to do so.

"Am I your opponent?" he grunted, his eyes fluttering shut as she began to grind against him in circles meant to torment them both.

She nodded. "There is always an opponent."

"Hmmm." Those gorgeous dark brown eyes snagged hers and held. "Then how does one…oh God, Esme…how does one win this fight?"

The way his breath hitched and his words came with difficulty only served to arouse her more and more. This man was powerful and in control and she was breaking him. Making his veins in his neck strain, making his face darken with pleasure and the exertion of trying to withhold his release as long as possible. She wanted it. She wanted him dripping down her skin, tattooing her with his pleasure.

"It doesn't matter," she whispered as she put one hand on each shoulder and leaned in closer to just brush his lips with hers. "Because I'm going to make you come, Finn. I'm going to win."

"Sounds like I win, as well," he said before he cupped the back of her head and drew her in for a deeper kiss.

She drowned in it and him, her body clenching around his even tighter. She was already on edge, her body needy from two orgasms that had almost altered her orbit they were so powerful. Had any other man in her experience ever done that?

It didn't matter. She wouldn't think about that. She didn't want to think at all and shoved it all aside to focus just on the pleasure, on the taste of him, on the warmth of his arms as they came around her and held her.

She was losing control all over again, the pleasure building deliciously between her legs at the spot where she ground against him. He lifted to her, matching her rhythm, pulling her to the edge. He seemed to sense when she was there, for he sat up, adjusting her into his lap, and latched his mouth onto her nipple. The sweep of his tongue over that sensitive tip was enough to send her to the stars all over again. She rocked against him, their hips colliding as the waves of pleasure rose and rose, never-ending, like the pleasure could be hers to ride forever.

But at last it eased, faded, and she collapsed against his shoulder, breathing as hard as she did after a difficult fight. He kissed her damp neck, whispering, "Such a good girl." Those words made her clench all over again and he laughed into her flesh. "I'll remember that. But right now, I think it's time for me to lose this fight. Or win it. I still don't fully understand the rules."

He shifted her onto her back and rose up over her, all without withdrawing from her wet sheath. He lifted one leg to balance on his shoulder, kissing her calf, and then he began to take her hard and fast. She shoved a hand between her legs, stroking herself as she watched in fascination as he went from man in control to something closer to beast. Oh yes, she wanted that beast. Wanted to feel the shift of him as his pleasure mounted, to hear his moans and gasps as she squeezed herself in time to his thrusts.

At last he cried out her name and then withdrew. He acted as if he would pump away from her, but she caught him, tangling her fingers in his and directed him so that his release splashed onto her legs, her stomach, one final proof that she had bested him. Although he was correct that they had both won here. A strange idea, really.

He collapsed over her, kissing her, stroking his hands over her. For a while, she let him, relaxing into the gentle strength of him, the soothing sensations of him holding her. Her body still tingled with the remnants of pleasure and what she wanted, more than anything, was to stay like this. In his arms and in his bed, for as long as he would allow it.

She opened her eyes and stared up, over his bare shoulder, at the wispy canopy draped over the big bed. This was exactly what she needed to avoid. She no longer belonged in this world. Playing at its edges was far too dangerous. She had what she'd come for, after all. Finn had promised not to speak to her cousin or anyone else about her whereabouts.

"Stay," he murmured against her neck, his lips brushing her skin as he spoke.

She shivered at the touch. This temptation was against everything she'd built. Everything she was now. But she found herself nodding.

"For a while," she whispered in return, and when he shifted a little over her, pressing his body against hers with the promise of pleasure still to come, she smiled.

What could a little while longer hurt?

CHAPTER 10

Finn lay on his side hours later, watching Esme sleep. The light from the dying fire spread a soft glow across her skin and he traced the shaft of it with his fingertips. They had made love until exhaustion had taken her, and normally he might crow about his prowess in this moment.

Only that exhaustion seemed to have at least something to do with what she'd confessed to him in the last twenty-four hours. Everything to do with the fact that she'd been running, she believed for her life, since her father's death.

He frowned at the thought. While what Esme had told him about her cousin and his behavior since the marquess's death was deeply troubling, he wasn't certain it amounted to murder. The very idea of it was shocking. Heartbreaking. Enraging.

Chilton had been the best of men. If someone had snuffed out his life, he hadn't deserved it. But whoever had done it did deserve the harsh hand of justice to slam down on him and make sure he paid.

Esme let out a little sigh and turned toward him. She opened her eyes and looked up at him, her expression softened by sleep. "What are you thinking about?" she whispered.

"How gorgeous you are in firelight," he said before he leaned in and kissed her.

She returned the caress, cupping his cheek with her hand and letting out a shuddering sigh of pleasure. But when she pulled back, she looked undeterred. "That's a sweet thing to say, but it's also a half truth."

He arched a brow. "And you can read me so well?"

She was quiet for a moment and caught the hand he had been tracing along her skin. They both watched as she folded her fingers around his. "Over the years I've learned to read men as much as possible."

He frowned at the reasons why she'd had to make such a study. Frowned at the idea that she'd ever been unsafe out in the world. Her cousin definitely deserved to pay for that.

"I was thinking that your cousin shouldn't be allowed to get away with murder, if he did indeed commit one. Nor should he get away with dislodging your life."

She glanced up at him. "But he did. And he will. People like him always do."

"Unless," he began, and then cut himself off.

She sat up a little. "Unless what, Finn?"

"Unless someone like him decides to intervene."

Now she sat fully up and inched away from him on the bed. He frowned at the loss of her touch and the way that her expression went guarded. "What are you saying?"

"I could investigate," he said. "I could push. I could find out the truth."

∽

It felt like an ice-cold hand had pushed into Esme's chest, wrapped around her heart and was now squeezing. She gasped for breath even as she tugged the coverlet up around herself.

"What happened to your promise that you would never speak to my cousin about me?" she snapped.

"I would *never* bring you up, Esme. I'm not talking about confronting him or revealing you. I said I wouldn't and I won't."

The edge of her fear faded a little as she stared into his eyes. As she'd told him before, she had learned to study men for their genuine character, to guard herself against attacks. But Finn looked earnest in his suggestion.

She felt a flare of hope she hadn't allowed herself in years. One she hated. Hope only caused disappointment in the long run. She couldn't let a pretty face convince her otherwise.

She folded her arms. "What do you think you could do exactly?"

"Insert myself. Everyone knows I was close to your father. If I asked questions about him, that wouldn't be unexpected."

"It would also be potentially dangerous if I'm right about my cousin's murderous heart," Esme said. "Why would you bother?"

He tilted his head, and for a moment it felt like he could see right through her. "Because I cared for your father."

She was surprised how that statement stung. It was foolish that it did. She and Finn barely knew each other and all they had shared was two nights of passion. Amazing passion, yes, but nothing that should make her wish that he thought of her in his plans for her cousin, not just her father.

"Well, my father adored you," she said, and ducked her head. "You were his favorite."

Finn slipped a finger beneath her chin and tilted her face toward his. "Yes, we were close, but in this case your remarkable ability to read others has not served you. I most definitely wasn't his favorite. During our talks, he would go on and on about you, Esme. He adored *you.*"

She hated that memories flooded her, along with tears that stung her eyes. She tried so hard not to think of her father because it hurt so much. But now she could almost see his smile, smell his tobacco, hear him laughing at some story she told him over breakfast.

THE HELLION'S SECRET

"Well," she gasped out. "Perhaps he did at that."

Finn took her hand. "I want to know the truth, too."

She nodded slowly. Of course he would. She'd opened a Pandora's box when it came to the demise of her father. Of course a man who'd cared for him wouldn't be able to simply close it and walk away. Why hadn't she anticipated that?

"I suppose," she said slowly. "That after more than two years, my cousin must believe he got away with whatever he did. I'm gone, no longer a bother and a reminder. No one has arrested him or even investigated him."

"He could have his guard down," Finn said. "My thought exactly."

She worried her lip. He wasn't wrong about that. "I don't know," she whispered.

She expected him to argue, or even to tell her he didn't care about her opinion. After all, he could do whatever he liked. He didn't need her permission. But instead, he just nodded.

"It's been an emotional few days for you," he said. "I understand why it would be difficult to make a decision about something that's brought you so much pain. Think about it. And when you're ready to discuss it again, send me word."

Her brow wrinkled. "You...you won't do anything until I say?"

"No. I wouldn't do that." He leaned toward her. "I think you'll find that I'm actually not as much an arse as I pretend to be. Though don't tell. I wouldn't want to ruin my reputation."

She found herself laughing. "Not after all these years building it up, I understand." She sighed. "Yes. I'll think about what you suggested. And now I should go."

He lifted her hand to his lips and she shivered at the warmth of his breath on her skin. What this man did to her. "You're certain I couldn't convince you otherwise?"

She shook her head. "I'm sure you could. But it's for the best if I take some time by myself, I think."

"I understand." He moved for the door. "I'll arrange one of my unmarked carriages to take you home. Take your time dressing."

He pulled a robe on to cover all those lovely grooves and valleys of his remarkable body, then exited into the antechamber where she assumed he would ring for servants. She stared up at the canopy of the bed again with all its rich fabric and expertly carved wood. Even the bed was from a different class than she was now.

And yet this man wanted to help her. Help himself, too, of course. But he wasn't forcing anything. All he did was give. Orgasms, a listening ear…an offer to punish the man who had stolen her world, her life, her father.

It was a bewitching thought that such a man existed.

Slowly she got out of the comfortable bed, stretching muscles that ached from wicked use over and over that long night. She found her gown near the doorway and wrapped it over herself, tying and buttoning the little hidden places where the dress came together and could be removed easily. One of the benefits of being Esme and not Lady Charlotte anymore. Lady Charlotte's gowns had not been something she could put on or take off herself. God, she hardly remembered Lady Charlotte anymore. That part of her had begun to die the same night as her father and been buried when she ran away.

She blinked at unexpected tears and went to the mirror to fix her hair as best she could when half her pins had disappeared to heavens knew where. When she felt at least somewhat presentable she took a deep breath and moved for the chamber door and the antechamber within.

Finn wasn't there so she took a moment to look around as she hadn't when she'd needed him more than she needed information. It really was a lovely room, filled with the personality of its owner. She smiled at the landscape painting she instantly recognized as an Ezra Pembroke piece. Did Finn know what else the man painted? Wicked, erotic portraits?

Actually, he likely did. Finn was no monk, that was certain. Though the number of books stacked beside a comfortable chair by the fire did imply he was also not just a libertine. She moved to them and looked at their spines. There were some histories of different parts of the empire, a collection of Shakespeare's sonnets and, most shockingly, a copy of *The Castle of Wolfenbach*, a wonderful, horrid Gothic novel she had adored as a girl.

She left the books and was drawn to the mantel, where a few miniatures were perched. She couldn't help but smile, for they were all of Finn's sister, Marianne. One from when she was a very little girl, another she looked to be around thirteen or fourteen and a more recent one. Esme had come out two years before Marianne, and Finn's sister had an unfortunate first few years after her debut, so they hadn't known each other well. But she'd always liked the bookish wallflower. She was kind, and Esme appreciated that now more than she probably had during her years in ballrooms and drawing rooms.

There was a light knock at the antechamber door and she turned toward it in surprise. "Yes?"

The door opened and Finn stepped in. He paused in the doorway and leaned on the jamb, his gaze flickering up and down her body. She warmed at the focus of his stare, the desire in it. Good Lord, but it was out of control to want someone so much. To be wanted in equal measure.

"You—you didn't have to knock. This is your room and you've seen me naked multiple times."

He chuckled as he entered, at last. "And I hope to do it again in the future. But that doesn't mean you surrender your right to privacy as you prepare yourself."

She shook her head. There were few men who understood that consent was something forever asked for and given. Fewer still in the class this man belonged to.

She motioned to the mantel. "I love these portraits of your sister."

He stepped closer. "Yes. I suppose I'll have a new one to add to the collection, as I'm sure she and Sebastian will pose for one after their wedding in ten days."

"That wedding helped you uncover my true identity," she teased.

He smiled down at her. "Your attempt to comfort me about my sister did that, my dear." He sighed. "I worry about her, but…"

"But?" she pressed.

He shrugged. "She and Ramsbury declare they are happy and in love."

"Do you not believe it to be true?"

He stared at Marianne's most recent portrait a moment, an expression of sadness in his eyes. "Sometimes I believe it. I see their connection now that my blinders have been torn off, certainly, and not just the physical. But love? I'm not certain I'd recognize it if it were there. I have not much experience with the emotion."

She shifted. He knew so much about her father, but she knew so little about his. Only what rumor had told her years ago. But rumor was so often wrong.

"Your parents weren't a love match, then?" she asked gently.

He stiffened and didn't look at her. "Very much not. My mother longed for it, though. Chased it. Rode every wave of that man's attention and crashed on the rocks when he withdrew. She was obsessed with how she could force him to see her. She had a breakdown right before my sister came out and died shortly after."

"Oh yes, I recall that. Your poor sister, not only losing her mother but having her coming out so tied to such a tragedy."

He nodded. "There were so many rumors about how our mother died, that was all people saw when they looked at her."

"How did your father take it, after all those years of dangling her on a string?"

He laughed but there was no humor to the broken sound. "My father was annoyed she'd ruined his night out with his mistress."

He trailed off and she couldn't help it. She reached out and took his hand, cupping it between hers as she stared up at him. He finally looked down at her and in that moment, in the soft firelight, he looked lost. How she wanted to find him, even if that was the most dangerous desire she'd ever experienced.

She released him and backed away. "I assume your carriage is ready for me?"

He cleared his throat. "Yes. All you need do is give my man your direction and he'll take you. If you're ready, I'll escort you down."

He held out an arm and she almost laughed. It was all so proper after a highly improper night together. But she took the arm, loving the shape of his muscular bicep beneath the silky fabric of the dressing gown he wore. Together they walked through the halls and down the stairs into the foyer. She braced to encounter his butler again, be stared at and sniffed at by someone who knew what she was.

But there was no one. It was just them. Finn stopped and turned toward her, cupping her cheeks gently. "This night was wonderful, Esme."

She nodded. "Yes."

He bent his head and his lips brushed hers, gentle at first, but slowly it transformed, becoming heated. It made her want to forget her promise to leave. It made her want to shove him down on the hard marble floor and feel him surrender to her, feel herself surrender to him, all over again.

So she stepped away, lips burning and breath short. "Goodnight, Finn."

"Goodnight," he said softly and then reached back to open the door.

She slipped out to the carriage that was waiting for her there and briefly gave her direction to the driver who held the door for her. She gave one last glance to Finn, watching her from the doorway, and then got in. The carriage began to move and only then did she flop back against the seat and draw a deep, full breath at last. The man seemed to keep her from doing that when she spent any time around him.

He had unmasked her in every way now. She had allowed it. But instead of offering censure, he offered protection. He offered assistance. She would have a great deal to consider now, a great many decisions to make.

And not all of them were about the investigation of her father's death. Because when she thought of Finn, it wasn't just of his offer to investigate her cousin. He made her think of passionate kisses, warm arms, pleasure and…and a future she had surrendered long ago. One she couldn't allow to come creeping into her thoughts and ruin the life she had now. It wasn't real.

Somehow she had to recall that.

CHAPTER 11

Esme had never been one to avoid a problem. It hadn't been a luxury she could have for many years. If she didn't face things head on, she could be put in a dangerous position. And yet, two days after her last conversation with Finn, she still hadn't been able to make herself think too hard about his offer to help her.

His offer to reopen a wound she'd tried to let heal on its own, despite the pain.

She shook her head and stood up from the settee where she had been trying to read and went into her room down the hall. She crouched down and pulled a small box from beneath the bed, then sat down on the rug, her back against the bedpost and sighed as she stared at it. It was a plain thing, something she'd bought for a few shillings on a whim. She opened it and stared at the items inside.

There was a swatch of cloth, rich and green that matched her eyes. It was from the gown she'd been wearing the night she'd fled her home, feeling the danger of her cousin's intent at her heels with every uncertain step. It had been torn and dirtied, eventually repaired. Then made over again and again until it was so worn out that there was no use trying to fix it anymore. She had enough other gowns by then, paid for by her own labor. And yet she'd kept one swatch of the worn fabric.

She removed it and fingered what was left of the fine silk. It made her think of Finn's dressing gown when she'd last seen him. Made her think of silk moving across flesh in the dark.

She swallowed and carefully unfolded the material to find the real treasures she kept safely within. There was a miniature of her father and an old enamel pendant that had belonged to her mother. The pearls that outlined the simple blue circle were worth something, but she'd never sold them even in her darkest hour as she tried to cling to what little she had left.

She picked up the miniature of her father and stared at it. It had been painted when she was very young, when her mother was still alive. His hair had still been dark, a little too long, curling around his forehead. His long nose had a little crookedness to it and she smiled at the imperfection he had always hated but she had loved for its uniqueness. His green eyes were the same as hers and were bright as he stared out at the artist with a warmth to his expression that was usually reserved for his family. Had he been looking at her mother at that moment? Or her, held in the arms of some friend or family member?

She gasped as a tear splashed onto her hand. When she reached up she felt dampness on both cheeks.

"Oh, dearest."

She glanced up to find Jane in her doorway. Her friend came across the room and promptly sat down on the floor beside her to put her arm around her. They sat like that for a moment, both staring at her father's small portrait.

"He was a handsome devil," Jane said at last.

Esme laughed. "He was. Lordy, but I miss him. It's so silly, I'm not the first woman to lose a father and I certainly won't be the last but—"

"You needn't minimize the pain," Jane said. "I didn't know my father at all and am probably better for it. But that doesn't mean you shouldn't mourn yours out of penance."

"I suppose." Esme turned her father's portrait over in her lap so she wouldn't have to look at his face for a moment. She drew a few breaths. "I've been thinking about what to do regarding Finn's offer."

Jane nodded slowly. Esme had told her friend all about everything the moment she got home. Jane had, surprisingly, not offered much advice. And now Esme needed it.

"What do you think I should do?"

"You know how I feel about your endangering yourself when it comes to that bastard cousin of yours. But…" Jane took a long, unsteady breath. "I think you ought to let the earl investigate."

Esme jerked her face toward her friend. "What? Why?"

"Because I've watched you rolling this over in your head for two days and you had the same lost expression you did when I found you. Because you've never gotten justice and if there's a chance of it in this world, you shouldn't walk away from it." Jane reached down and turned the portrait of Esme's father over again. "You should because maybe you could go home."

"This is my home," Esme said. "I already told you that no one in Society would ever accept me back."

"Perhaps not, but I would wager if this is resolved, if your horrible cousin is hung or transported and the next in line takes over, that you'll get at least a settlement. Even if it's just to cover up what was found. You could be set for life. You wouldn't have to do…" Jane waved a hand around the small room. "*This.* Or get black eyes for a living. Or lie on your back for it."

Esme rested her head back against the post and stared out at nothing as those words worked through her. "I suppose there is some part of me that wouldn't mind more stability. Though I don't hate this little home we share, even though the front window leaks air. I certainly don't hate what I do. I'm good at it. It's satisfying to know I can fight my way, quite literally, to freedom."

"But I like your face, Esme," Jane said with a laugh that faded quickly. "And we both know that what you do now will take it away at some point. That *everything* we do to survive chips away at our bodies and our souls."

Esme nodded slowly. "I suppose if that happened and I went to live the life of an eccentric with a dozen adorable cats in the countryside, you could come with me."

Jane laughed. "I've always liked cats."

"That's because you *are* a cat." Esme nudged her gently and Jane's laughter increased.

When she became serious again, she said, "Or perhaps you'll become an earl's wife. A countess, isn't it? I could carry your trains while I don't make eye contact with Lady High and Mighty."

Her friend meant it as a joke, but Esme tensed at the idea. Not so long ago, it would have been an attainable dream. To be Finn's, in his arms and life and bed forever. But now she had no business considering that. Not that she wanted it. Finn was temporary.

"You are terrible," she teased with difficulty and lightly slapped her friend's arm.

Jane became serious. "Truly, though. Let him help if he offers it. At the very least, you might get peace of mind."

Esme nodded slowly. Peace of mind sounded lovely. To turn the page fully on the death of her father, knowing she'd done all she could to avenge him.

"Very well. I'll reach out to Finn. I'll meet with him and discuss whatever it is he thinks he can do for me."

Jane lifted her eyebrows. "Yes. *Whatever* it is."

They both got up and Jane left the room first, giggling over her quip. But Esme couldn't. She was about to enter the most treacherous waters she'd ever encountered. She'd have to be careful not to drown.

Finn had known his sister for twenty-six years and Sebastian for almost as long, and yet the silence in his parlor as they sat together was as awkward as if they had all just met. He shifted in his chair and forced a smile at the pair on the settee. It was only relieved when a servant stepped in with the tea and placed it on the sideboard before quickly bowing out.

"Let me play hostess," Marianne said as she got to her feet and hurried to the sideboard.

"I'll help," Sebastian said, at her heels immediately.

Finn remained silent as he watched the two interact. He'd been skeptical of their sudden union, as well as the delicate position he'd found them in together at the country party. Ramsbury was attentive now, his eyes bright as he helped her. But Finn still feared for her. If she ended up married to him and had to chase him for his affections like their mother had…

Finn's stomach turned. That was why he still maintained distance from his friend, despite the upcoming nuptials.

And yet as Finn watched, he did feel the connection between them. He saw it in the way Sebastian smiled down at Marianne when she wasn't looking at him. He saw it in the way she blushed when their hands met as she passed over a cup to him. Or the way she said her intended's name, something gentle and intimate and so filled with love that it seemed rude to listen to them.

Ramsbury returned to Finn, handing over a cup prepared just as he liked it. The two of them settled back into their places and Marianne smiled. "The first reading of the banns seemed to go well, as well as the announcements in all the papers. Thank you for doing that, Finn."

He inclined his head. "Of course. I would do nothing less than publicly celebrate your union. From the comments I've received, it seems that on the whole, most are seeing this as a fetching love story."

"Good," Ramsbury said, and took Marianne's hand. "Because that's what it is."

Finn wrinkled his brow. He'd told Esme that he couldn't recognize love, but that wasn't true. When he forced himself to see beyond his own fears, there it was, right in front of him. And while he was happy for his sister and his friend that they had found it, he still felt an empty ache in his chest.

"I'm surprised Aunt Beulah didn't join us," Finn said, searching for small talk.

Marianne laughed and sent Ramsbury a side look that indicated some private little joke. "She is obsessed with my wedding trousseau and could not be dragged from stitching me handkerchiefs with what will be my new initials, so she stayed behind in our little home."

Finn wrinkled his brow. Their spinster aunt had lived with Marianne in the years when she had taken her own small home in London. He hadn't thought about what would happen after she was wed. Why hadn't he thought of that? It was his duty to do just that.

"Actually, we wished to speak to you about her," Marianne said, and patted Ramsbury's knee gently.

He smiled at her and then said, "We would like for her to join us in our home in London after the wedding. She's been a good companion to your sister all this time."

"And she adores Sebastian," Marianne said with a smile.

Finn nodded. "Y-Yes, of course. If she would be happy with that change, I'd support it fully. I can sell your small home after everything is settled and distribute the money as additional dowry if you'd like."

"Settle it on her," Marianne suggested. "As an extra allowance. You know how she wagers at cards with her friends—she could always use a little extra."

Sebastian nodded. "That's a fine idea. Marianne certainly will want for nothing."

Finn stared at his teacup for a moment. Everything was being taken care of without his input. The time for him to be his sister and his aunt's protector was over, it seemed. And just when Esme might need him. Was she correct that he would simply transfer his need to protect to her?

No. Wanting to save Esme, help her, had nothing to do with his basic instincts and everything to do with the way her eyes lit up when she looked at him.

They drank tea for a while, discussing the wedding and friends and whatever other topic came to mind. Finn tried to stay focused, but he found his mind wandering more than once. Over and over again Esme, to everything they'd discussed and done two nights before. He hadn't heard from her and he wanted to. Needed to.

"Do you still have Mama's emerald leaf necklace?" Marianne asked, drawing Finn from his musings.

He cleared his throat. "Yes, of course. It's with the rest of her things in the old wing. Why?"

"If you don't object I'd…" Marianne's voice cracked a little. "I'd like to wear it on my wedding day. I would return it, of course, afterward. It was meant for the countess and I'm certain you'd like to save it for whoever she ends up being."

Finn swallowed hard. It was too easy to imagine Esme in that necklace that would match her eyes so perfectly. His voice was rough as he said, "I would love for you to wear it. Do you want to fetch it now?"

Marianne nodded. "Oh yes, I do. Tomorrow we have my next fitting for my wedding gown and I wanted to try it so that my seamstress may lay the bodice correctly to display it to its best advantage."

Sebastian stood as she did, his face bright with a smile. "I cannot wait to see your gown."

"But you must," Marianne said with a laugh as she moved to the door. "It's bad luck otherwise. I'll have Bentley help me find it. Entertain yourselves, gentlemen."

Sebastian looked down at Finn when she was gone and shook his head. "I don't think I've ever seen you fail to rise when a lady exited a room. Certainly not Marianne."

Finn jolted. Was he not standing? God, he wasn't. He did now and smoothed his waistcoat. "How abominably rude of me. I cannot believe I didn't. I shall apologize to her later."

Ramsbury moved to the sideboard where the tea remained and bent to open one of the lower cupboards. He brought out a fine bottle of scotch and poured them each one.

"She doesn't care and you know it. Her only concern would be the one I share, which is that *you* are out of sorts. And you have been, even before our trip out to the country and all that transpired there. Still, I must ask, is your poor mood only related to that fact that you are still displeased with me about everything?"

There was true concern in his friend's tone as he handed over the scotch. Finn swirled it in the glass, staring as the amber liquid rolled around the edges without sloshing over. "On the contrary, when I see my sister light up as she does whenever you're near her, how can I be anything but pleased, despite the unfortunate details of your beginning?"

Ramsbury smiled and there was something so gentle about it. Something that changed his rake of a friend into an infatuated lover. Finn didn't think the other would ever return. He both mourned and cheered that fact.

"I truly do love her, Delacourt," he said softly. "You should not fear otherwise."

"I don't. I can see you love her. It's written all over your face." Finn forced a smile, but turned away to slug half his drink in one burning gulp.

"Then what's wrong?" Sebastian asked.

Finn crossed to the window and looked out at the garden below, but he didn't truly see any of the cool, green beauty. Not except to compare it to Esme's eyes. The garden seemed faded in comparison.

"It's nothing," he lied. "Just a silly distraction that I will get over soon enough."

"I see." Ramsbury was quiet a moment. "And what is her name?"

Finn pivoted away from the window to stare at his friend and found

Sebastian with his arms folded and a little smirk on his face. "I'm a very *recently* reformed rake, Phineas. I can still see the signs of a man taken in by a lover, or a potential lover."

Finn pursed his lips. Sebastian wasn't wrong, of course. Esme was nothing more than a lover, no matter how many of her secrets he had uncovered, or how many offers of help she took or didn't take. And yet that term felt dismissive. It wasn't enough to encompass the connection they had.

But he wasn't about to tell Sebastian that. Instead he shrugged. "She isn't anyone you'd know. Just a...it's just a lark."

That felt even worse to say.

Sebastian's smile faltered and his brows lowered. "No, it doesn't seem like a lark. You'd hardly be so troubled by a bit of fun like that. Or left so bleary eyed by one."

Finn rubbed a hand over those very eyes. "Perhaps it's more then. It's a conundrum, for certain, of most frustrating proportions."

"That sounds serious." Sebastian took a step forward. "What can I do to help?"

Finn stared at him. Even with the tension that had developed between them in the past few months, under any other circumstances he would have turned to Sebastian. Very few people in the world knew him better, or would have better advice. But if Finn revealed the truth of his problems, he would also be revealing Esme. "I promised the lady in question that I'd reveal nothing of her circumstances. I must keep that vow."

Sebastian nodded slowly, but his expression was intense. Like he could see something in Finn, something he didn't want to acknowledge, even if only to himself. So he turned away.

"If anything changes, you know where I am," Sebastian said softly.

"Sneaking into my sister's house at night, no doubt," Finn said with false glare toward his friend.

Sebastian tilted his head back to laugh but didn't deny the

charge. As he did, Marianne returned to the room and her face lit up to see them laughing together. "Oh, a joke! What is it?"

Finn snorted. "I'm sure Ramsbury will tell you later."

She wrinkled her brow but didn't press. "I admit, I'm happy to see you two at such ease with each other. I know our engagement, the circumstances that created it in the country, they strained your friendship. It has been the only mar on an otherwise joyful time."

Finn pushed aside everything else he felt and moved toward his sister, catching her hands in his. He looked down into her face and saw her joy and also her love for him. "Marianne, I free you from any worry about me when it comes to your union. No, I wasn't happy with…er…discovering you two in such a delicate situation at the country estate."

Marianne blushed and ducked her head, so Finn hastened to continue. "But I can see your happiness and that of my dearest friend. And as I was speaking to him a moment ago, I had this realization that your union will make Sebastian, a man I've always seen as a brother, into my brother in truth. When added to your own joy, how could I ever be anything but elated at that future?"

Marianne's eyes misted with tears. "Oh, Finn!" she gasped, and then tugged him in for a tight hug. "Thank you," she whispered. "Oh, thank you for saying that."

He squeezed her back. It had always been just the two of them. They were each other's only true family. He never wanted to risk that, to harm that. And being able to finally fully accept the union, to celebrate it, it lifted a weight he'd been carrying.

It also put into stark contrast Esme's situation. She, too, had only had one person in her life. And with her father's death, she'd lost everything. He grieved that on her behalf.

Marianne stepped away and then moved toward Sebastian. The earl had been watching the siblings interact quietly, but he smiled broadly as he wrapped an arm around Marianne and tucked her to his side.

"If you two are quite finished with this highly emotional display,"

Sebastian teased. "I think I must whisk the future countess away, for we have a dozen errands to run when it comes to wedding plans today."

Finn motioned toward the door and followed the couple into the foyer where the carriage was rung for. "You are assisting with the wedding plans, then? That is progressive thinking for a groom."

"There would be very few ladies I could plan with," Marianne said with a sad expression. Finn frowned. She had lost her closest friend a little over a month prior. He hadn't thought of how that must affect her joy as much as his previous attitude had.

Sebastian took her hand, lacing their fingers together. "And I like being involved. Watching Marianne's face light up when she finds the perfect fabric or some exquisite bauble for a table is my current greatest pleasure."

Marianne smiled up at him. "You tease."

"I do not," he said as the carriage arrived.

She said her goodbyes to Finn and Sebastian handed her up into the vehicle. She slid to the other side and began to look through her reticule for something. He was about to join her when a messenger rode up the drive. The young man swung down and looked between the two earls.

"Delacourt?" he asked.

"That would be me," Finn said, and held out a hand for the missive. It was in a very pretty hand, his full title written carefully above his address. He hadn't ever seen Esme's writing, but he knew it was hers and his heart began to pound into his throat.

Sebastian arched a brow and spoke quietly, so Marianne wouldn't hear him. "From the way your expression just lit up, I would wager your conundrum isn't always frustrating."

Finn glanced up. "No. She is not."

"Well, happy hunting, my friend." He stepped up into the carriage and leaned out. "I'm always here."

With that he shut the door and the carriage pulled away, leaving Finn still staring at the letter in his hand. He returned to the house and back into the parlor where his tea was going cold on the sideboard next to the scotch Sebastian had poured. He took a long sip of the second before he broke the wax seal on the back of the pages.

> *I'd like to see you to discuss your offer. I'm certain you must have had your driver pay attention to where I was delivered. You're too clever not to do so. Send me word as to when and where is convenient. Esme.*

Finn read the three sentences over and over, marking every shiver in the handwriting, every swirl of each letter. It was direct, with nothing flowery to it, but he could almost hear it being read in Esme's throaty voice. Whispered like a caress against his skin. He would see her again. As soon as he wished to do so, and however privately he wanted to make it. That was the thrill, even more than knowing she might allow him to help her uncover the truth about her father's death.

And that was dangerous. If he was intelligent, he'd turn this entirely toward his old friend. He owed Chilton this, he owed him more than panting after his wayward daughter, certainly.

And yet he knew, as he walked to his study to reply to her message, that the moment he saw Esme, he wouldn't be able to resist the electric current that bound them together. It was just too powerful.

CHAPTER 12

Esme felt nervous. It wasn't a sensation she often allowed herself to have. A lack of confidence, at least outwardly, could be dangerous in the world of boxing, even deadly on the streets. But at that moment she couldn't stop pacing up and down Finn's fine parlor carpet, clenching and unclenching her hands before her as she waited for his arrival.

It had been a day since she sent her note. He'd responded immediately, even though he'd asked her to come the following afternoon. There had been something disappointing about that. That he hadn't arranged to meet her the same day, same hour, same moment, she'd sent her letter.

But then again, they weren't courting. They weren't falling in love. They were in an awkward dance of passion and long-kept secrets. Nothing more.

And now she was here. In his house. His *estate*. Of course he would call her here for their meeting. His domain. It made sense—it was private—but returning to this place was another reminder that she was stuck between worlds. She hadn't felt that way for a long time, not since she first ran away and had to learn to survive from Ripley and Jane.

The door to the parlor opened behind her and Esme turned to find Finn standing at the entryway, staring at her. He blinked as his gaze moved up and down her frame, then he entered the room and closed the door behind himself.

"You are lovely," he said softly.

She glanced down at herself. "Thank you. It's my…it's my best dress."

She felt foolish now that she'd said that. The gown was serviceable, yes, but there was nothing fancy or unique about it. The fabric was a cheaper silk and she had sewn the seams back together a few times.

"It doesn't fit here," she continued. "But then neither do I and—"

He crossed the room to her in a few long steps and silenced her by cupping her cheeks in his warm palms and dropping his mouth to hers. The kiss was gentle, yet somehow still powerful and her spinning thoughts settled.

"You are *lovely*," he repeated when he pulled away at last. He motioned to the sideboard. "Tea?"

She bent her head and muttered, "Whisky."

When he laughed, she was surprised. She hadn't thought she'd said that loud enough to be heard, but it seemed he was paying attention. "I have that, too, though it's a bit early for me."

She shook her head. "Tea is fine. Two sugars, no milk."

He paused and looked at her over his shoulder. "Like your father used to take it."

"Yes." She nodded and marveled at the swell of pain that simple statement caused. But it was a good ache, somehow. Finn understood her father's loss. He knew him. And it helped to talk to him.

As he poured the tea, she worried a loose thread along the back of one of the chairs. "Did you…did you attend his funeral?"

He came to her with a cup, which she took and then sat when he motioned her to do so. He fetched his own tea, then sat in the chair beside her own.

"Yes," he answered at last. "I did."

She stared at the teacup for a moment. "I wasn't allowed. My cousin said I was overwrought."

His lips pursed and she saw the anger tighten his jaw. Anger on her behalf. Such an odd thing, for she hadn't expected to find a protector in a man like this. "Even if the man isn't a murderer, he's certainly a cruel arse. Who else had more reason to be overwrought? You two were so close."

"We were," she said with a faint smile. "He was unlike anyone I ever knew. A man with power, but also principles. A dreamer caught in the body of a marquess."

"A true gentleman," Finn added.

Their eyes met and for the first time it wasn't desire that hung between them, nor tension from the secrets she kept and he now knew. It was understanding. It was shared emotion. It was comfort.

"He was," she agreed.

He settled back in his chair and sipped his tea. "Chilton was the only man I knew who could discuss politics and the habits of bees, sometimes in the same breath. Always with the same passion."

She couldn't help but laugh and it felt so good. Her thoughts of her father were so often about his loss, about the circumstances, that she sometimes forgot the little joys of him. "Oh Lord, the bees! His hives were wonderful, I loved watching him put on all his layers and go out to tend them." Her smile faltered. "I-I made sure they went to a good home."

"They aren't still on the family estate?" Finn asked, his eyebrows lifting in surprise.

She shrugged. "Francis wanted to burn them. It was only the suggestion that they were worth something to sell that made him reconsider. I had to save them. Save something of *him*."

"Bastard," Finn said, and his brow lowered with even more anger.

She sighed. This was as good a segue as any to the topic she had truly come to discuss with him. She set her tea aside and leaned forward. "Do you…do you truly think you might be able to unmask Francis if it was what I said I wanted?"

He drew a long breath. "I don't know," he admitted. "It's in his best interest to continue to cover it up if he did do something criminal. But that doesn't mean he won't slip. He had none of your father's keen intellect nor his discretion, if I recall him correctly."

"No. He had none of my father's good qualities," she said with bitterness in her tone.

"You do," Finn said gently.

She cleared her throat. That observation felt too intimate. "Er, what would you do? How would you go about such an investigation, if you still wished to do it?"

He tilted his head. "I offered, Esme, and the offer still stands. I would need a reason to bump into him. I believe he maintains your father's membership at White's. I've always preferred Fitzhugh's, but I have my own membership regardless. I could find him there and strike up a conversation without it seeming too odd."

She worried her lip. She'd wanted this and she still did, but the idea of Finn walking up to her cousin, a man she believed capable of murder, was frightening. She felt defensive of him. "What would you ask him?" she pressed.

"Nothing."

She shook her head. "Nothing? Then what would be the purpose?"

He laughed. "I think it would be too obvious if I marched across a crowded club, grabbed him by the lapels and demanded he confess to murdering my friend."

She let out a humorless chuckle. "Oh God, but that sounds wonderful, though. To do that? To humiliate him in front of his friends, to put the idea out there into the world where it would be whispered about and questioned?"

"I wish I could do that for you," he said, and took her hand. He lifted it to his lips and brushed them to her knuckles gently, frowning at the light bruises there from her fight earlier in the week before he'd returned to London. Which she'd won, despite her distraction. "And perhaps one day I can. But for now I would need to put him at ease. Make him see me as a potential ally, not an enemy. Perhaps I'll even invite him to my sister's engagement party in a few days. It's become quite the sought-after invitation in Society."

Whenever he'd spoken of Marianne's upcoming nuptials, Esme had sensed a tension there. A sadness. But now he seemed lighter. Like a weight had been lifted from him.

"The engagement to Ramsbury," she said.

He nodded. "Yes."

"He's quite the catch."

His face immediately fell. "Please tell me you didn't ever have eyes for my friend."

"Never!" she said, though her chest puffed at what was clearly his flash of jealousy at the idea. "I had eyes for no one in my days in Society. I never really fit in, even before I had to run for my life."

"I've no idea how," he said, and pushed a loose curl away from her cheek. "You ought to have been the center of all attention."

She swallowed once again at the focused intent of his stare. There was the longing. The want that called to her own. She reached up to trace his lips with her fingertips. "You know, I have no way to repay you for this, Finn. Save one."

She let her fingers drag down from his lips, over his chin, across his neatly tied cravat and the center of his chest. He caught his breath as she inched lower, tracing his stomach and finally cupping his cock through his trousers. He was half-hard already and she went a little weak in the knees at the feel of him.

His pupils were dilated with desire, but to her surprise he caught her hand and lifted it to his lips again, kissing her palm this time. "Esme, if we do that again, it will be only for mutual pleasure. It's not a repayment."

She stared at him, this man who so flummoxed her with all he was. "Oh."

"But if you'd like to stay here for a while, then we could discuss whatever happens when I go to White's. Perhaps we could share supper while we do."

She shook her head. "You're going to go today?"

He smiled. "Yes. Right now. There's no time like the present, and if I'm going to deliver an invitation for the engagement ball, it's better to do it now than later."

"And you'd have me stay here? Wouldn't your servants talk? Judge?"

He shrugged as he stood and she followed him to her feet. "I doubt it. Even if they do, who gives a damn? Unless you're uncomfortable."

She was, in truth. She hated the stares of people who could see through her and there was no one who could judge more swiftly and likely accurately than a servant. But this was about her father. About justice. She would have to be brave.

"I'm fine."

"Good," he said. "You can make use of my library if you'd like. Or stroll the gardens. Play in the music room if you're so inclined. I'll be certain the staff knows you have free access to anyplace you'd like on the estate."

Her head spun at the ease with which he behaved. As if this was nothing. As if it was all normal and fine when it certainly wasn't. But she could find no argument against him when he was so confident in himself and his decisions. So she made none and simply nodded. He leaned down to press the briefest of kisses to her lips, then moved to the parlor door and rang the bell for his butler.

Leaving her standing in a parlor that she no longer belonged in, determined to wait for a man who could never be hers, who was off to uncover secrets that she'd sworn to keep to her grave.

And it was all very confusing.

When Finn had told Esme that he preferred Fitzhugh's to White's, he hadn't been lying and it was all coming back to him why he avoided the place. He stood in the large entryway, soft sounds of voices drifting from various parlors and game rooms, and sighed. So many here were pretentious or terribly dandified, there to see and be seen.

He supposed he was little better today, though. He had prey, after all. One he could only hope was actually in attendance.

"May I do anything else for you, Lord Delacourt?" the attendant said as he took Finn's hat and gloves.

"I am hoping to meet some friends today," he said. "I wonder if Lord Ramsbury or Lord...Lord Chilton are in attendance."

It was hard to say the second. He hadn't thought about the fact he'd be forced to refer to Esme's awful cousin as Lord Chilton. A name he associated with one so dear to him and to her.

"Lord Ramsbury is not here," the attendant said. Finn wasn't surprised. Normally Sebastian wouldn't set a foot in White's. He only asked so that his interest in Chilton wouldn't be too obvious. "But Lord Chilton arrived an hour ago. I believe he is in the reading room."

Finn inclined his head and made his way into the main rooms of the club. A few turns and he saw the reading room ahead of him, a place where gentlemen could read the newspapers from all over the world, as well as current books and political and scientific papers. He had a hard time believing Chilton would be interested in any of that, as he was no intellectual.

But he entered the room and did, indeed, find the marquess sitting by a large window, a paper in his hands, though he didn't seem to be reading it. Finn's heart began to pound and he took a few long breaths to calm himself before he looked around the room. There were two other gentlemen in the quiet area and he forced himself to acknowledge one with a wave and cross to say a brief good afternoon to the other.

Once that was done, his eagerness hopefully masked, he turned toward Chilton. The marquess was watching him now and he rose as Finn made his way to him.

"Good afternoon, Delacourt," he said, extending a hand.

Finn wished he didn't have to take it, but he did, shaking it firmly. "Chilton." It tasted as bitter as it felt to say it. "I feel I haven't seen you in an age."

Finn took in his foe in the moment they shook hands. He was a dandy through and through, wearing the highest collar Finn had ever seen, hair teased and twisted into a ridiculous pompadour. It was all fashion, no function, as Chilton's face twisted with discomfort when he tried to retake his seat in his stiff jacket.

In truth, the man didn't look capable of hurting a fly, let alone committing or orchestrating a murder. Could Esme be wrong about him? Not about his selfishness, but about the danger he posed?

"Will you join me?" Chilton asked.

"Certainly," Finn replied, and took the place across from him.

There was an intricately carved and painted snuff box before the marquess and he motioned to it. "Will you have some?"

"I've never taken to the habit, I'm afraid."

"Hmm." Chilton looked him up and down with a sneer. "I see." He opened the box, took a large portion and stuffed it up his nose with a great gasp of air. When he had shut it, he leaned back and said, "I don't normally see you at White's."

Finn shrugged. "Not often, I fear. You know how it is. One has memberships at White's and Boodles and Fitzhugh's and Ripley's…I can never find the time to fit them all in."

"A gentleman's work is never done," Chilton purred. "I swear, since taking over the title, I've never had more to do."

"Yes, the management of estates and tenants and—"

Chilton wrinkled his nose. "God, no! I don't give a damn about that. I have managers for such things and if they cannot resolve an issue, why should I? My tenants and servants should be happy they have a position at all."

Finn's stomach turned. He knew far too many men like this in

Society. Ones who didn't take their duties seriously. He might play, but by God, he refused to let those below him suffer because of it.

But he nodded. "I suppose when you inherited, your uncle had a great many good people in place to take care of things for you."

"My uncle," Chilton said with a short sigh and a more focused look for Finn. "If I recall, you and he were great friends."

"Yes. I'm sorry for your loss. He was the best of men."

"*Was*," Chilton said, and Finn thought he emphasized the word. But had he? Was he just chasing ghosts now, trying to find some hint of proof so that he wouldn't have to tell Esme he saw nothing to back up her claims?

Was he so focused on that now, despite their short acquaintance?

"You must be busy, yourself, with the upcoming wedding of your sister," Chilton said.

Finn blinked and forced himself back to the conversation at hand. The marquess was leaving him an opening for exactly what he'd intended to do. "Ah, yes. There is much to do," he said.

"What a coup for Lady Marianne. To land such a fine prospect after so long on the wall. I think most of Society must have given up on her, as well as you. Good that you didn't have to waste resources trying to force a union through financial and other means."

Finn felt every muscle in his body tense at that statement. It wasn't that others hadn't implied as much, that somehow his sister had lost her worth after years as a spinster. That she had become a burden on him. But few were willing to put it in such harsh terms.

He arched a brow. "She is a most beloved sister, my lord. I would have been pleased to support her in any way she lived her life, just as I support her in the wonderful future she will have with Ramsbury. It is a love match, it seems, and I am over the moon for her."

Chilton looked as though he didn't understand that concept. He shrugged. "It's certainly all the talk of Town."

"Yes," Finn said. "The engagement ball is in just a few days, at my home here in London. The invitation is impossible to acquire, what with all the interest."

Chilton's lips thinned. "I suppose Ramsbury is making most of the invitation decisions. Never liked me much."

Finn almost smiled. His friend had always had impeccable taste. "I don't know about that. Either way, if you'd like to attend, I could arrange it. As you said, your uncle and I were once close, I see no reason why the Chilton name shouldn't continue to be linked to mine."

There was a light that entered Chilton's eyes that immediately let Finn know that he had won his prize. How could this grasping man refuse, after all. A sought-after invitation? A way to get over on Ramsbury by showing up at his party? A continued relationship between two powerful titles?

It was everything a man like this could want.

"That would be very kind, yes," Chilton said.

"Excellent. I'll arrange it the moment I return home." He made a show of pulling his pocket watch from his jacket and frowned. "Speaking of which, I have something to attend to. I'm glad I stopped by here today and we were able to speak. I see great things in the future, Chilton."

They both rose and Chilton extended a hand again. They shook for the second time, a cold chill rolling up Finn's arm with the touch. When he left the room, he rubbed his palm against his thigh, wishing he could erase the memory as much as he could erase the touch.

And yet he had discovered nothing yet that said the man was anything but a grasping dandy, concerned with appearances and wealth. No worse than dozens of others in his position. And he had no idea how Esme would react when he told her that upon his return to the estate.

CHAPTER 13

Esme had felt uncomfortable the first little while she waited in Finn's house, but the feeling had faded when his butler had brought her some biscuits to go with her tea and had kindly left the door open when he left, almost like he was setting her free into Finn's world.

She finished her second delicious biscuit, downed the last bit of tea in her cup and finally got up. She exited the room and went into the long hallway to her left. There were many doors to either side of her all the way to the end and most were open, once again making her feel that there would be no judgment if she gave herself a little tour. She peeked into a few parlors, each painted and decorated in a thematic color and all lovely.

Though another door down the hallway was a music room. She stepped inside and drew a deep breath. There was a gorgeous piano beside a large window, a harpsichord and a smaller lute harp. She hadn't played any instrument in so long, but she found herself recalling nights where she and her father had played together. She wondered if Finn played or if he only observed while Lady Marianne did so.

She turned and crossed the hallway where she found a library.

This time she fully entered the space and breathed in the dusty heaven of the books. It was a wonderful room, with high shelves lined with tome after tome, a large fireplace that was currently unlit, and two tall ladders so that a reader could reach even the highest shelves, both on rollers so they could be moved to any place needed.

She could easily imagine herself perched in the window seat on a rainy day, lost in some story or poem. She blinked. That wasn't right. She had no place to imagine herself in this house. In this life. She'd left one very much like it and surrendered all claim she had to return. She and Finn were having an affair. There was nothing else to it.

She huffed out a breath and moved down the hallway again. It widened toward the end and was lined with a portrait gallery. She paused to look up at the endless faces of Delacourts past. Men and women who shared Finn's dark eyes, his strong hands, the hint of his smile. The last portrait was of his immediate family and she stared up at it.

The previous Earl of Delacourt stood ramrod straight, the young Finn at his side. She couldn't help but note how the earl's hand rested heavily on his son's shoulder, fingers slightly clenched as if he was pinching the boy. Lady Delacourt sat in a chair just in front of the two, holding a baby who had to be Lady Marianne. She was looking away from them, her expression taut and pained. Whoever had painted this had captured such a fractured moment. One laced with heartbreak that she knew Finn still carried.

And she ached for him. Both as the small boy in the painting and the man who had crashed into her world and blown her expectations to pieces.

She stared a few moments more and then let out a long sigh. Once more she was dipping her toes into waters where she certainly had no place. No matter how she kept reminding herself, it seemed impossible to keep that truth in mind. She saw Finn, thought of

THE HELLION'S SECRET

Finn, recalled Finn and…poof! All her best intentions and logical facts were gone.

"It cannot be that way."

She marched herself forward, toward double doors at the end of the hallway. They were cracked and she heard some commotion inside. When she ducked her head in, she saw she'd found the ballroom. Servants were readying it in a bustle of activity. They laughed and joked with each other as they worked, occasionally spinning around the big ballroom floor together before they picked up their duties again. The room looked lovely as they hung pale blue bunting and prepared a raised platform for the orchestra that would play for the partygoers. It seemed Finn had spared no expense to celebrate his beloved sister's future with his best friend.

She smiled slightly at that fact and the warmth it gave her. Lucky Marianne to never have to fear again.

"Miss Portsmith?"

She jumped at the sound of a voice behind her and turned to find Finn's butler, Bentley, at her shoulder. He had a few items draped over his arm. It looked like more of the bunting.

"I'm dreadfully sorry," she said, stepping back so she no longer blocked the door. "I was nosing around where I wasn't needed."

"Not at all, miss. Lord Delacourt made it clear you have the run of the house while he is gone." There was no indication how that fact impacted Bentley. He was too good to show a reaction. "We are preparing the ballroom, of course."

"For Lady Marianne's engagement ball, yes. I've heard the happy news."

"Happy, indeed," Bentley said with a slight smile. "Lady Marianne is vastly content, it seems. We all wish her nothing but joy."

She nodded. "You seem a comfortable household."

"Oh yes, miss. There could be no better man to serve than the earl." He shifted. "Is there anything you need, miss, before I get back to my duties?"

She glanced around the room, and as she did she noticed a high

119

balcony that surrounded the edge of the room. One that could look down on the dancefloor.

"Do guests really go up in those high verandas?" she asked, motioning to them.

The butler smiled. "Not usually. We don't encourage it. Three earls ago there was apparently an incident with a drunken attendee and a...well, stomach upset. All the servants know about it. Usually the passageways to the observatory verandas are left closed off during parties."

"I see." She looked up again. That would be a perfect place to watch the engagement ball surreptitiously if Finn did manage to obtain Francis's attendance. "I think I'll stroll in the garden to stay out of your way. Is there a best exit to do so?"

He held out a hand toward the line of French doors along the back of the ballroom that were already open wide to let the breeze in and cool the room while the servants worked. "This is the fastest exit. The veranda behind is quite long and wraps along the back of the home. There are stairs on the west side that lead straight to the gardens."

"Thank you, Bentley," she said with a small smile for him. Then she moved through the ballroom, feeling the fleeting glances of the servants on her as she left the house.

Outside she drew a deep breath of air. The knowing looks of the servants, as innocuous as they had been, still felt stifling. There was a part of her that felt the shame of their knowledge of her relationship to their employer. News of a woman spending time in his chamber, in his bed, had to have spread belowstairs. They would gossip about her while they worked now. And after. And for a while to come, she suspected.

She pushed her shoulders back and crossed the stone veranda to stand at the wall. After a few breaths, her worry subsided and she could enjoy the beauty of the gardens below. There was a lack of green in the spaces where she now lived. To find it, she had to go to parks, but this was a private heaven she couldn't resist.

She moved to the east end of the veranda and down the curving staircase where she met with a beautifully tended pathway that guided her into the garden proper. All around her were beautifully tended and trimmed bushes, neatly kept trees straining with soon to be ripe fruits and then there were the flowers.

Oh, the flowers. She almost skipped along as she looked at all of them. Blooms of pink and red and yellow turned their happy petals toward her, filled her nostrils with scents that smelled so fresh and sweet. There were roses and hyacinth, bluebells and lilies and everything in between. She stepped up to each bush and stem, leaning in to breathe them, smiling at the bees buried amongst the blooms. It all felt so right. Like home, but a home she'd lost and couldn't return to. It felt like a dream. It felt...like peace.

She sat down on the closest bench with a thunk. Over and over her mind kept taking her places it shouldn't be. Thoughts she couldn't entertain. Hopes and dreams she had killed and that had to remain dead or else they would haunt her. She had a life. It wasn't this one. It never could be.

Why couldn't she remember that when she was in this man's space? Or his arms?

She drew a shaky breath and looked up at the house, just in time to see Finn coming down the same stairs she had descended not long before. She watched him through the dancing light and shadows cast by the trees and dipping sun and couldn't deny the thrill his presence caused. One more outrageous thing she had to control somehow, some way.

"My lord," she said, rising as he reached her.

He stopped in his tracks and stared at her. "Are we back to *my lord*, then?"

She pursed her lips. "Finn," she said softly. "You've returned and are in one piece."

His brows lifted and the small smile that tilted his lips was far too attractive. "Were you worried about me, Esme?"

She wanted to say yes. To launch herself at him to ensure he truly was whole and well, but she didn't. Instead she stepped away.

Now his expression drew down with concern. "Was everything well in my absence?"

She nodded, for she didn't want her confused emotions to cause trouble for anyone else. "Oh, yes. Your staff was very kind and I was offered all the hospitality I could have asked for. But I *am* nervous to hear how it went. You were gone so long."

"I'm sorry to have concerned you." He motioned to the bench where she had deposited herself a moment before, and together they sat there, their knees forced close together by the narrow seat. "I did find your cousin at White's," he began.

She was glad to be seated because for a moment her world swam and she gripped the edge of the bench so she wouldn't pitch herself out of it. "You did?" she whispered, her voice almost not her own it sounded so odd and far away.

He leaned closer and caught the hand that didn't hold tight to the bench. He cupped it between his own and drew a long breath. She realized she did the same with him and the world calmed a bit.

"I did. We spoke briefly, and then I had to pretend other business there just so our meeting wouldn't seem suspicious to him."

She nodded. "That makes perfect sense, I should have thought of that. So what happened? How did you find him?"

"Selfish, boorish, every bit as unpleasant as I recalled," he said, but he did so slowly, as if trying to ease her into a thought she wouldn't like.

She pulled her hand away slowly and stared at him. "You found yourself uncertain of his intentions," she said. "You think him innocent of my charges."

His immediate surprise that she could read that in his expression and body language was almost comical. He shook his head. "I don't know."

It wasn't an unfair judgment, especially after what sounded like a brief encounter, and yet anger rose up in Esme's chest. No, not anger. Disappointment. She hadn't realized just how much she wanted this man as an ally. Wanted his support not just for an investigation, but to tell her that her beliefs about her father weren't just born out of heartbroken grief and a weakness. She wanted him to take her side.

And now that he wasn't, at least not wholeheartedly, her chest hurt and revealed even more of the weakness she had been admonishing herself for all day. She got to her feet and turned away.

"This was a mistake, I'm sorry to have wasted your time. I'll just go on as I was." She took a long step toward the house and ultimately escape, but he rushed to his feet and went after her.

"Esme!" he said, catching her hand.

She yanked her hand back and threw her elbow out to thwack his fingers away, then pivoted and set her body, immediately in a fighter's stance.

He stared at her, his breath coming hard and heavy, but he didn't move toward her. Instead, he took a step away, hands lifted to show he was no threat. A lie. All he was was a threat, perhaps not to her physical person, but to everything else she'd built and become.

"Please," he said, more softly now.

She was blinking at tears, hating herself for letting him see them. "If you want to take his side—"

"I'm on *your* side," he interrupted, and now he stepped up again, this time more carefully and took her hands in his. There was nothing aggressive about the motion, nor about the way he smoothed his thumbs across the top of her hands so gently. This time she didn't pull them away. "I've spoken to him all of once and the first impression he leaves is of a silly fop. Of course that could be false, he could be much more Machiavellian beneath. So I don't necessarily believe one way or another that he did something yet."

She pursed her lips. "When you put it that way it sounds… reasonable."

He let out a low chuckle. "Thank you. I don't think I've ever been accused of that before." His smile fell. "Esme, don't you think it would be a *good* thing if we determined that your suspicions about Francis are untrue? That your father's death was deeply tragic, but natural?"

The tears she had felt stinging her eyes now began to slide down her cheeks no matter how she tried to stop them. "I-I need it to be someone's *fault*," she gasped out. "I want there to be someone to blame."

His eyes softened and he drew her in, putting his arms around her, holding her against his chest as his hand came up to stroke her hair gently. She dug her hands into his coat, clinging as she was wracked by sobs she hadn't been able to release for years. It shocked her how they came, how she couldn't stop them, and how he quietly allowed them without comment, without discomfort. All he offered was kindness and understanding.

Eventually the pain loosened, released its harsh grip on her body and soul and she was able to stop weeping. She lifted her head from his now-damp coat and heat filled her cheeks.

"My apologies," she whispered.

He cupped her cheek, brushing away some of the remaining tears there. "I doubt you've ever fully been able to grieve thanks to your cousin's actions. You needn't ever apologize for how you feel, at least not to me."

He reached into his pocket and drew out a handkerchief, monogramed with his initials. He handed it over and she first wiped it over his jacket.

"I must at least apologize for the state of this coat."

He smiled. "Things are things. It's not damaged."

She tilted her head in wonder at him, then wiped her eyes and nose. When she had put herself back together a little, she sighed. "I didn't even allow you to finish your story. So you talked to my wretched cousin and made your first impressions. You planned to invite him to your sister's engagement ball. Were you able to do that?"

He nodded. "I was. You should have seen his eyes light up, the grasping fop. He was thrilled to be included in such a highly spoken-of event and he agreed to attend. So the next part of our plan is already in motion and we'll see where it leads."

She clutched his hand in hers. "Oh, that's wonderful. I'm sure his tongue will be loosened when he has a drink or two in him and is puffed up in his own importance."

"That's my hope, as well," he said. "I won't stop, Esme. I'll continue until I'm certain I've uncovered everything he may be hiding when it comes to your father. I promise you that."

She stared at him. There had been many men who had made her promises since her father's death, both when she'd briefly worked as a lightskirt and since. She'd never had any trust in them. But *this* man had already kept his word and she found herself believing that he always would. That she could trust him with her faith and hopes. Dangerous but oh so bewitching.

She inched closer to him on the bench and his pupils dilated as she rested a hand on his chest. "Thank you, Finn," she whispered before she leaned up and kissed him.

He allowed it, his arms coming around her, drawing her even closer. The brush of lips turned headier, hotter, as she traced the crease of his mouth with her tongue. He opened to her, letting her taste and tease him until her breath was short and all she wanted was to be closer to him. As close as she could be.

She drew back. "I want to go to your chamber."

He blinked and she could see him trying to process that demand. "I told you, there is no repayment."

"You also told me we could do this for mutual pleasure. That's all I want right now. So please, take me to your chamber."

He untangled himself from her arms and stood, a god of solid muscle and sinew towering over her and holding out his hand. Offering her heaven for a moment. She took it and together they walked back through the garden, up the stairs and into the house where that taste of heaven awaited her in the big chamber at the top of the stairs.

CHAPTER 14

Finn could hardly breathe as he drew Esme into his bedroom and reached behind her to shut the door. She put her back to him and turned the key, then flattened her palms against the hard surface with a shuddering sigh.

He stepped into her, wrapping his body around her from behind, tangling his fingers with her against the door as she rolled her hips against his.

She wanted him, that much was clear. She never hid it, never minced about it. It was fascinating and powerful to always know her desire that way. But beneath that desire, he also knew her emotions were still high. She had broken down out in the garden, allowing herself a grief that had torn at him like animal claws on flesh. She had protected herself so long, never allowed a moment to rest and feel.

He didn't want to simply sweep her up in desire and not acknowledge that what she needed most, perhaps had needed for a very long time, was tenderness. Peace. God, how he wanted to give her peace.

He pressed his mouth to the back of her neck, tasting and teasing the soft curve there. She whimpered and her backside pressed to him more firmly, grinding against his already hard cock in a way meant to force him into a loss of control. It was tempting, but he ignored the throbbing needs of his body and continued to focus on her.

He reached around to the front of her body and found the first button at the bodice of her gown. He slid it free, then the next, then the next. Enough that he could slide a hand into the warmth trapped between her skin and the fabric. She whimpered as he cupped her breast, massaging and stroking the delicate flesh.

"God, just lift up my skirt and fuck me," she moaned.

He removed his hand from her gown and gripped her shoulder, turning her so her back was to the door. He leaned in, caging her there, his mouth close to hers.

"No," he said firmly.

Her eyes went wide just as he kissed her, slowly, deeply, savoring her and not allowing her to rush, even as she tried to force his hand by sucking his tongue and grinding up on him. He pressed her back more firmly against the door and she made a little sound in her throat, frustration and desire mixed.

He ignored it and went back to work on the remaining few buttons along the front of her gown. When it was open wide enough he parted the fabric and looked down. The chemise beneath was worn and threadbare and she blushed at that revelation.

He didn't address it, but slid his hands beneath both the shoulders of her gown and the straps of her chemise and slowly lowered them at the same time. She lifted her gaze to his and held there, her breath short as he peeled the fabric away and bared her from the waist up.

He'd seen her like this before, of course, many times. But he was still dumbstruck by her beauty. By the perfection of those curves. He let her gown dangle at her hips and slid his fingers up her sides, tracing her ribcage and then cupping each breast.

She tilted her head back against the door with a little thud and let out a soft moan when he stroked his thumbs over her nipples. He kissed her as he caressed there lazily, tracing the hard peaks while he stroked his tongue over hers. She was still tense, making every effort to maintain control, but he could feel her wavering.

He drew his mouth away from hers, kissing her jawline, her throat. He sucked there and she lifted her hips. "Please."

He ignored the plea and nuzzled lower, tasting her collarbone, drawing between the valley between her breasts. Only then did he move to her right breast and gently suck.

Her fingers came into his hair, gripping there as she gasped with pleasure. He sucked a little harder, scraping his teeth gently across the flesh. The gasp became a whimper.

"Please," she repeated, but this time more softly, with less demand.

He continued to ignore it and instead tugged her dress, letting it fall to the floor in a pile before he slipped an arm beneath her knees and lifted her into his arms.

She wrapped her arms around his neck with a laughing gasp that he swallowed when he kissed her as he carried her to his bed. He laid her there, on his pillows, her red hair coming down on the stark white, and stared.

"You are so beautiful," he murmured as he crawled up beside her, placing one hand on her stomach and gently stroking her there.

She pulled him to her, kissing him once more, but her kiss was desperate and needy, still laced with tension. He almost laughed at her repeated attempts to regain control. She was a fighter at heart, he knew. Built to grab the upper hand and save herself.

But *he* wanted to save her. At least in this, at least today, he wanted her to be able to surrender. So he slowed the kiss, probing more deeply, gently until her hands released from their fists in his hair and she whimpered his name in the quiet.

Then he started on his path again. Down her body, licking and kissing every inch of skin he touched. He sucked the nipple he had left untouched at the door and she arched now, mewling out wordless sounds of pleasure that drove him wild. This was a test of his control as much as hers. He intended to pass that test.

He let his mouth drift lower, kissing her ribcage, her stomach. She lifted her hips, widening her legs, a silent demand. He continued on his own path instead, tracing his tongue over her hipbone even as his fingers pressed into the softness of her backside.

He moved lower, but not to the pussy she had spread out so temptingly before him. He could scent her desire and see it on the dewy folds, but he was in no rush. Celebrating her was the goal here, not simply slaking mutual desire like they were unthinking animals.

He kissed along the crease where her leg met her hip and then into her inner thigh.

"Finn," she gasped, lifting again to demand action. He laughed against her flesh and instead moved lower. Her stockings were held up by pretty garters and he caught the ribbon of them with his teeth, looking up at her as he tugged and loosened the bow. It fell away beneath her and he kissed the edge of the fabric. She twisted beneath him, hands fisting in the bedclothes. He pushed the stocking down, following the path with his lips. She had a hard edge to so much of her, developed as protection to a harsh world that had hurt her. But her skin was still silk. He tasted every inch, moving his lips over her knee, down her calf, against her ankle until he dropped the stocking over the edge of the bed.

He followed the same path back up her body, cupping the back of her now bare knee, kissing his way without any hurry. Then he shifted to her opposite leg.

"You are driving me mad," she burst out, and sat up, reaching for her garter to rush him along.

He laughed and swatted her hands away. "That's the point, my dear. And you will lie there and let me."

Her lips pursed and he could see how much she wanted to argue.

To retain control. If she pushed, he'd allow her to do so. But he hoped she wouldn't. That she *would* let him.

Their eyes held for a long moment and then she flopped back with an exasperated grunt and threw her arm over her eyes. "Fine. Do as you will."

"Oh, very erotic," he teased. "Let me see if I can make you say that in a much prettier way."

He leaned in and licked her thigh, just above the garter, tracing the line of silk ribbon with wet heat.

"Fuck," she gasped.

"No," he said, and licked again. "The same thing you said before."

"Do as you will," she moaned. "Anything at all."

His cock throbbed at her surrender and he untied the ribbon and kissed his way down her leg to remove that one, as well. As he discarded it, he rose up on his knees, looking down at her. She was naked now, spread out on his bed, eyes closed, breasts rising and falling with shallow breaths. And oh, God, how he wanted her.

She opened her eyes and looked at him. Her expression wasn't teasing, though, it wasn't playful or in control as it had been the other times they'd done this. There was something different about it.

"Anything, Finn," she repeated, softer and with a waver. "Please."

He nodded. He couldn't deny her. He stripped out of his clothing, tossing each item off the bed without giving a damn where they landed or the shape they would be in later. She watched through a hooded glance, and he loved how she responded to him. The way she licked her lips like he was some treat.

When he was as naked as she was, he placed his hands on her thighs, widening her further as he lowered himself, rubbing his cheek on the tender flesh, drawing in a whiff of her desire for him. She smelled so good, he wanted to drown in that scent. He wanted to make it part of him.

He pressed his thumbs to the outer lips of her sex and she gasped and lifted to him. He spread her open and then licked her, gently at first, just tasting her, slipping along the line of her and enjoying how she moaned. He took his time, learning every part of her, tasting her desire increase, feeling her thighs quiver when he swirled his tongue around her clitoris. Oh, he wanted her to come. Yes, he did. But he wasn't going to rush, no matter how mad she drove him.

So he didn't. He took his time, teasing, edging her to the brink and then backing away from her clitoris. Over and over he built her heat then let her cool, and all the while he devoured her and reveled in her taste and the feel of her dripping against his chin. She was remarkable and wild and oh, so responsive as she rose with him, rocked with him.

She was shaking now, even when he backed away from her clitoris, her breath almost nonexistent. But the tension, at least the nonsexual type, had bled away from her.

At last he swept his tongue over her in earnest, stoking the flame of her pleasure instead of just teasing it. She rolled against him, her head thrashing against the pillows, and then she went stiff and he felt the waves of her pleasure against his tongue. He drew her through it, holding her hips tightly, never letting up the torment as she jerked beneath him.

It was only when she went weak that he relented. He sucked her one last time, then traced a path up the apex of her body, covering her for a kiss. She dug her fingers into his hair, stroking her tongue over his like she was savoring the flavor of her pleasure.

She locked one leg around his hip and his cock fell into place, notching against her sex like it was made to do so. He drew back, holding her gaze as he shifted his hips and took her slowly. Her sex still fluttered as he glided inside and dropped his head to her shoulder with a little moan of his own.

"Is it my turn to torment you?" she whispered, some of the wicked confidence back in her tone.

He laughed against her neck. "You torment me just by existing, Esme." He drew back and thrust. "You haunt my dreams. I wake up sweating, hard as stone and wanting you." Another thrust. "I touch you and I'm lost." Another. "I want to learn all the ways to make you gasp and cry out." Again. "You drive me mad and I never want it to stop."

She lifted against him as he spoke, their bodies grinding with every thrust. Her pupils dilated every further, her fingers dug into his shoulders. He kept thrusting, slow and steady, wanting more of her, all of her. And she gave it, almost levitating off the bed as her already sensitive body fluttered with pleasure a second time.

The grip of her was almost too much. It streaked sensation up his cock, into his balls, through every nerve ending, across every inch of his body. He was, as he had said, lost to her. Lost to this. Lost to them. Normally that would have terrified him. He wasn't a man who gave control with any more ease than she did, but with her it was impossible not to surrender. He rocked harder, faster, loving how her thighs gripped him, how she moved with him like powerful ocean waves. They crashed against each other with growing intensity, their mouths meeting and clashing, tongues tangling until he couldn't find where he ended and she began.

With a powerful burst of wild pleasure, he managed to withdraw and spent while her fingers tangled with his and they stroked his sensitive cock together. When he was finished, she lifted his hand, licking his fingers, whimpering with continued pleasure until he dropped down to kiss her and their legs and arms entwined in peace at last.

When he rolled on his back, she followed, half covering him, kissing his throat, tracing his chest with her fingers. He had no idea how long they lay like that, quiet in the dying firelight in his chamber, basking in the glow of sex and pleasure and connection. Not just physical, but deeper. He knew it was deeper. It didn't even take him off guard anymore.

"You know I found my way into your ballroom when I was exploring your home earlier," she said at last.

He looked down at her, stroking her hair away from her lovely face. "You were exploring?"

"You said I might."

"Yes, and I meant it. Did you like the house?"

She laughed. "How could anyone not? It's beautiful. One could tuck themselves away in any parlor or other chamber and just live comfortably forever."

He took in a shaky breath at that idea. That she might fit herself into the life he'd built. *Forever.*

"The servants have been busy in the ballroom preparing for Marianne and Sebastian's engagement soiree," he said.

"Yes. It's beautiful in there. It will be a magical event, just as your sister deserves," Esme said. "I realized I'd never been in your ballroom. Not even before I ran away. It has those lovely little observatory balconies."

Finn swallowed. He wasn't about to tell her how many assignations had been had in those balconies over the centuries. He could picture having her there now, her trembling fingers wrapped around the balcony edge, her body flush against his as he took her. They would both try to be quiet as people gathered below, completely oblivious to what wicked things were happening just above their dancing heads. God, how he wished he could.

"Yes. They're rarely used now, but they add a bit of whimsy to the room, I think."

"They would also make a very good place for a person to hide during an event. To observe without being seen." She smiled at him broadly, as if she were proud of herself for this thought.

He wrinkled his brow. "I suppose. Who would be spying on an event, though?"

"Me," she said. "When I attend your sister's ball, I could sit unseen up there and observe my cousin myself. It would be perfect, Finn."

He sat up and stared at her. The idea that she would potentially endanger herself by being exposed during his party made a cold hand of terror wrap around his heart. He shook his head. "No, Esme. Absolutely not."

If the moments after they made love had been lazy and calm, now Finn's face twisted with emotion that put Esme immediately on guard. His tone was tense, unbendable as he utterly refused her very good plan.

"What do you mean *no?*" she asked, sitting up herself and staring at him.

"I mean it would *never* work. What if you were recognized either by your cousin or by some other person who knew you before? The circumstances surrounding your disappearance were and remain of great interest. If you reappeared there would be no keeping it secret. *He* would find out."

She tilted her head. She'd initially thought he was just being heavy handed, but now she could see that wasn't it. Finn looked... afraid. For her. This was about protection. Who had last offered her such a gift? It had to have been Jane and Ripley. But this felt different. It felt wonderful and terrifying all at once.

"I wouldn't be out in the middle of the ballroom filling up a dance card, Finn. I'd be hidden, as I said. I could even be disguised."

He caught her hands and held them gently, but firmly. His gaze was the same, locked on hers, willing her to bend to his demands. "Esme, I don't think you understand—"

She pulled away and got out of the bed. She grabbed for her dress and held it up before herself, shielding her nakedness and wishing she could do the same to cover the emotions that bubbled up in her. Ones she couldn't share with someone like him. With anyone.

"*I* don't understand?" she snapped. "Do you forget yourself? You can speak to simpering misses in such a fashion, but not me. I've experienced far more danger in my life than you could imagine."

He took a long breath and she saw his sorrow for her softening his frustration. He got out of the bed, doing nothing to cover the beautiful body that had so pleased her just a little while before.

"I know," he said. "I apologize. When I say this, it isn't to dismiss your experience. I know you have seen and done things I couldn't fathom."

Did he judge her for those things? She couldn't fully tell so she folded her arms and lifted her chin.

He continued, "You've been through so much. My true fear is that you might be so focused on your hopes to uncover the truth about whatever your cousin's involvement in your father's death that you won't think of your safety. One of us must think of your wellbeing if that's the case."

She blinked. He was saying *he* would tend to her wellbeing. That he would protect her even if she refused to protect herself. But she couldn't depend on that offer. It wasn't real and it certainly couldn't be long lasting. If she learned to lean on him, it would make standing on her own so much harder when he was long gone and on to more appropriate lovers and loves.

"My safety isn't your concern, my lord," she said softly. "Not truly."

He stared at her for a moment, his expression hardening with that dismissal. "Perhaps it's not at that. But I'm telling you that you *will not* come to this ball, Esme. You will *not* use my home to endanger yourself when I'm perfectly capable of handling my end of our bargain."

She set her jaw, but he had done the same and so they stared at each other, two stubborn people unable to bend toward each other when they were both equally certain they were right.

"So that is the end of the discussion?" she asked.

He nodded. "Yes."

"Very good, my lord," she said, and pulled her chemise from the tangle inside her gown before she tugged it over her head. "Now if you will allow me to dress, I'll be on my way."

His nostrils flared slightly and for a moment she thought he might argue. He might continue this conversation or ask her to stay. Soothe things with his kiss and his hands and his body.

Instead he inclined his head. "As you like. Let me arrange for your transportation back home."

He left then, shutting the door behind him none too gently. She huffed out a breath, but the anger she had expressed didn't last. She tried to cling to it, but it was replaced by sadness. Defeat.

And also an intense determination to do whatever it took to obtain resolution to this matter. Even if it meant defying the man who had just spun her world off its axis.

CHAPTER 15

While Ripley's boxing club was stuffed with rich fops during the morning and early afternoon hours, the late afternoons were closed to his membership and open to those who truly made their living at the sport. Today Esme stood outside of one of the raised rings, watching two young women spar. They were both much younger than she was, probably just barely eighteen, if not even younger. God, she could hardly remember those days. Hers had been so much different, raised in a world far removed from this one.

That world she didn't belong in, even if she couldn't stop thinking about one infuriating earl who haunted her dreams. It had been two days since she'd last seen him, since their argument where he had denied her his permission to spy on his sister's engagement ball and his meeting with her cousin. Afterward, he'd sent her away with a promise to reach out to her when it was over. And a kiss. One searing kiss.

She jolted from her distracting thoughts and shouted out to the women in the ring, "Oy, keep those hands up. Never forget you're in a fight."

The two young women both adjusted their stances and continued.

"I could say the same to you."

She turned to find Ripley coming toward her. His dark hair was mussed from his own training sessions with some of the other fighters scattered across the gym. He unwrapped his hands as he reached her.

"What do you mean?" she asked, refusing to meet her old friend's dark eyes.

"You're distracted. I've seen it for a while now. You don't fight distracted, Esme. That's how you end up dead."

She shook her head. "I'm not in a fight," she muttered.

He arched a brow. "You're always in a fight, you know that. Better than most."

She took in a long breath. He wasn't wrong. Her life was a fight, she had grown accustomed to that. Finn had been a distraction to it. Her thoughts of him, those images and feelings that intruded in her dreams and her waking hours, that took the edge off of her. It had to stop.

Even if the idea stung.

"I know," she said softly. "I know."

He turned away and she watched him smile broadly as Jane approached. "There's my Janie."

Jane's cheeks darkened in an uncommon blush. "If you keep promising to make me yours, be careful or I'll take you up on it someday."

Ripley chuckled as he strolled away and left the two women alone.

"Someday you're going to have to make good on all those promises you two tease each other with," Esme said with a false smile.

Jane looked over her shoulder at Ripley. He was standing at a different ring now, speaking to one of the fighters, but he glanced back at Jane and winked.

"Maybe someday," Jane said. "I mean, who wouldn't want to steal a little bit of that?" She handed over a towel. "But you realize he's right, don't you?"

"Oh good Lord, you two aren't my guardians. I don't need you parenting me." Esme snatched the towel and began to tangle it between her hands.

"Don't you?" Jane asked. "How do you figure that when you're planning to be so reckless tonight?"

"Please don't tell me you told Ripley about my plans to sneak into Finn's home tonight and observe the ball. The last thing I need is for him to get involved, I'm sure he'd have a great deal to say about me fucking a man who is a member of his club, not to mention all the rest."

"*I* have a great deal to say about it," Jane said with a shake of her head. "That earl of yours isn't wrong when he tells you that exposing yourself to Society is an enormous risk."

Esme stared at the tightly corded ropes of the ring. "He isn't mine."

Jane was quiet for what felt like a very long moment, then she said, "That's what stood out to you? That I told you he was yours?"

A glare from the corner of her eye was all Esme could muster. "You are blowing all my reactions out of proportion. I know exactly what this situation is, Jane. I know what I can and cannot expect and what I must and must not do. I'm not a fool. I cannot depend on some man to determine my fate. Even this one who hasn't proven himself to be anything but—"

She cut herself off and Jane raised her eyebrows. "Oh, Esme."

"Don't," Esme said, and hated how her voice became choked. "Please don't. I'm going to his ball tonight, and I'm tired of arguing about it." She pushed the bottom ring rope down and ducked under the top one to join the other women who were sparring.

Jane shook her head and as Esme stepped up to one of the other women to begin her own practice session, she heard Jane say, "It seems the worst danger might be him, not anything else."

Esme ignored her, but in her heart she knew those words were true. She was becoming increasingly attached to Finn, and that could lead to nothing but pain, heartbreak and potentially worse if she couldn't regain some control over herself.

∼

Finn had always enjoyed a ball. Unlike his unlucky sister, he had been popular from the first time he stepped out as a man, always surrounded by friends and admirers. He was a proficient dancer and a practiced flirt, so ladies always flocked to him, filling his time with mindless conversation. And sometimes after the balls, he'd been able to manage encounters with willing widows or bored ladies who were desperate for pleasure outside of the bounds of their awful marriages.

None of it had ever meant anything, but tonight as he stood in his ballroom, there was a great deal of meaning to everything.

First, it was his sister's engagement gathering. She was currently surrounded by cooing ladies, all of whom seemed to hang on her every word as she spoke about her long friendship turned love with Sebastian. If the couple had feared a scandal over the sudden engagement, it seemed they would not have it. Sebastian's utter and obvious devotion to her had squelched any talk about wallflowers forcing marriage upon unwilling rakes.

And so, Marianne had a celebration instead of a refutation of changes against her character and worth. Finn couldn't have been more pleased.

That would have been his only emotion had he not kept looking at the door, waiting for the arrival of his second reason for this gathering: an excuse to connect with the current Marquess of Chilton. The man was late and more than fashionably. If he didn't come, well, Finn would have argued with Esme for nothing. There should have been more to it but there it was.

He hated that they'd quarreled. Hated that she'd hardly looked at him when he said goodbye. Hated that they hadn't interacted since that moment. He missed her, strange as an idea as that was. Missed her touch and her company, but also her smile and the sound of her voice.

As he pondered that thought, he felt someone touch his elbow and turned to see that Marianne had approached him as he brooded. She smiled up at him, face lit with pleasure and happiness.

"Do you have a dance for your sister?" she asked. "Or have the debutantes forced their claim on you for the entire night?"

He didn't tell her he'd been studiously avoiding anyone who looked as though they wished to dance, but smiled. "I'll always have a dance for you."

He took her arm and guided her to the floor where they began to twirl in time to the music. Marianne was quiet as they did so, studying his face with a worried expression.

"You don't appear happy, Finn," she said at last.

He made himself smile. "For you? I'm over the moon."

Her hand gripped his a little tighter. "Thank you. But what about *you*?"

"What do you mean?" he asked past a suddenly dry throat. He didn't want to reveal too much to her about his current dilemma. It wasn't safe for one and he wasn't certain he could make her understand for another.

She shook her head. "Phineas, I'm not blind, you know. I can see you've been troubled for a while."

"You and Sebastian might have had just a little to do with that, you know. A brother can only take so many shocks to the system, even if they lead to great happiness." He said it in a teasing tone and was pleased that she blushed and smiled.

"I admit our imprudence in the countryside adding to your overall discomfort was something I'd thought of. But…but it's more than that, isn't it? Larger than us. Isn't there *anything* I can do to assist you?"

The music had begun to filter away and the couples were

bowing and curtseying to each other before they filed off the floor. Finn caught Marianne's hand and lifted it to kiss her knuckles gently.

"Be happy. I promise you that there is nothing in this world that helps me more."

She touched his cheek before she took his arm so he could lead her from the floor. As he did so, an announcement echoed from the ballroom door.

"The Marquess of Chilton."

The partygoers paused and looked toward the newcomer, then returned to their conversations as the other man entered the fray. Finn couldn't help but track him, his heart beginning to pound.

"I didn't realize Lord Chilton was invited," Marianne said with a slight wrinkle of her nose. The same one she always got when she smelled something unpleasant. "You and Sebastian aren't in his circle, I don't think."

"No," Finn said, trying to master his tone so his interest wouldn't be marked and discussed. "I invited him. A late addition." Her disgusted expression didn't change and Finn laughed. "You don't like him?"

"No." She smiled up at him in return. "He isn't a very pleasant man. He's always rude and too loud. And there is something about him that makes me...nervous. Not in a good way."

Finn glanced toward his quarry again. It was odd that he'd never sensed a feeling of discomfort around the new marquess. But then again, he wasn't a woman. He wasn't under threat.

"You were close to his uncle, though, weren't you? The last marquess seemed a far superior man," Marianne continued.

Finn nodded. "I was. The man took me under his wing after I inherited and was never anything but kind and helpful. Far more of a father than our piss-poor paternal figure."

Marianne's expression grew sad. "I'm happy you had someone like that in your life, Finn. Is that why you invited the nephew? As some sort of recognition of the uncle?"

He nodded, for it was a good explanation. Better than to tell her he'd been tupping the long-missing Lady Charlotte in secret. What would his sister say to that? "I think I owed it to Chilton to make some effort. This was a sought-after invitation but a large enough gathering that his presence wouldn't be uncomfortable or odd."

Marianne watched the gentleman again. Chilton had moved to a small group of men and was talking in a rather animated fashion that seemed to be off putting to his audience. She shivered. "You know I always liked Chilton's cousin, your friend's daughter. Charlotte? Though I didn't know her very well, as she was a bit older than I was."

Finn tensed. Esme had mentioned Marianne a few times, but he hadn't thought to ask Marianne about her in return. This was an opportunity to do just that.

"Her disappearance is still one of Society's greatest mysteries," Finn said as cautiously as he could.

Marianne glanced up at him. Now she worried her hands before her. "Yes. I know there are many theories on that score."

"Such as?"

She sighed. "Her cousin has always implied she left to pursue an imprudent affair on the continent. An attempt to ruin her reputation in absentia."

Finn nodded slowly. "I've heard the same from time to time when the subject came up. Do you believe it?"

He didn't know why he needed the answer. Needed to know what the gossip was amongst the ladies who had once called Esme acquaintance and friend. But he did.

"I don't know. There are friends of hers who say they've never heard from her again after the disappearance. Not a letter, even to people she was very close to. Perhaps that's merely indicative of her truly taking to a new life. Or…or…"

She trailed off and shifted with discomfort.

"Or?" he pressed.

She swallowed. "There are those who think she might be dead.

That everything her cousin has said is a lie, meant to cover up his misdeeds. Not that he has to. His position seems to have protected him, and not her. As is the way of Society in a great many instances."

Finn bent his head. The statement gave some credence to Esme's belief that her cousin was dangerous. If the other ladies of the *ton* even hinted at it in gossip, that meant a great many of them had experienced that flutter of intuition that the new marquess was not a safe companion.

"You are pale as paper, Finn," Marianne said, and gripped his hand in both of hers. "Are you well?"

He didn't have a chance to answer when Sebastian crossed the room to them, his gaze focused firmly on Marianne rather than Finn.

"I am here to steal my love for a dance," Ramsbury said, holding out a hand to her.

Marianne's concerns seemed to have floated away as she laughed up at her fiancé. "We have danced two times already, Sebastian! We shall cause a scandal at this rate."

He shrugged. "Oh no, what will happen? Will we be forced to marry?"

She shook her head at Finn. "He's a cad."

Finn forced a smile at their teasing. "You knew that before the bargain was struck, my dear. There is no escaping now, not that I think you wish to do so for one moment. Now off with you two. Scandalize away."

Sebastian winked at him before he whisked Marianne to the dancefloor and spun her around, holding her too closely as he murmured words to her that made her blush. Finn sighed and turned his attention back to Chilton. He had removed himself from the company of the group he'd been socializing with earlier and now he stood alone, watching a small circle of women chat.

Finn smoothed his waistcoat and drew in a deep breath. He'd orchestrated this man's arrival here with a purpose. It seemed now was the time to pursue it. He just hoped he would have something to report to Esme when it was all over.

CHAPTER 16

Esme crouched on the floor of the balcony perched high above the ballroom, peering through the slats at the crowd bobbing below. The gathering had been nothing but a success, just as she had expected it would be when she'd first stumbled upon this magical room days prior and seen the hard work being put into the decoration. Despite her purpose in coming here, sneaking into the house, forcing her way past a lock to this hiding spot, she hadn't been able to keep herself from being lost in the ball, at least for a while.

It had been years since she had gone to such an event. She'd always enjoyed a ball and had danced and laughed and flirted without a care in the world. She could scarcely recall that carefree girl she'd been in those days, the one who hadn't truly known loss or fear or desperation.

She blinked at stinging tears and focused her attention on Finn. He looked dashing in his formal clothes and certainly the ladies in attendance noticed. He'd been the center of attention all night, smiling at the attendees, talking with the chaperones. If he wished, he could pluck any flower from the garden of debutantes and make her his bride. Society would celebrate as he went forth into his expected future. Once he did, he would probably never look back at her at all.

That shouldn't have stung, but it did as she watched him talk to his sister for a moment. Marianne had been glowing since she'd entered on the arm of her fiancé, the devastatingly handsome Earl of Ramsbury. If the way they looked at each other was any indication, they were truly a love match. What a thing.

Finn stepped onto the dancefloor with Marianne and they took an elegant turn around amongst the crowd. She smiled at how lovingly Marianne looked at Finn. It was good he had that. He deserved it. He was a decent man, at the heart of it. His refusal to accept that she would come here to observe the ball wasn't about being cruel, she knew that. It was to protect her.

Even if it wasn't his place.

The song finally ended and the siblings made their way to the edge of the floor where they continued to talk for a moment. Esme noted the way Finn tilted his head, the way he stood with his shoulders pushed back—she noticed every detail about him. It was impossible not to when she knew that body so very well and wanted it even more. What would it feel like to dance with him, to go back in time and meet him when she wasn't touched by loss and fear? Would he have held her close, splayed his fingers across her back? Flirted shamelessly and made her toes curl in her slippers with things she hadn't even begun to understand then?

She blinked to clear those thoughts away and heard the butler's voice at the ballroom doors. "The Marquess of Chilton."

She pivoted so fast she nearly deposited herself on her arse from the squatted position she was in. For a moment she searched for her father and when she saw her cousin her chest hurt. But Francis was here! He had come at Finn's request.

She hadn't seen him since she ran, and she flinched. He was wearing her father's diamond pin in his cravat. She recognized the glint of it in the lights of the ballroom and she gripped her hands into fists at her sides. Her mother had given her father that piece—it was not part of the inheritance of title.

She stared as he moved into the crowd, being greeted by those around him as if he weren't a monster. How could they not see that he was a monster? Why did they shake his hand and bow their heads toward him with the same respect that had been afforded her wonderful father? It was so desperately unfair.

She glanced at Finn and found that he was now alone and also staring at Francis. Even from a distance, she could see the difference in his stance. He looked like a fighter now. Good. She needed him to be a fighter as he slowly crossed the room and found her hateful cousin.

The two men greeted each other and she watched them speak. It all looked very normal and even friendly except that Finn had tucked a tightly clenched fist behind his back. Her cousin laughed at something Finn had said, slapped his arm like they were old friends. She wanted to vomit.

Oh, how she wished she could hear their words. To listen in so she could parse out if Francis said anything of importance that Finn might not catch. Even if he claimed he didn't, he had to need help. And she needed to be part of this plan. Needed to be the one to see her cousin's downfall if they could prove he was the villain she believed him to be.

Finn leaned in almost conspiratorially and then motioned to the ballroom doors. Her cousin nodded and together they exited the glittering hall, leaving behind Finn's guests and the safety of the eyes around them.

Her heart was pounding as she got up and hurried for the stairs that led away from the balcony. She burst into the hallway behind them and drew in a few long breaths. She had no idea where the two men might go for whatever private conversation Finn was arranging. She just knew she had to find them.

She rushed down a servant stairway to the same floor as the ballroom and the other parlors and chambers there. Most doors were closed as she rushed through, keeping half an eye out for servants or partygoers she would be forced to hide from. At last she turned down a side hall and saw a light flickering from one of the rooms. From her earlier self-guided tour, she remembered it being Finn's study. Of course he would take her cousin there. It was his domain and private. The perfect place to press him.

She edged closer to the door and leaned in toward the crack. The two men were sitting by the fire already, drinks in hand and a bottle on the table between them. She pushed the door just a fraction so she could hear better and held her breath as she waited for some explosive piece of evidence to be revealed that would prove her fears and perhaps change the course of her life.

∼

Ever since he and Marianne redecorated it after his father's death, Finn had loved his study. It felt like *his*, a full reflection of himself. But now, sitting in his favorite chair by the fire, he was only uncomfortable because he was seated across from Esme's cousin and all he wanted to do was slam the man through a wall.

He was so very small, the new marquess. Since they'd left the ball together for this private discussion, he'd hardly drawn breath, talking endlessly about vulgar topics like money and the attributes of the ladies in the hall not thirty paces away.

He was nothing like his uncle, certainly. And Finn despised him for that and for everything he'd done to steal Esme's choices and make her feel she had to run to save her life.

"I must say, this is a fine whisky," Chilton said, chugging another big gulp.

Finn leaned forward. He knew the man had already had two glasses of wine in the ballroom and now nearly an entire tumbler of whisky. Esme had said he'd edge around the topic of her father's death when he was in his cups, so perhaps that was the path to Finn's discovery, as well.

He topped off Chilton's glass. "It is," he agreed. "Your uncle agreed, it was his favorite when he'd come to call."

Chilton had been smiling, but now that fell and his gaze narrowed. "Did he? I had no idea." He took another long sip, taking half of the refilled glass rather than savoring it.

"He also liked his billiards on those nights," Finn pressed. "We were fairly evenly matched, though I was driven to best him. Perhaps you and I could play some time and determine if you also inherited his skill at the game."

Chilton emptied his glass in a gulp and refilled it himself this time. "I've never been much for billiards. And I don't like comparisons between my uncle and I."

Finn nodded. And there it was. The animus he'd sensed when they'd discussed the late Chilton earlier was back in the edge to the new marquess's tone. Good. That meant he was getting under the man's skin a fraction.

"I can understand that," Finn pressed carefully. "He would be a hard man to live up to."

Chilton's grip tightened on his glass. "Not as hard as some might think."

"Hmmm." Finn fought not to glare at this man who could so easily dismiss a person who had been so good and decent. "Well, perhaps I place my own feelings on the matter. I find I struggle with his death even now. It was such a sudden, unexplained illness that seemed to come from nowhere."

Francis lifted his gaze from his drink and looked at Finn, holding his stare evenly now. There was a flicker to his look, an edge that put Finn on edge in return. "Yes."

"He was never one to get ill."

"And yet he did," Francis said with a shrug. "I suppose he should have been more careful."

"Careful?" Finn repeated and felt his brow wrinkle. "How could he have avoided such a fate?"

There was a shadow of a smile that moved over Francis's face, but he didn't answer the question. "Is that why you brought me here then? To whinge about my late uncle?"

"It is an undeniable tragedy," Finn said, ignoring the nastiness to the other man's tone. "And then it was followed by the sudden disappearance of your cousin. What was her name?"

"Charlotte," Francis said, and his gaze now held Finn's firmly. "Did you know her, to be so impacted by her disappearance?"

"No. My sister mentioned her tonight when you entered the hall. I'd all but forgotten about her, to be honest. I saw her father mostly at his club or at my own home here."

"Oh yes, Fitzhugh's," Francis said with a scoffing laugh. "My uncle certainly never gave a damn about appearances."

Finn set his jaw. "You seem to have disdain for the man."

"How could I not? He was a weak-hearted fool, always wasting his time and money trying to fix broken wings." Francis had finished another glass of whisky and poured again. His words were becoming slurred now, but he kept on. "And the way he spoiled that little bitch of a daughter of his."

Finn gripped the arms of his chair harder. He wanted so badly to come out of it and slam a fist into this man, but that would do him no good. "But you must have concerns about her whereabouts," he pressed.

Francis shrugged. "Why? The little hellcat probably ran off to fuck every man on the continent. I could care less if she's alive or dead."

The rage was building now, burning in Finn's throat. He might have done something about it. Might have moved on this piece of utter shite, but there was a soft sound from the hallway that drew his attention. A little gasp.

He jerked his head toward the door and saw it was farther open than it had been when they entered. He thought he saw a flash of movement there. Francis, of course, wasn't paying enough attention to notice, which was good because Finn had a sneaking suspicion he knew who had been lurking there.

He pushed to his feet. "You know, I ought to return to my guests. But I would love to finish this conversation another time."

The other man looked him up and down. "Certainly a friendship between our two houses could be very powerful. If you'd wish to continue that, I'm amenable."

Finn swallowed back bile and motioned to the door. "I'll let you find your way back to the ballroom while I take care of a small matter before I rejoin the party. I'll send my man with an invitation later in the week."

"Very good." Francis started up the hallway toward the ballroom and when he was out of sight, Finn pivoted toward the parlor that was next to his study.

He pushed into the room and looked around. The fire in here was cold and the curtains were drawn. It appeared empty, but as the light from the hallway hit the room, he thought he saw the slightest motion behind the curtains.

He closed the door behind himself and crossed the room in a few long steps. He yanked the curtains apart to find Esme standing in the moonlight, her fist cocked back. He only just lifted his arm for a block as she swung.

∼

Esme hit the muscle of Finn's forearm rather than his cheek as she swung with her full might. She was just as pleased. She'd only swung because she wasn't certain it was him who'd come into the room rather than her cousin.

He caught her arms and tugged them down at her sides, holding her there with his superior strength as he pushed her back into the well of the window.

"I said no," he growled, his face close to hers.

She panted as she stared up at him, his expression positively feral in the shimmering moonlight. That was what was under the sleek façade of an earl. She'd felt it when he made love to her. She saw it now in his anger toward her. Both made her shiver with arousal she shouldn't feel.

"You have no right to say anything," she said back, pushing at his arms.

He refused to release her. "Don't I? I am trying to *help* you, Esme!"

Now she pushed harder and broke his hold, pivoting on her back foot and spinning away from him into the main area of the room where she'd have more space to maneuver. "Are you? I stood in that hallway and watched as you did *nothing* while he disparaged my father."

He threw up his hands. "In order to build some trust with the bastard. It took all the control I could muster not to rip the man apart piece by piece when he spoke so harshly about your father and about you."

She flinched. Yes, he'd said horrible things about her, as well. She'd let them slip off, rolling from her like water because she couldn't bear to listen to what he'd likely told everyone she'd ever known or cared for. That Finn included her in his rage toward her cousin was…comforting.

And what he said about building trust made sense, damn him. She folded her arms. "I…can understand that."

"Well, thank you very much," he said with sarcasm dripping from every word. "But none of it is the fucking point. How long have you been here?"

"In the hallway?" she asked, lifting her chin because she knew that wasn't what he was asking.

His eyes fluttered shut out of frustration. "Please."

She shrugged. "I slipped in through the servants' entrance while everyone was busy with final preparation and immediately snuck up to the balcony. The door to it was locked, as you said it would be, but I picked it."

"You picked the lock," he repeated. "I don't know whether to be impressed by all this or even more exasperated."

"I was correct about what I said before. No one even knew I was up in the rafters, watching them dance and play without a care. I was perfectly safe."

"And when you followed me and the man you believed murdered your father? The one you were so afraid of that you bolted from your life and home like a spooked rabbit?"

She clenched her hands before her. She really had no response to that charge. It had been reckless, something Jane and Ripley would have railed at her about, as well.

Finn stepped closer. "What if he'd seen you?" His voice was ragged. "What if he'd heard you like I did? I said I would handle this, Esme."

She shook her head. "And why should I trust you? I don't even know you."

"Don't you?" He closed whatever small remaining distance there was between them and now he invaded her space completely. Her mind and soul, as well. "Well, I know you. You are hard as steel thanks to everything you've gone through. You're a fighter in reality, a fighter in every way that the word could be defined. But you've spent years taking care of everything for yourself and now *I am here*."

All her breath had left her lungs with that assessment that struck her to her core. Now she stared at him, unable to stop shaking. "Why?"

His expression softened slightly and he reached out to cup her cheek. His fingers, still clad in gloves, traced her jawline. "Because of your father." He drew a short breath and shook his head. "Because of *you*, Esme. Because I can't not be here. I look at you and I *must* be here. I'm not walking away. Please, please trust me."

He was too close and yet somehow not close enough. Her world was spinning and she gripped his forearms in a wild attempt to find purchase. But touching him only brought need, harsh, undeniable need that filled the holes in her left behind by loss and sorrow and fear.

She lifted on her tiptoes and caught his cheeks. She tugged him to her, finding no resistance, and then she kissed him. There was hunger to his kiss the moment it began and he crushed her closer, his mouth devouring and pleasing and driving. She moaned against him, unable to think or bargain when they were staggering together toward the settee in front of the cold fire.

He fell first, seating himself, and she straddled over him, lifting against him as he cupped her to him and ground her down to feel his desire for her. She whimpered, increasing the kiss, rubbing him like a cat in heat, needing his touch the same way she needed breath, no matter how foolhardy an admission that was.

He seemed to know it. He pushed at her gown and chemise with a curse that was muffled against her lips. Together they fought the straining buttons of his trousers and then his cock was free to brush against her inner thigh.

She moaned with pleasure and lifted, positioning him against her entrance before she took him in one slick heavy thrust. They gasped together, foreheads touching, bodies lifting and falling in unison. He cupped her closer, she rode him recklessly and found herself at the edge so swiftly that she could scarcely believe it. What this man did to her…it was unbelievable.

She came with a gulping gasp he caught on his tongue, and he lifted to meet her jerky thrusts of her hips. He increased his tempo from below, his neck straining, his hands gripping her. Then he slid her back gently and came between them, spilling himself beneath her skirts as they both cried out with pleasure.

His fingers gripped looser on her skin as their breath matched and his arms came around to hold her closer. "Go to my chamber," he said softly, his words tickling her neck. "Wait for me there. We can discuss this situation further after the ball."

She stiffened at the order, there was no denying that's what it was, but fought her urge to refuse him just for the sake of keeping control. That hadn't gotten her anything but his intense frustration in the end. And to be truthful, she was tired now. Wrung out emotionally and physically. She needed space from everything that happened tonight before she faced off with him again and tried to keep distance from everything he stirred up in her mind and soul.

"Esme," he whispered, lifting his gaze to hers.

"Yes," she murmured before she dropped her lips for another long, drugging kiss that made her want to just take him back into her body and never let him go. At least when they were tangled in each other, everything made sense.

She stood and he stuffed himself back into place, swiftly becoming the proper earl again as if he hadn't just made her quiver around his cock thirty feet from the ballroom where the world celebrated his sister's engagement.

She smoothed her skirts, feeling the wet heat of him against her skin, loving that it was her secret beneath her clothes. She moved to the door and together they peeked out into the empty hallway. She gave him one more glance before she tiptoed away to the backstairs where she could creep into his room and regroup.

She had to for her own sake. Because this man was like quicksand and she was starting to want to stay in the mire even if it might swallow her up in the end.

CHAPTER 17

Never before had a night gone by so slowly. Every remaining moment of the ball had felt like an eternity. In the end, he'd all but kicked out the last stragglers, feeling his sister and Sebastian watching him with every move he made. They had both made it clear they thought something was amiss with him. Neither was the type to stop pushing. Eventually that might cause problems, but he'd convinced them to leave without pressing. And now he was alone, climbing the stairs to his chamber where he knew Esme waited for him.

Waited to resolve what felt like the unresolvable.

He opened the chamber door and moved through the antechamber to his bedroom. Because he had given the order for the servants not to bother with their nightly rituals for his room, the fire had burned low and it took a moment for his eyes to adjust to the dim light. When they did, he caught his breath.

Esme lay tucked up on her side on the bed, her red hair splayed out on his pillows and her hands bunched around her throat. She was fast asleep and didn't stir, even when he moved closer.

She looked younger in sleep, with all the troubles she'd carried lifted, at least in her dreams. He could almost see her across a room at a ball just like the one he'd just hosted, laughing with her friends, dancing with her father. Dancing with him. Why hadn't he ever asked her to dance all those years ago? Would things have been different for her if he had?

He shook his head at those wayward thoughts, but they wouldn't leave his mind. They were stuck there, like a throbbing wound, pulsing with answers to those questions.

If he'd made an effort to get to know Esme back then, he would have found her to be as brave and interesting and wonderful as he found her now. He wouldn't have been able to resist her, because she was irresistible. And in the ranks of Society where they had belonged, that would have led to only one conclusion.

He would have courted her. He would have fallen in love with her. He knew it because as he looked at her now, tucked into his bed, there was no doubt he had done the same in the weeks they'd been acquainted. He *loved* her.

That staggered him and he sucked in a sharp breath and steadied himself lightly on the edge of the mattress. Love had never been a positive in his life. Finn had avoided it with intense focus. Truth be told, he'd feared it.

But now he…didn't. He just felt it, warm and powerful and unyielding. It was part of him, just as she had become a part of him.

And yet she might never let him in. She might never accept what he felt because of what she'd gone through, what she'd lost, what she believed she could never have again. That realization hurt worse than anything he'd ever experienced in his thirty years on this earth.

He put a knee into the mattress and reached out to touch her arm. She immediately put up her hands with a gasping burst of breath, on the edge of a fight that broke his already fragile heart. The things this woman had endured.

"Esme," he said softly. "Esme, it's me. I'm here. You're safe."

She stared at him, almost unknowing for a moment as dreams faded to reality and then she nodded and relaxed. "I'm sorry. I didn't mean to sleep."

"I'm glad you did. The party dragged on for a long time," he said, and leaned his hip on the high edge of the bed.

"Was it successful?" she asked with a yawn, her hand coming out to trace his fingers gently.

He shivered at the touch. "Yes. It was lovely despite my anxiousness for it to end. My sister is very happy."

She smiled up at him. "And that means *you* are happy. She's so lucky to have you, Finn."

"I'm the lucky one to have her. We went through so much together and lost so much."

"Your mother, you mean?"

He looked at her. He'd told her a little about the loss of his mother. She had been supportive, but hadn't pressed. Now he felt compelled to say the rest.

"Yes. It was hard on both of us. She'd longed for my father for years, exuberant with any attention. Brokenhearted with every slight. And there were many slights. At some point it destroyed her. She could talk of nothing else, think of nothing else but him. If we would try to help, she'd scream at us. Poor Marianne got the brunt of that, especially after I came of age and lived in my own home."

"That's terrible."

"One night Marianne showed up, eyes rimmed black from no sleep and begged me to help her. She told me our mother had passed the edge of hysteria at last, despite my sister's efforts to hold her together, and was in a full collapse. Of course I came at once."

"You must have been devastated."

He nodded. "I tried to intervene, tried to convince her to come back to us. But we watched her refuse to eat or drink, watched her wither away for days, weeks. My sister and I asked her to live for us, to live for her children."

He stopped talking as pain closed his throat. Pain he had been pushing away for years now, trying not to feel that and the helplessness of those horrible days.

"She couldn't," Esme said softly, and her gentle voice brought him back to the present.

He drew a shaky breath. "She couldn't. Or wouldn't. Or both. Instead she died for a man who wouldn't even come see her when I finally found him holed up with whatever mistress had caught his eye and begged him to do so."

"He wouldn't see her?" Esme said, and sat up.

"No. He was a cruel bastard who didn't give a damn about anyone but himself." He shook his head. "I'd always known it, but that day was proof. He laughed in my face and sent me away. It was horrible."

"No wonder you were so drawn to my father. He was the very opposite of such a man."

He nodded. "Yes. I'd known of Chilton over the years, been friendly with him. But after my mother's death, he truly became one of my closest friends. One of my dearest confidantes. I cherished every moment with him."

She touched his face. "I know he felt the same about you. I do recall when your mother died, of course. But how old were you?"

"Twenty-one." He bent his head. "A man and yet I might as well have been a boy for all the good I did."

She cupped his cheeks. "You couldn't have changed the broken heart of a woman who was clearly troubled. Or the cold heart of a cruel man. But you did the next best thing, which was ensure that you didn't lose Marianne. You two are clearly close, I saw that tonight as I watched from above as you interacted. You're a good brother."

He flinched. "Am I? Sometimes I don't know. I became very protective after Mama's death. After Marianne's disastrous coming out afterward. I closed in the walls around her and told myself it was to make sure no harm came to her. But I think now that I did her no favors."

"Why?" Esme asked.

He shrugged. "I couldn't see what she truly needed thanks to the blinders of my fear for her well-being. I tried to keep her in a box of my control. When she escaped it, it led her to be a little reckless." He shook his head. "I found her in a very compromising position with Ramsbury during the country party."

Esme's eyes went wide and then she smiled. "Good for Marianne."

He coughed out a laugh at the unexpected response. "I suppose one could see it that way. It's all led to her happiness in the end."

"Then perhaps you needn't beat yourself up about any further."

He stared at their hands, their fingers folded together against the sheets. "I could have lost her."

"But you didn't. Whatever you tried to do, you accepted their love in the end. You celebrate it. You cannot be expected to be perfect, Phineas."

He jerked his head up at her use of his full given name. At her suggestion that he didn't have to be what he'd always been, the only way he knew to earn love. "I still could have been better. With her. With you."

She let out her breath slowly. "I got upset with you tonight after you found me out, but I realize that it wasn't fair. This situation is difficult for me. I was lucky enough to have a father who loved me. One I could depend on and when he was ripped out from under me, I had to learn to only take care of myself. I wish I'd had a sibling like you are to Marianne, someone to protect me like you did her."

He cupped her cheek and she leaned into his palm, her green eyes soft in the low firelight. "I'll protect you."

Those same eyes fluttered shut and her mouth set, making his heart sink. "I want to believe that," she said. "To sink into it like a warm bath. But when this is over...I know I'll only have me to depend on again. I can't take the loss, so I must avoid ever feeling it."

When this was over. She meant the investigation they were conducting into her cousin. But she also meant this thing between them. She was already halfway out his door, back to the life she'd been forced to choose. The life she didn't believe could ever include him.

It stung like fire. But she had been pushed and forced and harmed for far too long for him to try to prod her now. If he wanted her to trust him, to believe him when he finally confessed that he loved her, he had to continue to earn that trust every moment he was with her.

He drew her in and kissed her gently. He wanted to wash her away on his desire, to connect with her the only way she ever truly let him. Instead, he lay down beside her, pulling her back to his chest and wrapping his arms around her to hold her. She let her breath out in a long, trembling sigh.

"I'm not giving up," he said, his voice muffled against her hair. God, her hair smelled good. "Tonight Francis was on the edge of drunk and it led him to speak imprudently about your father and you. As enraging as that was to hear, it also encourages me to think that he could be driven to whatever the truth is if I ply him with enough alcohol to bring his guard down entirely. If I make him believe I'm an ally, or at least a potential person he could use for his own advancement."

She turned her face slightly to look at him over her shoulder and he could see how much those words meant to her. How much she *wanted* to believe he would live up to them. "Thank you, Finn."

He nuzzled her neck gently and she shivered. "Will you stay with me?"

She was silent for a moment and then she cuddled back more firmly against his body. "For a while. Just a little while."

CHAPTER 18

Finn sat in his study three days later, staring at some of the arrangements for his sister's wedding, but he hardly saw the words and numbers swimming on the page. Just as he had been since the ball, he was distracted. Esme took up too great a share of his mind for him to have any other main focus.

Things had shifted between them since he realized he was in love with her. Not only had that feeling grown with every moment he spent with her, but she had changed too. She came to him at night, they shared supper and long talks, and then they made love, over and over until he was weak from her.

But she never stayed for more than a few hours. And she never let him too close beyond her body. If he edged toward anyplace she felt he didn't belong, she offered pleasant distraction, or she slipped away into the night, leaving him aching for her body and soul.

There was a light knock on the study door and he lifted his head as Bentley entered the room. "You have a missive, my lord."

"About the wedding?" Finn asked. "They come fast and furious with the ceremony tomorrow. Put it with the pile, I intend to start going through all of it just now."

"Er, I don't believe so, my lord." Bentley stepped forward, the note outstretched. "This is from Lord Chilton. You asked that if anything arrived from him, to interrupt you with it."

Finn was already on his feet and he took the letter with shaking hands. "Yes, thank you, Bentley. Thank you."

"Is there anything else I can do, my lord?" Bentley asked.

"No. Just continue with the arrangements for tomorrow. I know Lord Ramsbury and Lady Marianne intend to join me for supper tonight, so make sure you have some of her favorite madeira available, separate from the cases for the wedding party tomorrow afternoon."

"It is already done, my lord."

"Excellent." Finn managed a warm smile. "I can always depend on you, old friend. I appreciate it."

The butler blushed a little, but then stepped out of the room and left Finn. As soon as he was alone, Finn tore the wax seal free and unfolded the letter.

Delacourt,

I realize you must be busy with final preparations for the wedding, but I've been thinking about our last conversation and would very much like to see you at your earliest convenience. This afternoon, if you've time.

Chilton

Finn's jaw set as he read the words over and over, looking for some clue within the swirl of the man's handwriting that would say he was a killer. In the end, he set the letter down on his desk and walked to the window.

He should reach out to Esme and let her know about this development. They had agreed he would wait to contact Chilton, himself, until after the wedding, even if the waiting made things uncomfortable for them both. But she would want to know Francis had made the first step, himself.

Of course, when he did that, she would rush to decisions. She would want to come along with him, to insert herself into the answers they sought. Endanger herself.

But if he went alone, he could handle Francis in whatever way he saw fit. She might be angry, but wasn't an apology better than asking permission? It didn't feel better, but that was the saying after all.

He moved to the door and rang the bell and Bentley reappeared momentarily.

"Have one of the footmen ready to deliver a return message to the marquess in a moment. And I'll be following not far after, so my horse should be ready at one."

"Of course, my lord," Bentley said.

Finn returned to his desk and got out all his writing instruments, forcing his hands and mind to settle before he began to write his short return message. This was a long chess game, a marathon, not a sprint. And since he intended to play it to a win, he had to be in no hurry.

Whether Esme would agree with that decision was another story.

∽

It had been over two years since Finn had been in the Chilton house. He'd normally met Esme's father at Fitzhugh's club or in his own home, but from time to time he'd call here. Now he stood looking around at what had once been a sophisticated parlor. Once, because now it was decorated with a garish, ostentatious eye from the overly stuffed chairs to the truly ugly crystal animals along the mantelpiece.

Gone were the serene paintings of estate grounds and favorite dogs and horses, replaced with portraits of the current marquess.

Francis in his finery. Francis standing with a gun and a dead stag's gory head. Francis in military regalia, though Finn didn't think the man had ever served.

He was still rolling his eyes when a throat cleared behind him and he turned to find the marquess, himself, had entered the room.

"Good afternoon, Chilton," Finn said, extending a hand and swallowing back the disgust that still came any time he had to refer to this man by the title.

"Delacourt," Francis said, and motioned to one of the chairs Finn had already found far too uncomfortable to sit in while he waited. "I'm glad we could arrange this meeting this afternoon. I know you're busy."

Finn sat. "I am. My sister's wedding is just tomorrow and the gathering after the ceremony is to be held at my home here in London."

"Well, that is the duty of the servants, I suppose. Glad I never had a sister, what a lot of wasted blunt on weddings and trousseaus and such."

Finn tilted his head. "Yes, and with your cousin gone, I suppose you are free of all that."

There was a slight twitch to the other man's lips. "Well, I would have worked out a way not to pay for that hoyden even if she hadn't run off. Why should I have to provide for such a woman?"

Finn shrugged even though he was gripping one hand against the seat arm. This man was truly a demon. "I'm pleased to provide for Marianne. I suppose it takes all kinds," he said.

"I suppose. And she matched well enough with Ramsbury. He has a fine fortune, after all. Very well played on your part, or hers if she forced the match somehow."

Oh, it was getting very difficult to keep himself in order now. He felt his lips thinning as he pressed them tightly before he said, "This cannot be a topic of interest to you, my lord. It barely ranks as a topic of interest for me."

"No, of course," Francis chuckled. "I actually did have a purpose in asking you here."

"Oh?" Finn didn't have to feign surprise, he truly felt it. "And what is that?"

"When we spoke last week, I had the impression you might want to carry on the link your house had to Chilton. Would that be true?"

"Certainly," Finn said. "Men of power must stick together, mustn't they? We likely share some of the same interests, when it comes to financial dealings or other things of that type."

Francis eyed him more closely. "And my uncle didn't turn you off of me before his death?"

Finn wrinkled his brow. "Turn me off of you? What do you mean?"

"Well, it came to my attention before his...his *untimely* demise that he had occasionally tried to poison others against me."

The turn of phrase this man had picked was difficult to ignore. "Poison is a hard way to go, I hear," Finn drawled. "But no, he never spoke much to me about you."

That much was true. He'd had a sense of the late Chilton's tension when he spoke of his presumptive heir, but never had gone into much detail. However, if he were turning others against Francis...that was certainly a motive for murder, alongside the inheritance of title and fortune that would follow the previous marquess's death.

"Interesting," Francis mused, Finn thought more to himself than to Finn. "I *do* have financial interests that I'm trying to find partners in developing. If someone like you were to come on board with them, it would certainly lend credence, wouldn't it? And benefit us both in the end."

"Such as?"

"I have an interest in independent country banking, you see. Holding investments, loans, that type. There are already several in my circle who have bought in."

Finn arched a brow. The country banking system was all

privately run and often corrupt. There had been stories of charlatans who stayed in one village just long enough to take the funds of the locals, then disappeared into the night with whatever they had collected, leaving destitution and destruction in their wake.

"Hmm, that can be tricky business," he said coolly.

"Not if you're on the right end of it." Francis chuckled.

Oh yes, if Finn were going to place a wager, he would have put it on the new Marquess of Chilton being involved in some kind of fraudulent banking. Why the last marquess had never warned Finn off, he had no idea.

"An interesting notion." He leaned back in his chair. "Perhaps you can give me more information in the coming days. Is there anything else you're thinking about?"

"I know someone who is running supplies to and from the continent."

"Past the blockades?" Finn asked.

"For the right price, one can make a fortune on such goods," Francis said. "We could go in together on it. You'd have to do nothing at all, just collect on your investment."

Finn almost laughed. Anyone who promised that was *definitely* a charlatan. "And your uncle was aware of these ideas?" he said. "I never would have imagined he'd be so bold."

He didn't mean bold, of course. He knew the late Chilton never would have been so criminal. But bold made it sound like he approved on some level. Like there was bravery involved.

Francis's mouth twisted. "My uncle was a coward. Turned me down flat when I asked for money for some of these things just before his death. Even threatened to go to the authorities. When he was finally gone, the deed done, I was ready to access my due. But there's a great deal in entail, forced into places where I cannot easily access it. I want more. And now that he's no longer there to stop me, why shouldn't I have it?"

The deed done. Those three small words rang in Finn's head, even though he doubted Francis had even known he'd said them, he was so busy railing in general. But they implied the man had done something. Done exactly what Esme feared. It wasn't evidence, but it put Finn closer to the edge than ever.

"I'm sorry for your misfortunes," he said softly.

Francis stopped going on about the injustices he had endured and glared at him. "Don't take a high and mighty tone with me, Delacourt. We're equals now, you know."

"It wasn't meant to be high or mighty, Chilton," Finn said.

The room was silent for a moment, thick with tension now. Francis folded his arms and said, "After your sister's engagement ball, you weren't alone."

Finn sat up a little. "I beg your pardon?"

"A lady was with you. I don't think she was a doxy, there was something in the way she moved that felt familiar. Well heeled." Finn's world was spinning now but he managed to stay in place and keep his expression as calm as he could. "So if you think you're better than me, I might remind you that you also have some secrets, don't you now?"

"An interesting road to take if you want my help and friendship," he drawled. "Attempting to blackmail me over a one-night lover."

"But she isn't just for one night, is she? I've seen the same lady coming and going to your house ever since. In an unmarked carriage that I believe is from *your* stable."

"You're spying on me," Finn asked and he couldn't quite control his tone anymore.

"A man has many ways to make allies, or force them." Francis leaned back in his chair. "But only if he must. Perhaps you need to think about your options when it comes to what I've suggested we partner in, yes? We can speak again after your sister's wedding."

Finn rose to his full height and glared down at Francis. "It seems I have a great deal to think about. Good day, sir."

He didn't shake hands or wait for a response. He simply pivoted on his heel and exited the room, signaling for his horse as he came out of the house and down the steps. He had trouble seating the animal as he thundered from the drive. All he could think about was the fact that Francis was spying. He'd seen Esme, even if he didn't fully realize who she was.

 To protect her, Finn had to go to her as soon as possible and inform her of this turn of events. And he had a very good idea of where she might be. He just didn't know how she would respond to where he'd gone, what he'd done and what he now knew about a man who was looking more and more like a killer.

CHAPTER 19

Esme's head snapped back as her sparring partner, a young fighter named Rose, landed a punch square across her jaw. She staggered and was only not deposited on her arse because they were fighting at fifty percent strength.

"Good punch, Rosie!" Campbell Ripley called from the side where he was coaching the session. "And oy, Esme, put your damned hands up. This is why you don't fight with your mind somewhere else, girlie."

Esme lifted her hands higher and just barely kept herself from glaring at Ripley. "Just been doing this for years," she muttered to herself. "Not like I know what I'm doing."

Her opponent's eyes went wide, but Rose said nothing, and they just went back to circling. Esme forced herself by sheer will not to let her mind wander and the rest of the session didn't produce any further unexpected result.

When it was over, she patted the other woman on the shoulder. "You've a good cross, Rose, and even your half-strength is powerful. If you want it, I think you have a future."

Rose's eyes widened. "Thank you, Hellion. That means a lot comin' from you."

Esme forced a smile and ducked out the ring, unrolling her hand wraps as she reached up to touch her tender jaw. She would likely have a bruise there by tomorrow. Bollocks it all.

She felt Ripley approach behind her and chose to ignore him. He was going to have things to say and she wasn't certain she had the energy to have that particular conversation.

"I'll stand here all day, Es," he said after a moment had passed. "I'm not so easily put off."

She faced him and looked up into his harsh, yet handsome face. "What are you on about?"

He arched a brow, the one with the stripe of a scar across it. "I'm also not a fool, Hellion."

She sighed. "What do you think you know, Ripley? I don't like games."

"Who is he?" he said, and folded his arms across his broad chest.

She stopped fussing with her things and pursed her lips. "Who is who?"

"Whoever is making you blush when I ask the question. Whoever is making you forget yourself in the ring and just about everywhere else right now."

She shook her head. The fact that her distraction was so obvious to Ripley didn't bode well. She shrugged and hoped she could put him off, but before she could answer the door to the fighting area opened and Finn stepped into the room. She stared at him, watching him before he saw her. She had no idea why he was here during this time that Ripley usually had his club closed to gentlemen. She couldn't imagine it was a good reason.

But despite her fears, she drank in the sight of him. He was so beautiful. So perfectly handsome in every way. She knew that body, that mouth, those hands and all they could do. Not just offer pleasure, but comfort. Support. They could make her want things she'd given up on having a long time ago.

"What the hell, Esme?" Ripley growled, his tone lower now as he caught her arm and forced her to look back up at him. "The Earl of Delacourt?"

She blinked. "What?"

"I have eyes." He shook his head. "I can see you looking at him across the room, a room he very much shouldn't be in, and you look like you just saw your favorite dessert."

"Bugger off," she muttered, and shook her arm free from his gentle grip. "You don't know a fucking thing."

"Does he know who you really are?" he snapped.

She opened and shut her mouth, but couldn't find the words.

Ripley threw his head back and cursed a streak that would have burned the ears of most ladies clear off. "He does. I can see it written on your face. He's an *earl*, Esme. You had to run from that life. How could you ever go back and be safe?"

He was only saying all the things she already knew, but Esme's eyes stung with unbidden tears nonetheless. She let out a shaky sigh. "I don't know. I-I can't."

Ripley's expression softened as if he understood something in that moment that he hadn't before. Then he patted her shoulder, pivoted on his heel, and started across the room toward Finn.

~

Finn found Esme at last in the big room, standing beside a ring in a black leather corset over a thick-strapped chemise that went to her knee. She was currently barefoot with her red hair frizzy from exertion, one hand still wrapped from where she must have been sparring.

He caught his breath at the sight of her, here in her element, watching him across the room. She looked like a goddess, as irresistible beside the ring as she was in his bed or would be in a ballroom.

But before he could move to her, he also noticed something else. Campbell Ripley, the owner of the club and his own boxing teacher, heading toward him, shoulders thrown back and the look of an angry bull on his face.

Finn squared his shoulders as Ripley reached him, setting one foot back out of habit and adjusting his hands at his sides in case he was about to have his own fight.

Ripley's gaze moved up and down him in a moment. "Well, you aren't a useless student, are you, my lord? Your stance is good."

"I'm wondering if I'll need to use it with you coming across to me like that," Finn said cautiously.

Ripley jerked his head back toward Esme. "You know who she is?"

Finn chest tightened. It seemed Ripley was here to protect Esme from him. She'd said several times that the boxing master had helped protect her when she first ran from her cousin. For that, Finn couldn't be more grateful. But seeing this man, who was properly considered handsome, come to her rescue like he had a place to do so made Finn…

Jealous.

"Oy, answer me," Ripley snapped. "You know who she is?"

Finn nodded. "I do. Do you?"

"I know exactly who she is," Ripley growled. "I saw what she was like after she ran, I protected her all those years ago from a man of power just like you."

"Not like me," Finn said with a shake of his head. "But like *you*, all I want to do is defend her. Help her."

"Oh, how lovely, a *gentleman* who likes to go around saving ladies who have virtually nothing to fall back on. That always ends well when they run out of interest in them," Ripley said, and there was something bitter in his tone that made Finn wonder what personal attachment he had to that story.

"I'm not going to run out of interest, Ripley."

"That's what they all say," the other man grunted.

Finn looked at Esme. She was still standing across the room, watching them, but she made no move to join them. It was as if she was seeing how this would play out. If Finn would be put off and abandon her, perhaps.

"I've known you a long time, Ripley," he said, calming his tone. "I respect you, and for the fact that you've helped her and continue to help her, I can only feel friendship and gratitude."

Ripley's brow knitted but his mouth had begun to relax a fraction. "You didn't look none too grateful a minute ago."

"Because..." Finn drew a long breath. He hadn't intended to say this out loud for the first time to a man who was no more than an acquaintance, but sometimes in stories about knights, they had to pay a toll to cross a bridge. Pass a test to reach the princess, didn't they? "I'm in love with her," he said softly.

Ripley stared at him for a moment that felt like it stretched a lifetime. "Does she know that?" he asked, gentler now.

Finn shook his head. "I think we both know she isn't in a place to accept that from me. Not yet."

"No. Her shell is very strong, life led in your high society made her so." Ripley glanced back at her and then back to Finn. "Would you love her enough to let her go, if that was what was best for her?"

The pain that ripped through Finn at that question was almost enough to drop him to his knees. But he managed to maintain calm. He had been clinging to the notion that somehow he could work this out, get Esme out of danger and then find a way to welcome her back into his world. But Ripley was only presenting an option that Finn knew was very much also available.

He might never find a way to bring her home. She might not want to come home after everything she'd endured. She might not want Finn and all his life entailed.

"If I had to, if it was what she wanted or what was best for her, yes." His hands tingled and he shook them out at his sides. "I'd walk away."

A long silence stretched between the men and then Ripley stepped aside and motioned his head toward Esme. "Go on, then."

Finn blinked in surprise, but moved toward her regardless. She shifted to stand a little straighter as he came near, and he felt her reading him in that scant distance that separated them. She saw through him, too, for the first words out of her mouth when he reached her weren't about why he was there or whatever had happened between him and Ripley.

"What's wrong?" she asked instead, reaching for his hand.

He swallowed hard. "You may be in danger, Esme," he said, and watched how her eyes went wide, flashed with a fear she immediately tried to control. "Will you come with me?"

～

Esme hadn't argued when Finn asked her to go with him. She hadn't fought him as they loaded into his carriage and rumble off away from the boxing club and back toward…well, she assumed his home. Where else would he take her?

She stared across the vehicle at him where he sat watching at her, his fist lifted to his mouth. She could bear this no longer. "Tell me what happened." she demanded.

He nodded. "Yes. Yes. Earlier this afternoon I went to meet with your cousin."

Her head began to spin as she tried to digest that information. "You what? Why? And why didn't you tell me that this was your plan?"

"Esme." His tone was even.

She blinked as reality became clear. "Because you thought if you did that I might follow. What happened to being trustworthy, Finn? What happened to not keeping me out of a situation that involves only *my* well-being in the end?"

He caught her hand as she'd done his in the club and held it gently. He leaned forward, his dark eyes bright with earnest concern and…and something else she feared to see in them.

"I was never going to keep it a secret for long," he said. "Look into my eyes and know that's true."

THE HELLION'S SECRET

She did and she could see it. God help her, she believed him. Because she wanted to or because he was really true…well, that was something likely still up for debate.

"You said in the club that I was in danger," she whispered. "How?"

"Francis invited me to join him, said he wanted to renew the friendship between my house and your father's," he said. "But when I didn't respond immediately to his offers to join in his financial… well, no one could call them less than schemes, he moved to a different mode of convincing. He moved to blackmail. He's been watching my house."

Her lips parted and she felt like her throat was closing. "But…but I've been coming to your house."

He nodded. "He's seen you do so."

"No!" she almost screamed, and pushed herself back on the bench of the seat like she could escape the horrible words he'd just said. All her fears rose up in her chest like demons and words fell from her mouth in a jumbled mess. "No, no that cannot be true. It can't, not after all this time. He can't know I'm in London, he can't know where to find me. No, no, no-"

Finn lunged toward her and fell to his knees on the floor at her feet. He cupped her cheeks gently, smoothing his thumbs over her skin. "Please, please listen to me. Please, Esme. Please breathe."

She fought to do so and blinked at the tears that stung so strongly that she knew she couldn't keep them from falling.

"He doesn't know that the lady he's seen is you. I'm almost entirely certain because I don't think he'd be able to keep that to himself when he spoke to me about it. He thinks I have some lover, a lady based on the way she holds herself."

She continued to shake, but her heart rate started to slow with that information. "He thinks…he thinks you're bedding some innocent debutante or friend's wife, then?"

He nodded. "Yes. It's not that I don't think he'd pursue the matter, try to determine who she is…*you* are. But the lover is only a

177

means to an end for him. Still, I don't want you out of my sight while he's got this on his mind. I don't want you endangered if he starts to follow the threads he's uncovered."

"Oh God, Jane!" Esme burst out. "If he finds out where I come from, he'll find Jane."

"We'll send word to her," he soothed gently. "And if she needs a place to go I'll provide it."

Esme worried her hands before her. "Send word to Ripley," she suggested. "Jane won't go anywhere unless someone forces her. Ripley can do it."

"I will." He cleared his throat. "Though I expect a punch in the face the next time I see him for dragging him into all this."

"*I* dragged everyone in all this," she corrected, and sucked in another shaky breath. "And I know the person damaged by it most is you. What about the danger to *you*?"

He shrugged. "He threatened me, yes. But it's not something I can't handle. In truth, he revealed a great deal about himself, and about your father's relationship toward him in the process."

"Such as?"

"He's involved in illegal activities and your father was aware, refusing to invest or make any inheritance available before his death, and threatening to reveal Francis to authorities, the scandal be damned."

Her lips parted. "I-I had no idea. He never said a word to me."

"I suppose he didn't want you to worry," Finn said. "But that is certainly a motive for murder. Not only would Francis have access to at least some of the funds he so desperately desired, but there would no longer be the threat of transportation or even hanging."

"His crimes are so bad?"

"Fraudulent behavior and treason, plus the murder if he did commit it." He shook his head.

She wrinkled her brow at his troubled expression. "You look upset about this, beyond your concern for me. Why?"

He smiled at her slightly. "Leave it to you to see that." He sighed.

THE HELLION'S SECRET

"Francis also let it slip that your father was warning friends off of investing with him. Telling them he was a bad bet. But he...he never told me that. I wonder why. Did he think I wouldn't care about your cousin's bad deeds, that I might be open to them?"

She stared at him, and in that moment all her feelings for him, all the reasons she had tried to keep herself separate, became so perfectly clear. Finn was wonderful, he was good and decent, he was everything she'd ever dreamed of when she still dreamed of marrying and living happily ever after like some princess in a fairytale.

And she was in love with him. Deeply and powerfully and passionately, despite all the reasons why they could never be together.

She cupped his face in both her hands, tilting it up toward her as he continued to kneel at her feet. "If my father didn't tell you, it's because he knew you to be an excellent judge of character all on your own. He knew you would see Francis for what he is the moment he tried to recruit you, just as you did. Because you are too good a man to ever trade your scruples for money or power."

His eyes widened at that passionate defense of him, then he lifted up on his knees slightly, bringing his face equal with her own. "Esme," he said softly. At that moment, the carriage slowed and he glanced at the door behind them with a sigh. "We've arrived. I made special arrangements for us to be taken into a back entrance and the vehicle brought to a door so we can enter my home directly without being seen."

"To keep me safe," she said.

He nodded. "I'll also arrange for a few guards for the property who will be certain no one tries to enter, and my servants will be very clear on that score, even for my sister's wedding. Only those who were invited."

She flinched. There were details to be worked out, of course. She couldn't stay holed up with Finn forever, no matter how lovely that idea sounded. But for now, the idea of letting him protect her, even for a while, was so powerful. Just as her feelings were powerful, overwhelming, heartbreaking and life changing all at once.

"I'll do as you like," she said.

He looked surprised that she would agree, but when the door was opened, he pushed back, exited the carriage first and after looking around, handed her out and almost immediately through a door into the back part of his house.

His servants waiting there looked utterly confused and he held up a finger to them as if to say, "One moment," before he took her arm and led her to a parlor toward the back of the house. Away from the front windows by the street, of course. Because she wasn't safe there.

The reality of that sank in as he kissed her hand. "I've some explaining to do and other preparations to start. But please, have a drink or I'll have them send tea in."

"A drink is fine," she said past a suddenly dry throat.

He nodded and then slipped from the room and closed the door behind himself. Leaving her alone with feelings, confusion and fears that now began to grip her with an icy fist she couldn't dodge, no matter how good a fighter she'd trained herself to be.

CHAPTER 20

It took far too long for everything Finn needed to arrange to be begun. He'd had explanations to make, even if they weren't the complete truth, and protection to arrange. He'd asked for the countess chamber, which was empty and attached to his own, to be prepared for Esme. He didn't want to assume she would want to sleep in his bed every night, but he needed her close. Needed to be able to crack open her door and hear her breathing.

When it was all done, it had been nearly an hour since their arrival home. He made his way back toward the parlor where he'd left her, but as he reached it, he heard grunting inside, and thumping. His heart leapt with fear as he threw the door open.

Only to find Esme on the settee, raining punches down on one of the cushions of the couch. She glanced up when he came in, her cheeks flaming red and tears streaming down them.

"Finn," she said.

He crossed to her in a few long steps and sat down next to her, dragging her into his arms. She was trembling, the hard exterior she'd developed to protect herself cracked by the reality of her situation.

"I'm sorry," he whispered against her hair. "I shouldn't have left you alone so long, not after everything I told you."

She was breathing heavily, but she managed to gasp out, "I needed to be alone. I needed to—to feel it."

He held her closer, marveling at her strength, which never seemed to cease. "What can I do?"

She leaned back. "You are prepared to disrupt your life, on the eve of your sister's wedding, and you ask what more you can do?"

"For you?" he asked as he brushed back a lock of hair that had gotten caught on her cheek in the track of a tear. "I would do anything."

She leaned her forehead against his shoulder and he was quiet so she could compose herself. "I need to fight," she finally said.

"I-I beg your pardon?" he said.

She lifted her head. "Please. It's how I found my peace and my safety all those years ago when I ran from my cousin. It was the only way I felt like I knew who I was again, and right now I need to know who I am. I know you spar with Ripley, so you can do this with me. I *need* to fight."

"You want to fight me?"

"Not fight…hard. Spar then," she said. "Please."

He pursed his lips. There had never been a time in his life where he thought he'd agree to swing punches at a *lady*, but he could see how much she needed this. And he understood. Sometimes it took something physical to fully purge the hurts. It was part of the reason he liked boxing, too.

"Come," he said, getting to his feet and offering a hand. "I've a small practice space. We can spar as long as you'd like."

To his surprise, she lunged from her seat and wrapped her arms around his neck, hugging him with all the considerably might in her body. He cradled her close.

"Thank you," she whispered against his neck. "Thank you for not arguing, for understanding."

She began to release him and though he wanted to stay that way with her forever, he let her. Their fingers tangled as he led her from the room and down the hall to the parlor where he'd set up a small sparring space with a ring and weighted bag where he sometimes practiced punches.

She smiled up at him, her fear momentarily faded by the place. "I didn't find this when I was touring my way around your house before. It's impressive."

"If you like this, you'll have to see Ramsbury's sparring area. It's huge—sometimes he even hosts fights there."

Her smile fell. "I'll never see that, Finn. You know it."

She walked away and began to work on the buttons along the front of her gown with her back to him. She'd only thrown it on when they left Ripley's, so when she dropped it around her feet and kicked it away, she was still wearing her sparring outfit from earlier in the day.

"I'll need to arrange for you to have more clothing brought here," he said, trying not to stare as she sat on the edge of a chair near the ring and unfastened her boots.

She glanced up. "You really want me here."

"Until we can figure out how to end this, I need you to be. Please."

She pursed her lips. "You sent word to Ripley already, yes?"

He nodded. "The first thing I did."

"Well, I'll write to Jane, as well. And I'll ask if she can bring some things here, perhaps tomorrow during the bustle of the wedding so her arrival won't be marked."

"She saved you, you said. And you obviously wish to protect her. If she's so important to you, then I very much look forward to meeting her."

"*I* look forward to you unwrapping all that propriety, my lord," she said with an arched brow. "Unless you intend to fight in your cravat and waistcoat."

He smiled at her cheek, and in the same moment, marveled at her transformation. Gone was the woman who had clung to him in his parlor, mobbed by fear. She was the Hellion now. She held herself with casual confidence as she watched him, stood with guarded readiness. She was glorious and she broke his heart. He loved her for making this part of herself to survive, and he wept for the circumstances that had forced it.

"Stop staring, Finn. It's my turn to ogle you."

He laughed and shed his jacket, then stripped open the buttons of his waistcoat. She folded her arms and jerked her head toward him, indicating she wanted the shirt off.

"So pushy," he chuckled, but he was unwinding his cravat as he did so. He stripped open the buttons of his shirt and then tugged it over his head.

She let out a little sigh. "Much better."

"Is it?" he asked before he sat to remove his own boots. "Do you want to wrap your hands?"

"I will and I warn you, I plan to swing."

He inclined his head. "Very good." He grabbed for wraps and she moved to the edge of the ring, holding out her hand. He caught it and brought it to his lips, kissing the palm and then the inside of her wrist.

"We can have that kind of sparring match later," she teased, her voice a little more breathless.

He nodded. "I look forward to it."

He wrapped her hands swiftly and then did the same for himself. Finally he joined her in the ring and they stared at each other for a long, charged moment.

She stepped up and let the back of her knuckles drag along the center of his chest. The fabric of the hand wrap stroked his skin and Finn drew in a sharp breath. She smiled.

"I'm going to throw hard punches," she said. "I need to. But if it's too much, tell me."

He tilted his head. "I've watched you fight, Hellion. I know what you're capable of. I'll try to keep up."

Her eyes widened and dilated, filled with arousal. Then she smiled, stepped back and they both shifted to a fighting stance. They circled for a few seconds and she darted her fist out, but without heat or purpose. She was measuring the distance, measuring the quickness of his reaction. He was impressed with her. Many men he'd trained or fought with never did so—they just rushed in like wild dogs and it never ended well.

"Are you going to fight, my lord, or just stare?" she asked sharply.

He circled and she followed. "I'm still struggling with the idea of hitting a lady."

For the briefest moment, her confidence faded. "I'm not a lady anymore."

He wanted to argue on that score, but it would do no good. "A woman, then. *You*. I don't want to hurt you. I would do anything in this world to never, ever hurt you."

She stopped circling and stared at him, her eyes wide and filled with emotion he so desperately wanted to name as matching the love he felt for her. But she wiped it away and instead glared at him. "Respect me enough to spar, Finn. Please."

He sighed and began to dart his hand out, trying to find the right distance where a fifty-percent punch would land more like ten percent. She rolled her eyes and swung at last.

He blocked most of the punch with a quick raise of his arm, but she grazed his chin in the process and he was surprised at how much it stung.

"Too hard?" she asked with an innocent blink of those big, green eyes.

"Pretty hard, Esme," he said. "I'm impressed."

"I've fought men before," she said as she threw another punch, but he could tell she reduced the strength of it. He blocked it more easily and returned the punch, just grazing the leather corset around her midsection.

"You have?" he asked, eyes wide. He was distracted enough that he didn't block her punch and grunted when she hit him across the shoulder.

She winced like she hadn't meant to hurt him and adjusted her stance. They went back to circling. "When most women enter the fight game, they have to start on the streets. Back alleys, men who want to see your tits out, who want to see two women bite and scratch like they're going to fuck."

Finn shook his head. "I've heard of such exhibitions. How did you feel about that?"

"I hated it. Ripley hates it too, but it's the way most women make their name. Then they can exit into the more lucrative and professional fights." She swung and he dodged, but only barely. He was endlessly impressed by how fast she was. "Sometimes in those street fights, they pair a man against a woman. Again, it's really about eroticism, but they often let us use weapons, you know because we're so frail and unmatched."

She said those words and threw hard. He took the punch against the flat of his hand and shook out the sting that followed. "Fuck, that's extraordinary, Esme."

"Thank you," she said.

"With weapons? Like what?"

"Cudgels, knives. One woman used to fight men with two swords. It was very impressive, until she unmanned a bloke who once harmed her sister. Then she went to Newgate."

Finn shook his head. "You must have been stunned by such violence when you started."

She nodded. "I was. I'd been so sheltered my whole life. Oh, I was too brash and bold, it was why I never made a match in my debut years. But I'd never been struck. I'd never hit anyone in my life. At first it was terrifying, but it became empowering. I felt strong the first time I won a fight. I felt like I was able to be in control."

She swung again and this time he caught her fist and tugged. She fell forward against his chest and looked up at him, her bright eyes shining and pupils immediately dilating.

"I like a lady who takes control," he said softly.

She smiled up at him and then pivoted, breaking the grip of his hand easily. She took a few steps back. "Perhaps we need a street fight, eh?"

He arched a brow. "Oh? Do I need to go get you a sword?"

"No, I'll go bare with you," she said with a saucy wink. She gripped the midsection of her chemise and tugged. He realized as she pulled it free that she was wearing two pieces. Her top was a chemisette and as soon as she freed it from the leather she tugged it over her head, leaving her bare from the mid-waist up.

He swallowed hard at the sight of those gorgeous breasts against the dark leather.

"I think I might like street fighting," he murmured as they fell back into a fighting stance. This time when she struck out, her punch was no longer hard. She barely brushed his chest, letting her cloth-covered knuckles drag down his skin again.

He sucked in a breath and stepped in closer. "I've heard some grappling is part of women's fighting, as well. More often than men's."

She nodded. "Oh yes. Sometimes we…"

She trailed off and launched forward, catching his arms. He did the same and they moved around the ring together, eyes locked.

"And a takedown is very easy in this position," she said. Before she even finished the statement, she swept her leg against his. He didn't have enough time to adjust and he toppled backward. She came down over him, straddling his body, and pushed his arms back up over his head, holding him down.

"It seems," he said with a little smile he couldn't hold back. "That I am at your mercy, my sweet little Hellion. So how shall we fight now?"

The idea that Finn was at her mercy was a potent one, even if Esme knew it wasn't really true. Despite her skills, he was a far bigger and stronger person. It he wanted to put her on her back, he could. If he wanted to hurt her, he could.

But he wouldn't. She knew that down deep into her soul. This man would never hurt her. And that made her feel safe in ways she hadn't felt in a very long time.

She shifted, grinding down against him. She felt that he was half-hard already and smiled. "I don't think I want to fight anymore, my lord."

"No," he whispered, his voice rough with desire. "Than what do you want to do?"

She leaned down, continuing to hold his hands above his head, and kissed him. He groaned deep in his throat and lifted to meet her. Their tongues tangled and dueled, in a whole new kind of fight that set her body on fire.

"I want that tongue somewhere else," she whispered when she pulled away.

His dark eyes widened with desire, and then he pulled each hand away from her. He pushed at her skirt and smiled when he lifted it away and showed her to be naked beneath. Then he cupped her bare hips, his fingers pressing into the skin, and slid her up his body.

She realized with a start that he wanted her to ride his tongue like this. And oh, she wanted to. Wanted to use him, draw all the pleasure she could from him, forget with physical acts that were just as powerful as fighting.

She slid up his chest and perched herself over his mouth, where she hovered. He laughed and tugged her flush with him, and then the only sound in the room was the wet lap of his tongue on her. She bunched her skirt in her hands, watching him work at her as she began to ride him. There was no hesitation, he delved into the act of licking and sucking her with nothing but attention and enthusiasm. He swirled his tongue around her, latched his mouth at her clitoris and rocked her hips harder. She rested her hands back on his sides, tilting herself for better access and surrendered to sensation. It was a gift he gave, an act of love that nearly shattered her as much as he would soon shatter her with pleasure.

"Let go," he murmured against her skin.

She closed her eyes, focused on what he was doing to her. The way his fingers clenched against her skin, the way his tongue swirled, perfect pressure applied to the most sensitive place in her body. She listened to the catch of his breath, the way he moaned as if making her weak was his favorite pastime. And she spiraled in on the building pleasure between her legs, the expert way he built every brick in a wall he intended to pull down.

When it fell, she arched back, crying out his name in the quiet as she jolted her hips over his mouth and let the pleasure wash away everything else in the world. It was only him, it was only her, it was only this.

He drew her through the crisis, his hands clutching her tighter against him, never allowing escape. Only when her elbows buckled, when she collapsed back in a heap across his body, did he relent. She felt him shift, untucked her legs from beneath them. He moved over her, his hands coming into her hair, his mouth finding hers. She tasted her release on him, sank into the warmth and heat of it and of him.

"If this is where sparring with you leads, I'll do it any time," he whispered against her mouth.

She smiled. "Only with you."

"Good." The kiss deepened and she lifted her hips against him, needing to feel him inside of her. He ground down, the rough fabric of his trousers not hiding that he was hard now.

He shifted her onto her stomach and she whimpered as she lifted herself up in offering. He stroked her from behind and then she felt the bare thrust of him pushing against her wet sex. She collided back and took him inside in one harsh thrust.

"Fuck," he grunted, and then he caught her hips and any illusion she had of control was gone.

He took her hard and fast, their skin slapping, their moans intertwining in the quiet. As she supported herself with one arm, she shoved her other hand between her legs and arched against her fingers. He moved faster as she gripped him, taking her pleasure as he lost himself in his.

When she came a second time, he let out a loud cry and then she felt him withdraw and the heat of him splashed across her skin.

Together they collapsed on the floor of the boxing ring, his body half-covering hers, his hands still stroking over her as they panted together in release.

"There is nothing like you," he said as he kissed her shoulder and cradled her back against his chest.

She rolled to face him. "You can't mean that."

He nodded. "I do."

"You're too good at that to not be experienced," she argued.

"But you're *you*," he said, as if that should explain his words. "And when I'm with you, everything falls away but us. Yes, there's pleasure, but there's more. You must know there's more."

There was an edge to his voice now and she stared at his face, taut with tension that had nothing to do with passion. She swallowed. "Finn—"

"I'm in love with you, Esme," he said softly.

The words hung between them, as loud as an canon blast, as quiet as a whisper. She could hardly breathe as she looked at him and saw that he wasn't playing a game, he wasn't lying to gain advantage. He meant what he said. This man loved her, despite all the obstacles, despite the fact that there wasn't a way for this to work out.

He loved her.

She wanted to answer, even though her spinning mind couldn't formulate a response. But before she could, the door to the parlor opened and into the room came Finn's sister, Lady Marianne and the Earl of Ramsbury. They were talking and laughing together until they saw Esme and Finn, and then they both stopped short, staring.

Finn shifted in front of her, shoving her chemisette back to her so she could cover herself.

"What the hell are you doing here?" he barked out.

His sister was now looking at them through her fingers, but she lowered them as she said, "Lady Charlotte?"

CHAPTER 21

In the years since Esme had fled her house, fled her life as Charlotte, she had never come close to being revealed. Well, with Finn, of course, but that felt different. She'd been in rooms with men of power, men who'd known her father, even men who had asked her to dance at balls or paid her attention during promenades at the park.

But she'd worn a mask then, and despite her terror at first, had quickly realized that people only saw what they wanted to see when they looked at others. As a woman who fought, quite literally, to feed herself, she was beneath them. So they didn't see a daughter of a marquess.

But now Marianne stared at her, her eyes wide as Esme smoothed her wrinkled chemisette and shoved her skirts lower over her calves, and *she* knew.

"I-I—" Esme began, though she had no idea what she could possibly say to respond to this. It was as if all words and thoughts fled her mind in her absolute terror.

"You're mistaken," Finn snapped, and got up, tugging Esme behind him and continuing to block her with his body. "What are you doing here?"

"We were invited," Ramsbury said, his expression one of both shock and respect. "Remember? The wedding is tomorrow? Family gathering to celebrate? Last-minute details?"

"Damn it," Finn grunted. "Is it that late in the day?"

Marianne stepped closer, straining to look past her brother toward Esme. "I'm *not* mistaken," she said. "You're Lady Charlotte, the Marquess of Chilton's daughter. Finn, you only asked about her a few days ago at the ball when her cousin entered the room. Is *this* why?"

"Finn," Esme whispered, gripping his arm.

Then she thought of his face when he said he loved her. Because of that, he would destroy himself, wouldn't he? She knew that was the kind of man he was. She loved him in return, so she couldn't let him.

She stepped around him and inclined her head toward Marianne. "You're no fool, my lady," she said softly. "I cannot deny my identity."

"Esme!" Finn said. "You owe them no explanation." He glared at the others. "She owes you *no* explanation."

Marianne's eyes widened, though Esme wasn't certain if it was because of her desire to know what the hell was going on, or because of Finn's strenuous defense of her. But then Marianne drew a breath, sent a glance toward Ramsbury, and her expression softened. She held Esme's stare a moment and then nodded.

"I apologize for...for pressing. But of course you owe me nothing. I would never force you to give an explanation, despite my utter shock at seeing you here. Forgive me."

Esme's lips parted. "I couldn't judge you for the shock. I know my disappearance caused a stir."

"That's an understatement." Marianne smiled at her. "All I can say is that I'm so happy you seem to be unharmed. I admit I feared for your safety sometimes over the years."

A blink at tears was all Esme could manage at that statement. As part of her survival, she had pushed away the thought that she might be missed, worried over, by anyone in her old acquaintance. She'd had to cut all that away. The soft welcome in this gentle woman's gaze reminded her of all the relationships, friendships, she had lost.

Marianne held her gaze. There was no judgment in her stare, even if intense curiosity remained. "It's been a long time, my lady. I hope you'll join us all for supper."

Esme's head spun. "I…I could not. I've nothing to wear and after what you just saw, you cannot possibly wish to break bread with me."

Ramsbury let out a sharp laugh. "Oh, Delacourt has seen worse. Now we're even."

Marianne leaned back and elbowed him in the ribs, her cheeks flaming.

"Ouch, love," he said with an indulgent look for her. Then he smiled at Esme. "Please, you really should join us."

"If a gown is truly the sticking point, I've many items still here in my old room. I think we could find one that would fit." Marianne stepped closer. "Please?"

Esme looked briefly at Finn. He shook his head gently. "You don't have to do anything you don't wish to do," he said softly.

No, he'd never force her in any way. She sighed. "The damage is done." She looked at Marianne again. "I-I would appreciate the lending of a gown, my lady." She stepped from the ring and swept her own simple frock from the floor. She wrapped it around herself, fastening it carefully before she looked at Marianne again.

"I'm so pleased," Marianne said and then grabbed for Esme's hand. "Come, we'll go right now. It will give the gentleman a moment to talk."

She was already dragging Esme across the room, toward the door. Esme could have easily broken the grip, but there seemed no point. This was happening now.

So she gave one last look toward Finn over her shoulder. It was evident they would continue their truncated conversation later.

Which meant she had to find some way to respond to his declaration of love for her.

One that wouldn't leave them both broken in the end.

∼

Finn let out a long sigh as Marianne and Esme left the room together. If his sister had thought she was being subtle with her hard looks at Sebastian, she certainly hadn't been. And poor Esme just seemed...blank. Stunned.

It wasn't the way he'd wanted what they'd shared in the ring to end. Wasn't ever how he'd wanted her to look after he confessed he loved her.

He shook his head and ducked out of the ring, grabbing for the shirt he'd discarded earlier. As he tugged it over his head, he moved toward the sideboard. "Drink?"

"It seems we both need one," Ramsbury drawled.

As Finn pulled out glasses and uncorked the bottle, he could hear his friend moving around the room. When he turned back, he found Sebastian had gathered the remaining items of his clothing scattered at the ring and placed them over the back of a chair. He held out a hand and took the drink Finn offered.

"You know I'm just going to pester you until you tell me everything. We could skip that part if it would trouble you less." Ramsbury sipped his drink.

Finn let out his breath on a shaky sigh. "I know you will. But in this case, there is nothing to tell."

An arched eyebrow was the response. "I beg your fucking pardon, but your sister and I just burst into a room where we found you in the half-naked arms of a much-discussed missing heiress. How is there *nothing* to tell?"

Finn flinched at the pointed question. He'd known Sebastian for most of his life. They'd bonded at school, become close as brothers. Aside from a few of the details about his mother's death that he hadn't shared with anyone until Esme, he'd never shied away from discussing anything with his friend. Right now, he wanted so desperately to tell Sebastian everything. Despite his playful and rakish act, Finn knew that if he told him every detail, he'd have nothing but unmitigated support from the earl.

And advice. He'd have advice that he feared he desperately needed. And yet he couldn't.

He swallowed. "Her story is complicated."

"I assume so," Ramsbury said cautiously. "What with her disappearance and all the rumors around it. And yet she's here. In London. And apparently with you."

"But it's not *my* story to tell. I'd never betray her trust in me, no matter how much I want your counsel and support."

Sebastian's lips parted and he stared at Finn like he'd never really seen him before. His expression softened and he stepped closer. "You're in love with her."

"Am I so obvious?" Finn asked after he took what felt like the longest pause to gather himself.

"Only to someone happily suffering from the same affliction," Sebastian said with a small smile. "I see it in every part of you."

"Yes, I am," Finn admitted, and glanced toward the ring. "I had just told her when you timed your interruption so perfectly."

Sebastian chuckled. "I'd apologize, but again, we *were* invited."

"I suppose you were."

"Do you think she loves you?"

Finn set his drink down and ran a hand through his hair as he thought of Esme's expression when he'd admitted how he felt. The way her breath had caught, the way emotion had entered her gaze and her fingers had clenched against his chest just a little harder. He thought of all the ways she had trusted him when it wasn't her nature to do so after all she'd been through. The way she tried to protect him, even to her own detriment.

"I've reason to hope," he whispered, because he feared if he declared those hopes too loudly that they would dissipate into the wind and vanish forever. "She looks at me sometimes and I see...I see..."

"Everything," Sebastian finished for him softly.

He looked at his friend and saw in that instant how deeply he loved Marianne. It was a comfort to know she would be loved like that. That Sebastian would be. They were the two people he'd cared for most deeply until Esme. He wanted them to be happy.

And yet when he saw the certainty of his friend's affection in comparison to the endless doubt of his own, it stung all the more. Because he could have, *they* could have, something just as beautiful and permanent, but only if she allowed it.

"Yes, I see everything," he said softly. "But she isn't the same person she was when she was Lady Charlotte."

"I noticed you called her Esme," Sebastian said.

"It's her name." He gave no further explanation for that statement. "And she'll fight. She may not be able to accept my heart or my life or my protection. Even if she wants all of it, she may still walk away."

"I'm sorry." Sebastian squeezed his bicep gently. "Can I help?"

Finn gave a humorless laugh. "Are you suddenly so serious and sincere?"

"When it comes to my best friend, my brother...soon in more than heart, in actual name...most definitely." There was no teasing to those words.

"I-I'm sorry I bucked the idea of you being with Marianne," Finn said softly.

Sebastian's forehead wrinkled at the change in subject, but then he shrugged. "I was...oh, that's an odd thing to say...I *was* a rake. Very proudly so for a very long time. You wanted to keep her safe. I understand now, just as I understood then, why you would see me as a danger to her. But now I take on that duty, myself. It is, in fact, one of my greatest pleasures that I'll stand by her side and slay any of her dragons for the rest of my days. And I hope that Esme can allow you to give all of yourself to her just as freely and joyfully. You're a prize, you know."

Now Finn couldn't help but snort out a laugh, even though he realized Sebastian was being entirely serious. "Oh, don't go soft on me now." He slung an arm around his friend's shoulders. "I can't take it."

"And I can't take you being so undone," Sebastian chuckled, the tension in the room broken by their teasing. "Look at you, you're a mess. Go ready yourself for supper. I'll do my best to put you in a good light for the lady, though God knows it's a challenge."

"God knows," Finn said as he slugged his friend lightly in the arm, gathered up his things and headed for the door.

But even though they were playing, he feared Sebastian might have actually hit upon a truth that would break Finn's heart in the end: that there might be no positive light that would be enough to break through the shell Esme felt she had to put around herself.

And that would be the loss of his life.

CHAPTER 22

Esme smiled as she looked around the soft pinks and yellows that decorated Marianne's old room. There was a sweetness to the chamber, with its ragged toys lined along one windowsill as if they were old friends, the remnants of girlish days past. It made her wonder what had happened to her own old stuffed bear toy, Mr. Nix. It was likely her rotten cousin had burned him, along with everything else she'd ever owned. A depressing thought, indeed, to be erased from history so easily.

Marianne came into the bedroom from the dressing chamber with a few gowns draped over her arm. "These are older, of course. I've lived in my own home for several years, but we needn't be the most fashionable for a friendly family supper. And I honestly always liked the higher waists from the gowns three years ago. They're a little lower now and I always feel they hit me wrong."

"They could not," Esme said with a smile she didn't have to force. "You are so utterly lovely in that yellow, I cannot imagine you look anything but perfect in whatever you wear."

Marianne blushed and set the dresses on the bed, then smoothed her skirt. "Oh, that's very kind."

Esme found herself taking a step toward the gowns, drawn in by the beautiful fabrics and the fine cuts. She had almost forgotten what those things were like. She touched the silk of a dark green dress and jerked her hand back. Her palms were too rough for such a thing, it seemed, but the fabric was so lovely, with little swirls and in the slightest lighter green than the main color.

"I wouldn't even know what was in fashion anymore," she murmured.

"You'd be fashionable and beautiful in a sack, I think," Marianne said, and stepped in to spread the dresses out along the bed to show them off more fully. "Oh, how I used to envy how lovely and confident you were."

"Did you?" Esme shook her head. She had put all those memories away to protect herself.

"Of course I did, Charlotte," Marianne said.

Esme flinched. "I go by Esme now."

She waited for that sentence to be questioned or her request to be refused, but Marianne only inclined her head and squeezed Esme's hand. "Forgive me, *Esme*. I used to stand on the wall with my friend Claudia and we'd always talk about how you were one of our favorite diamonds of any season. Not only did you shine, but you were never unkind."

Tears suddenly stung Esme's eyes and she turned away so Marianne wouldn't see. "Th-thank you. I remember Claudia. How is she?"

Marianne's lower lip wobbled. "She…she died very recently."

"I'm so sorry," Esme whispered.

There was a moment's pause and then Marianne gently filled the silence. "That first gown you admired is such a pretty green. It almost perfectly matches your lovely eyes. Would you like to try it on? I could help you."

Oh, Esme hadn't thought of that. Someone would need to help her with her gown. With just the one exception, she had made gowns that were easy for her to manage herself. When Jane wasn't present, she had no one to depend on and she didn't want to have to do so. But in her old life, in Marianne's life, there were maids and friends to help.

"I'd be grateful for the assistance," Esme said, and began to unhook her dress.

She realized she still had her leather corset beneath and her cheeks heated. It was for fighting, a layer of protection during sparring and the like. But to a woman like Marianne, especially when she had seen what she'd seen in the ring earlier, it must have seemed scandalous. She unlaced it hurriedly and set it aside.

"You—you must be shocked by everything you encountered today," she said softly as she stepped into the gown while Marianne held it.

Marianne's little laugh as she moved behind Esme to fasten the dress surprised her. "I won't say I *expected* to find my brother like that, no. But as Sebastian said, it makes us even."

Esme bent her head, her cheeks heating further. After all, she knew exactly what Marianne meant. Finn had told her about his shock in finding his sister and best friend in a highly compromising position before their engagement.

"I can see by your expression that Finn told you about it," Marianne said, finishing the last button and coming around to look at her. "Oh, that fits you perfectly, Esme. Like it was made for you. Look at yourself."

She stepped aside and Esme stepped to the mirror and caught her breath. She could almost see herself five years ago, entering a ball on her father's arm, her greatest care then was if she could avoid some gentleman who wasn't her favorite dance partner.

"It is beautiful. Are you certain you wish me to wear it?" she asked with a quick glance toward Marianne.

"I wish you to have it if you'd like. It's been sitting in my wardrobe for years, and I never looked half so fine in it. It should be on the shoulders of a woman who looks so well in it."

"I couldn't—" Esme began.

Marianne waved her hand. "Would you like to try on any others?"

Esme glanced at the other gowns. There was a lovely powder-blue dress, another in raspberry pink that caught her eye, but she didn't want to be greedy. She also didn't want to open the door to the past too much. She didn't want to miss this when it was over, or always stare in the mirror when she was back to herself and wish she had fine things. It was best not to wish for items…or people… that were so out of reach.

"This is perfect," she said.

"Good. Now I'm not the best at fixing hair, but I am tolerable. Would you like me to try? If not, I can find a maid, though I doubt Phineas has anyone on staff who has much practice since I left."

"If you don't mind," Esme said.

Marianne motioned to a seat at her old dressing table and began opening drawers. "I think I left some things…oh yes, a brush, some pins, it will all do nicely. How clever of me to have done so."

Esme tried to relax as Marianne began to brush out her hair. It had been a lifetime since someone else did that and she almost purred at the glorious feeling.

After a moment, Marianne said, "I suppose when you said I must be shocked, you weren't just talking about finding my brother and you so…entangled. You mean seeing you after all these years."

Esme opened her eyes and looked in the mirror so she could examine Marianne's expression behind her. There was no unkindness or morbid curiosity to her face. But then, she didn't think this young woman could feel those things. She truly was compassionate and nothing more. No wonder her brother and her fiancé so adored her. She was lucky, and so were they. It made Esme's heart ache.

She swallowed past those thoughts. "It must have taken a Herculean effort to wait so long to ask me."

In the reflection of the mirror, Marianne met her gaze with a smile. "It's rude of me to press."

"You'd be odd if you didn't have thoughts about my sudden reappearance." Esme shrugged. "Especially since I know my cousin has said some things about where I went."

Marianne's lips pursed as if that angered her on Esme's behalf. "All I care about is that you are well," she said. "When you disappeared there were many fears from your friends and acquaintances."

"And those awful rumors."

Marianne shook her head. "Well, there will always be rumors, I think. I refuse to stop living to avoid them. Not ever again."

Esme blinked in surprise. Ladies of this kind were often ruled by rumor and gossip, fearful of courting it. And yet Marianne didn't seem to care. She began to carefully twist Esme's locks to fashion them into a pretty style. The quiet hung between them a moment and Esme braced for Marianne to press her more on her past, her disappearance.

"Perhaps in time you'll feel comfortable enough to tell me. I can wait." Marianne pressed a pin between her lips and her voice was slightly muffled when she asked, "Was there anything you have wanted to know since you left Society? Any people you've missed and wanted updates about?"

Esme's lips parted. Once again, instead of being grilled for information, she was being offered kindness and some semblance of normalcy. It was almost overwhelming.

"I...I was close friends with Gillian Highgrove, the Viscount Highgrove's second daughter," she said.

"Oh, Gillian," Marianne said with a wide smile. "You'll be pleased to know she fell madly in love with Gregory Parson, the grandson of the Marquess Culpepper."

"He was very handsome—she always liked him," Esme said. "So a love match!"

"Indeed." Marianne laughed. "They occasionally shock the world by kissing on the dancefloor in the middle of balls."

"And she was always so proper," Esme gasped.

"Love changes everything."

They giggled together as Marianne continued her work, chatting about friends and even a few rivals. It felt so normal and lovely to talk like this with a friend that Esme actually relaxed with every moment she spent with Marianne. Even though, in her heart, she knew it was all an illusion. But she was going to enjoy every moment of it while it lasted.

∽

Finn entered the parlor where everyone else was gathered before supper and nearly fell over. Esme stood at the fireplace talking to Marianne and Sebastian, and she looked so beautiful that he couldn't breathe. The dress she wore was green—it must have been one of his sister's gowns, but he certainly didn't remember it. It looked like it had been made for Esme, clinging to her lovely curves before it fell across the long lines of her body. Her red hair was twisted and curled in a very pretty, if simple fashion. She was stunning.

He crossed to her in three long strides, hardly noticing how the other two stepped away to allow them a moment.

He took her hand and she stared up at him, eyes soft in the firelight. "You are so beautiful, I can hardly find words," he said.

She glanced down at herself, cheeks pinkening. "Yes, it seems the costume still fits."

"It's not the costume, Esme. It's you. Only you." He glanced at his sister, who now stood at the sideboard with Sebastian, letting him pour her a drink while they talked with their faces far too close. "Did my sister pry?"

"No," Esme said with a smile toward her. "I know she's curious, how could she not be, but she was nothing but kind, just as I recalled her to be." Sebastian began to twirl a lock of Marianne's hair around his fingertip and both of them looked away at the same time. "Er, what about him?"

"He's the best friend I've ever had and occasionally the deepest thorn in my side," Finn admitted with a little laugh. "He asked. I didn't tell him."

Her brow wrinkled. "Why?"

"Because it's not my story."

Her expression softened and she took his hand and squeezed it gently. The door to the parlor opened and Bentley stepped into the room. "Supper is served, my lords and ladies."

Finn smiled at her and then held out his elbow. She stared at it for a moment, but then slid her hand into the crook and they led the way to the dining room up the hall. It all felt so right, so normal, so perfect.

Because it was a small gathering, the foursome had been placed together at once end of the large table. Finn was at the head, Marianne to one side with Sebastian beside her and Esme to the other. She shifted a little as they settled into their chairs, her discomfort at having the wondering eyes on her clearly bothering her.

Food was brought out and Finn was pleased that neither Sebastian nor Marianne brought up anything about her past. They talked of the usual things: weather, books, a play they'd gone to see, and occasionally the wedding the next day. They were both so relaxed about that, so sure, that it made Finn's continuing uncertainty about his earlier confession of love all the sharper.

And they tried to include Esme in the talk. She answered questions about books admirably, but many of the topics were about things she was no longer connected to. And with every question, he saw her face draw down.

Finally, after three quarters of an hour, she set her fork on the edge of her plate and let out a long sigh. "You are both very kind to steer away from the awkwardness in the room that is my being here. But I know you must have questions that I think no one has yet answered."

Finn stiffened and reached out to cover her hand. It was very cold, the only indication of how fearful all this made her. He met her gaze. "Esme, you don't have to. It's *your* story."

She gave him a sad smile. "No, it's become *ours*, at least this part. And because it involves you, because it might endanger you, I think it's only fair to include those you love most in what has come to pass."

"Endanger?" Marianne said softly. "What does that mean? How would Finn be endangered?"

Finn felt Esme's pain, throbbing just below the surface. He hoped, prayed, she could feel his support just as keenly. If she would spill herself out, he at least didn't want her to feel alone when she did it. She'd been far too alone for far too long. She deserved a champion, and by God he would be that as long as she allowed it. If that was the only way he could show his love, have it received, then it was what he wanted to do better than anything he'd ever done in his life.

He only hoped he could.

CHAPTER 23

Esme felt Finn's hand tighten on her own as she drew a shaky breath to begin her story. For a brief, horrible moment, she wondered if he might not be embarrassed by what she might say. If his reluctance was about himself, not her. But when she looked at him, when she saw his warmth and love for her as plain as the wonderful nose on his handsome face, that fear faded.

Slowly, she told her story. About her father's horrible and sudden death, about her suspicions surrounding the circumstances, about her cousin's cruelty. She watched as Sebastian and Marianne went through the emotions of horror on her behalf, anger for what she'd endured.

"I know my cousin has said I ran off to whore my way through the continent," she said, her cheeks burning hot. "Or marry some inappropriate charlatan. But in truth, I ran to escape what I feared were his continued murderous plans."

"You ran to save your life," Ramsbury said with an awe to his tone. "Brave of you."

She blinked at that kindness. "Th-thank you, my lord."

"Sebastian," Ramsbury said softly. "My lady."

She winced. She hadn't been addressed as *my lady* in an age. "Esme is fine."

He smiled at her with a nod. "Esme."

"How did you take care of yourself?" Marianne asked.

In any other woman, Esme might have thought Marianne was trying to force her to admit some shame. But Marianne was too sweet for that. By the way the men exchanged glances, she could see Sebastian had guessed some of it without having to be told the specifics. But Marianne had been sheltered and Esme didn't want to say that she'd survived on her back for a time, just in case the other woman might not like her as much. Her future husband would surely tell her soon enough.

Another reason why a life with Finn couldn't be possible.

"I-I box," Esme admitted. "I go by Hellion."

Sebastian had taken a drink and now he choked on it, his eyes widening as he set his glass aside. "*The* Hellion?" he repeated when he had his breath.

"Even *I've* heard of the Hellion," Marianne said. "You're a champion, aren't you?"

Esme nodded. "I know it's shocking, but I was lucky to make wonderful friends who protected me and helped me find a way to take care of myself after a life of being sheltered from any kind of work."

They both stared at her, surprise so plain on their faces. She wondered if they would shun her now, kindly of course, but firmly in the end. Perhaps it would be easier. They'd warn Finn against her, it might help him see that loving her couldn't be enough.

Only that wasn't what happened. Marianne reached across the table and grabbed her hand in both of hers. She squeezed gently. "You are so wonderfully courageous, Esme."

Sebastian nodded. "I'm glad to know all this because now I can help."

"Help?" she repeated with a blank look at Finn. "Why would you help? *How* could you help?"

"The why is simple," Sebastian said. "I like you. I like him, despite himself. And the how is...perhaps more complicated. I'm your servant, Esme. And I've always been yours, Finn, for any duty you'd ask of me. I would like to add that I have developed a friendship of sorts with the Duke of Willowby in the last year or so. We were both interested in the same investment situation and ended up having drinks a few times at Fitzhugh's. I'm under the impression that he was once was, if not still is, involved with the War Department. I would think he would be *very* interested the kind of activities Finn suspects your cousin of being involved in. Not to mention the potential murder of a peer."

"Truly?" Finn said with a shake of his head. "I never would have guessed it."

"I think that's how he got the limp," Sebastian said. "He's very undercover about it all. It's fascinating. But if you'd like, I could inquire if he might be interested or know parties interested in such information. I'd keep your name out of it, Esme, if you like."

There was a flash of hope that tore through her at the suggestion and she glanced at Finn. If they could stop her cousin then...

But no. That would end the imminent danger, perhaps, but a return to Society, after all she'd done and been, still felt impossible.

"If your cousin was gone, would you be safe?" Finn asked softly.

She nodded. "The next in line is an even more distant relation. He's never been anything but decent. He's rather a bore, actually. I doubt he'd hurt a fly."

Finn smiled. "I'll buy him a drink. I think he might become my best friend."

"Ouch," Sebastian muttered with a teasing wink that Finn rolled his eyes at.

"I think you should take Sebastian up on his offer," Finn said, leaning closer to her. "But you're the one who must decide."

"If Francis is dancing around your doorstep, there's no choice but to take care of this," Esme said. She looked at Sebastian. "Please do reach out to the duke. And if Willowby needs to discuss details with me I'll...I'll do it." Her cheeks flamed at the idea of her personal heartbreaks on display for even more prying eyes.

But to save Finn, she would do it.

"I'll reach out tonight," Sebastian said. "Willowby and his duchess, Diana, are attending the wedding gathering here tomorrow. I'm sure he'd be happy to discuss it further then and get more details."

"Oh, yes," Marianne said. "We could all meet with them privately at some point during the party."

Esme frowned. "At your wedding gathering? That is too much to ask, I don't want to ruin anything!"

"You wouldn't," Sebastian said and then he smiled as he settled a hand on Marianne's. "You *couldn't*."

She ignored him. "I-I shouldn't allow this, to drag even more people into my problems." Her feelings began to overwhelm her, guilt and hurt and anxiety. In a moment she wouldn't be able to control them, so she pushed back from the table. "I'm sorry. Clearly I'm overwrought. I should leave you to your family. I shouldn't have intruded here at all."

The rest were starting to rise, but she fled the room before anyone could tell her to stop. Before they could offer more of themselves in sacrifice for her: a woman who didn't belong in their lives, who could only cause trouble for them in the long run.

And she hated herself for it.

~

Finn watched Esme dart from the room with helplessness washing over him. He returned to his seat with a thud and covered his eyes with one hand. Her fears, her beliefs about what her future could and couldn't hold...they were so powerful.

"This is what you meant earlier," Sebastian said softly.

Finn let out his breath slowly. "Yes. She's had to run, had to fight, for so long. She can't believe there could still be a place for her in my world."

Marianne looked off in the direction Esme had departed. "I cannot imagine what she endured, without protection from the very person who should have been thinking of her welfare. I was and am very lucky to have you, Finn."

He smiled at her and took her hand. "Do you like her?"

"Oh, yes. I do. I always liked her from afar, but up close she is wonderful. There is a steel that goes through her, a strength I very much envy."

"You have a great deal of your own strength," Sebastian said as he put an arm around her.

She smiled up at him, adoration easy in her eyes. Finn wished it could be so for him, that he and Esme could somehow overcome the obstacles that separated them as Sebastian and Marianne had.

Theirs were far more complicated, though.

"Be patient," Marianne said. "As you said, she's had to run for a long time, never trusting anyone, perhaps even herself. It's her habit. But she wouldn't be here, she wouldn't have trusted you and the people you surround yourself with, if she didn't have some desire to stay. Give her every reason to do so and I pray she'll come around. That she'll see she has a future."

"You are very wise," Finn said, and smiled.

"I know we intended to stay beyond supper and enjoy ourselves," she said with another glance at Sebastian. "But I think it would be best for us to go. It will allow you to check on her without the pressure of guests awaiting your return."

"And I can write my letter to Willowby as soon as we get home," Sebastian said.

Finn arched a brow. "*We?* Are you implying that you and my sister will be spending the night together, before your wedding tomorrow?"

"Oh, stop," Marianne said with a laugh that warmed Finn's world. "You two are ridiculous."

They all rose and Finn led them to the foyer where the carriage was called for. As they waited, he smiled at the pair. "Love looks good on you both and I'm truly joyful for you, despite all the rest of this trouble. Tomorrow will be the happiest of days."

Marianne was almost bouncing as she stepped forward to kiss his cheek. "I cannot wait."

"Nor can I," Sebastian said. The carriage arrived and he helped her up and then turned back to shake Finn's hand. "We'll resolve this one way or another, you know. You're not alone in facing it."

"That means a great deal. Good night." Finn patted Sebastian's shoulder and then watched as he took his place next to Marianne and off the carriage went.

For a moment Finn stood in the cool night air. He stared up at the stars above with a sigh. If he could only wish on one and fix all this for Esme, he would do it. He would pull all the stars down if he could save her from her fears and her past and whatever she felt was stopping her from the life she wanted.

But he couldn't do that. So he had to go up and talk to her instead. To face whatever she'd say about his confession of his heart. Even if it broke that same heart. Even if it broke all the dreams he was beginning to have about a future with her.

∼

Esme stood at the window, staring down at the moonlit garden below. It was a beautiful view and a beautiful room, even if she was still startled by the fact that Finn had chosen the chamber his future countess would one day inhabit. It seemed so desperately unfair to sleep in the bed of a phantom who would at some point join the life of the man Esme loved.

There was a light knock on the door from the direction of the antechamber and she turned and folded her hands before her. "Please, come in."

The door opened and it was Finn. She'd known it would be, but she caught her breath nonetheless. He'd removed his jacket and cravat and rolled his sleeves to the elbow. He no longer wore boots, either. There was something so intimate about seeing him like this in this room. The barefoot, undone earl before her wasn't meant for her. He belonged to some other person, a lady with far less burden to bear.

"Did your sister and Ramsbury go?" she asked.

He nodded. "Yes. He'll write his letter to Willowby tonight."

She swallowed, forcing back the hope that could break her if it wasn't realized. "I'm sorry I made a fool of myself in front of your family."

He stepped fully into the room and crossed halfway to her before he stopped himself. "Please, hush. They understand your situation, your difficulties."

She almost laughed. "How could they ever? How could they ever truly make a place for me at their table now that they know what I've done, what I've been?"

"Because I love you."

She shut her eyes and wobbled. His earlier declaration had never stopped ringing in her ears and now he repeated it, making it clear that it wouldn't be something they could pretend away. That she could ignore until she'd convinced him not to be so foolish. "Please don't say it again."

He took another step. "But I must. I've fallen in love with you, Esme. I tell you this not to pressure you or hurt you, but because I cannot keep it to myself. It swells, it takes over, it lights up my life. I wake aching from it and for you." His breath caught a fraction and she couldn't stop staring at the earnest emotion on his wonderful, beautiful face. "Could you ever feel such a thing for me in return?"

She bent her head. She should tell him no. She should set him free. But that wasn't what was going to happen. She wasn't strong enough in the end. Or perhaps her own feelings were just *too* strong.

"I wish I could lie to you and say no," she said, meeting his gaze. "I wish I could protect you and tell you I feel nothing for you. But I can't." His face lit up and she had to fight the tears that welled up in her. "You look happy, but this is no celebration, Finn. I do love you in every part of me. And I love you enough to know that I'll destroy you if I survive whatever is about to happen and then imprudently try to put myself into your life."

"No," he said, and he moved to her at last, taking her hand, drawing her to his chest.

She looked up at him. "Please, you're no fool. The scandal of my return to Society would be intense. If anyone ever found out I'd been a lightskirt or the Hellion, and they likely would, it would be even bigger and more out of control."

"I don't care," he whispered as he traced her cheek with his fingertips.

"You *should*," she said, and stepped away even though leaving his arms felt like tearing herself in two. "And even if you somehow truly don't, I *do*. I don't belong in your life anymore. I'm not Lady Charlotte. And I don't want to hurt you."

She could see a thousand arguments on his face and she braced for a long night of them. Of growing anger and resentment that would sting like fire, but perhaps in the end would save this man. But instead of launching into those arguments, he put his arms around her and held her close. He kissed the crown of her head and let out a long sigh.

"Right now I think it's best to focus on Francis and removing the threat he poses," he said, his voice muffled by her hair. "The rest will come after."

She lifted her face to his and stared up at him. Her love for him was so powerful in that moment that she feared she might be the one convinced in the long run, even if she knew it would hurt him. He smiled at her, something so gentle, and then he bent his head to kiss her.

She lifted to him, whispering his name as she cupped his cheeks. He drew her to the bed that would be for his wife and as they fell against it, sweetness turning to something with more heat, she pretended, just for a while, that it could be her.

CHAPTER 24

The wedding was as beautiful as the bride, and Finn smiled as he watched Marianne all but float from one group of well-wishers to the next. She's always been shy, pushed to the wall where she had languished for many years, but now she looked…confident. Happy. Sebastian had somehow awoken that in her, given her the support to find herself.

"Isn't she stunning?" Sebastian asked as he approached over Finn's shoulder and offered him a drink.

He took it. "She truly is. Congratulations, Ramsbury. Sebastian. Brother."

Sebastian flashed a wide grin at him even as his eyes sparkled a little with what shockingly looked like happy tears. Then he cleared his throat. "Willowby and his wife are here. He approached me a few moments ago and said he wished to speak to you about Chilton. And to Esme if she is up to the task. Where is she, anyway?"

"She intended to hide out in my chamber today. At least that's what she told me. But I wouldn't put it past her to sneak around and spy on the festivities."

"I wish she could have joined us. Shall I introduce you to the duke and duchess?"

"Please," Finn said.

Sebastian moved them through the crowd, responding with smiles to the felicitations given from every corner. At last they reached two people standing beside the refreshment table. Finn had known of the Duke of Willowby, of course. They were close enough in age that he'd seen him at balls and the like. But they'd never formally met, he didn't think. After all, the man had been missing from Society for a long time. Rather like Esme, actually, though he had apparently been working for the Crown during those years.

Still, he wondered if the two might connect over what it was like to walk away from all they'd known.

"Your Graces, may I present the Earl of Delacourt, my new wife's brother. Delacourt, the Duke and Duchess of Willowby."

Finn inclined his head out of deference to the duke and gave a larger bow to the duchess. They were a handsome couple, no one could deny that.

"Delacourt," Willowby said. "I'm pleased to make your acquaintance. It's odd how one can circle another for years and not ever truly meet."

"Indeed, I was thinking the same thing," Finn said. He shifted slightly, trying to stay focused on small talk when what he wanted to do was dive immediately into how Esme could be protected. "Thank you for coming. It's a happy day."

"Yes, the couple seem more than content," Willowby said. "You and Ramsbury have been friends a long time, I think. It must be wonderful to have him as a true brother."

"It is," Finn glanced at Sebastian. "Though I prefer not to say that too loudly, as any compliment gives him the worst swollen head and he'll be insufferable for days."

Sebastian laughed, as did the others, but then the duchess nudged her husband. "Lucas, the poor man looks as though he might burst. He's trying to be polite, but certainly you must put him out of his misery."

Willowby gave her a half-smile. "My wonderful wife is correct. I don't want to drag out any discomfort you might be feeling. I've been told by Ramsbury that you are dealing with…a delicate situation. One that likely isn't best to be discussed in open company such as this. Is there someplace more private we could meet?"

Finn thought of Esme, pacing the carpet in the countess suite upstairs. The idea of bringing her through the entire house, risking her being seen, wasn't a pleasant one.

"I have an unorthodox suggestion for a meeting place." He leaned in and said to Sebastian, "Give me a few moments to speak to Esme, then will you bring them to my chamber? We'll meet in the antechamber there."

"Of course," Sebastian said. "And then I'll leave you to it, Marianne and I can keep the guests entertained so no one looks for you."

He squeezed his friend's arm before he bowed to the couple. "Ramsbury will show you shortly. Excuse me."

He hurried from the room and climbed the stairs two at a time. He had scarcely taken a step into his chamber when Esme burst from the countess side of the suite and rushed to him.

"Is everything well?" she asked, her eyes wide.

He nodded and caught her hands. "It is. Have you been worried?"

"It seems all I do is worry now," she said with a humorless laugh. "All my hair shall fall out at this rate."

"That would be a sad day, for I love your hair. But you'd be just as beautiful bald, I think," he said gently. "Sebastian's friends the Willowbys are here. They want to discuss everything with us and I thought up here would be the safest, if you're open to it."

She drew a shuddering breath and then nodded. "Yes. Yes, it must be done."

"Good, they'll be here momentarily," he said, and then caught her hand and drew her to him. "I wish you could have been there today, standing at my side after I gave my sister away."

"I'm sure she was lovely," Esme said as she rested her head on his chest. He smoothed his hand over her hair and for a moment there was peace in the chaos. But it ended when there was a knock on the door.

"There they are," he said, and briefly kissed her before he took her hand in both of his and they faced the door together. "Come in."

He felt her tense as their little peaceful oasis was invaded by strangers. She forced a smile though and went to Sebastian, her hands extended. "Congratulations, my lord. And please give Marianne, *Lady Ramsbury*, my very happiest wishes."

Sebastian took her hands and squeezed. "Thank you, my dear. Now I'll leave the introductions to Delacourt and go stand watch on our other guests. No one shall trouble you."

He slipped away and then they were alone.

"Your Graces, this is—" He broke off and looked at her as he realized he didn't know how to introduce her formally under these circumstances. "Esme."

She pursed her lips and some of the color drained from her cheeks. "I-I go by my middle name," she explained. "It's—"

"There's no need to explain," the Duchess of Willowby said gently as she extended an elegant hand. "Esme is a beautiful name."

"I knew your father," the duke said with just as much gentleness. "He was the best of men."

"He was," Esme said.

"Why don't we sit?" Finn suggested.

"There's tea," Esme said, and moved to the sideboard. "Finn's— *Lord Delacourt's* servants have been too kind in taking care of me."

"We're fine," the duchess said as she took one chair and the duke the other next to her, which left the settee for Finn and Esme. He thought they'd done that as a kindness, so he could be close to her and support her if she needed it.

She sat and he gently placed a hand on her knee. She seemed surprised he would do so in such company, but she didn't pull away, so he took that as a win.

"I say we dispense with any small talk, as this is a serious issue,"

Willowby said. "I believe Ramsbury may have informed you that I once worked for the War Department. Is that correct?"

Finn nodded. "He did."

"I worked in internal investigation," he continued. "Traitor spies, smuggling, the like."

Finn glanced at Esme and saw her eyes were wide. This man would truly be the best person to help them since that was exactly what they suspected Francis was involved in, at least partially.

"My father worked alongside Lucas," the duchess supplied. "And I've also helped him with his work."

He smiled at her and in that moment their connection was powerfully clear. Finn squeezed Esme's knee gently and she covered his hand with hers.

"Obviously, Ramsbury discussed some of the information about your cousin, the new marquess," Willowby continued. "But I'd like to hear it from you directly. If it's not too painful, will you tell me everything you know. First you, Esme. And then you, Delacourt. Leave out no detail. We need to hear it all."

~

By the time Esme and Finn had told the duke and duchess everything about the situation with Francis, an hour had passed. It was a strange thing. She didn't know these people, had no connection to them, and yet she didn't feel wary around them. They asked good questions, they listened carefully, and it was plain they wanted to help her.

At last, she leaned back against the settee back, exhaustion overwhelming her and sighed. "And that is all."

The duke got to his feet and paced to the window, his serious expression unchanging. While he stood there, the duchess got up. "Let me get you tea, Esme."

Esme blinked. "Oh no, Your Grace, I couldn't ask—"

"You didn't ask," she said with a little smile as she waved Esme off and went to the sideboard. "And you must call me Diana. We'll be friends, so I insist."

She blinked at the idea the duchess would want to be friends with someone like her, even after hearing what had happened and all she'd done to save herself. But she liked the woman, she *liked* the idea of being her friend.

Finn leaned in and put his arm around her, gathering her to his side. "I am forever in awe of you, Esme," he said softly, so only they could hear the conversation. "I only hope I can live up to the bravery and grit that is at the heart of you."

"It's easy to feel brave with your hand on my knee, giving me all your support without even saying a word."

"I'd love to do that for the rest of your life, the rest of mine," he said.

She jerked her face toward his. "What?"

"You know what I'm saying," he said, perfectly calm and certain. "I'm not going to ask you here, in this most unromantic setting. But I want a future, Esme. I'll do everything in my power to make sure it's possible. *Everything.*"

Diana returned with the tea and handed over the cup before she smiled gently at the two of them and then moved to stand with her husband. They talked for a few moments. It was all very serious and Esme shivered.

"What do you think they'll say?"

"I've no idea. The duke especially is hard to read," Finn admitted.

"He is. It must have served him well when he worked for the War Department full time." She shook her head. "It still boggles the mind to think of a man of his position doing such a thing."

"A rare thing, yes." He kissed her cheek. "But the world needs rare things."

The duke and duchess returned together and retook their seats. Willowby leaned forward, elbows draped over his knees and his attention focused intently on Esme. "Thank you for bearing my having a moment to think about everything you've revealed. You've been very honest, and I don't want you to think that it hasn't been appreciated. I know how hard it can be to tear oneself open and bleed for a stranger. You are remarkable."

Esme shook her head. "All these compliments will have my head spinning, Your Grace. I only hope that what I've told you can be of some use to you."

"I very much think it can," Willowby said. "Diana and I discussed it, and I think it's only fair that I give you some information in return for your honesty."

Esme caught Finn's hand and held it tightly. "Please."

"While I'm no longer a full-fledged spy, Diana and I still engage in fieldwork from time to time," he began. "And I've heard of your cousin before. Obviously some of these schemes he's been involved in before your father died. It's been hard to fully connect him to the banking, and those fraudulent behaviors are, sadly, harder to pursue. The victims often don't want to admit they were taken in. But the smuggling is more dire. And as for the murder…" He trailed off and held Esme's stare.

"You don't believe me?" she whispered, and hated how her voice cracked.

"I understand you have felt that way, that no one believed it or cared. But it's more that I hesitate to say what I must say next because it will sting. I already felt that your cousin might have been involved in your father's death."

The world began to spin and she felt Finn's hand grip hers tighter, grounding her. "You did?"

"As Delacourt determined in his conversation with Chilton…let us call him Francis, so we aren't confused."

"Yes, please," Esme replied. "I hate hearing him called by my father's title."

"Your father was warning people about Francis, threatening his schemes. Your cousin wanted that to stop. He'd made comments to several people about it. And there's evidence that he—"

He broke off and Esme got up. "What did he do?"

"He purchased a large quantity of arsenic," Diana explained, also rising and crossing to her. "It's a deadly poison."

Esme's knees wobbled and Diana reached for her even as Finn jumped up to steady her. She wanted to pull away from them both, run from all of this, even if it was what she'd believed all along.

"How would you know if he'd been poisoned?" she gasped.

Diana shook her head. "Esme—"

"Tell me!" she exclaimed. "Please."

Diana glanced back and Willowby and said, "He would have experienced intense stomach and chest pain."

Esme nodded. "He did."

"And sickness to follow."

"He vomited over and over, until it was just blood," she whispered, and tried not to picture it.

"Difficulty catching his breath."

"Yes."

"And darkening of the skin, as well as perhaps a faint scent of garlic," Diana said.

"All of those things. Everything." Esme tried not to burst into tears. "I saw it, his servants saw it. He became ill, but recovered after a few days. Then it returned, worse than before, and he died writhing."

"I'm so sorry," Diana said. "But these are the things that make us think he was poisoned. We did interview two servants who were released from your cousin's employ after he inherited. They told us just as you did."

"If you know this, if you believe it, why haven't you arrested him?" she asked. "If he bought a large quantity of a poison and all this followed, how could that not be enough?"

Now Willowby rose. "It might be," he said. "It likely would be.

But Chilton cannot be at the heart of this larger conspiracy. He killed to continue his role, but I fear he's a cog in a wheel."

"You won't move on him because you care more about smuggling than the death of my father?" Esme burst out, then pushed her hand against her mouth. In her upset, she had lashed out against not only a man who was trying to help her, but one who had a great deal more power than she did.

But Willowby's expression only gentled. "I care a great deal about the death of your father and the threats against you. With your help, I hope we'll be able to catch him for *every* misdeed your cousin ever committed."

"Help you how?" Finn asked.

"If he wants your partnership, Delacourt, your investment, to the point that he's willing to threaten the faceless lady he thinks is your lover, then his desperation may be at a peak. I'd like for you to invite him here, discuss it with him. Let Diana and I be close by, or another agent he might not recognize take part in the discussion."

"I'll do that," Finn said without hesitation.

"No," Esme said, turning toward him. "This man killed my father, caused his death in a barbaric way. I don't ever want you near him again!"

"Love," Finn began. "If he's gone, none of us will be in danger anymore. You, me, anyone else he's taken in through the abuse of your father's title. *That* is worth the risk."

When he said that, she knew it was true. This was to save him, as much as herself. She drew in a shaky breath and looked at the Willowbys. "You'd protect him?" she whispered.

"With my life," Willowby answered without hesitation and with such confidence that Esme immediately believed him.

"Very well. I cannot argue," she said.

"Diana and I will go now and make some arrangements. May we return early this evening, after the party has ended, and we can decide how to best proceed?"

"Of course," Finn said. "Speaking of the party, I would wager it's on the edge of ending now. I'll go down and say goodbye to my guests, not leave the impression of anything odd happening, just in case there are prying eyes watching."

"Good idea. I'll go down with you," Willowby said.

"I'll follow," Diana said with a smile for Esme. "But I'd like to say a private goodbye to Esme."

Esme stiffened and glanced toward Finn. "To me?"

"Yes, if that would be agreeable."

"Of course, Your Grace. Diana."

Willowby held out a hand to Esme and when she took it, he held it firmly. "On my life, I shall do what I can to make this right. For you, as much as for your father or anyone else."

"Thank you," she whispered.

The two men departed together, with only a brief backward glance from Finn, and that left Esme with Diana. The duchess tilted her head. "Take a breath, I promise I won't bite."

Esme did so and realized afterward that she had hardly drawn one since the duke and duchess entered the chamber together. "You and your husband are so kind," she said at last. "I will be forever in your debt."

"You are in no one's debt," Diana said. "Now then, when this is resolved, what do you plan to do?"

Esme shook her head. "I don't rightly know, to be honest. I was stripped of all financial support. I've saved a moderate sum from my own work, but it wouldn't be seen as a fortune by anyone. I would hope the next Marquess of Chilton might provide my living back to me, or at least a portion, given the scandal. If he did, I think I would…I would leave London."

Diana held her stare a moment. "Leave *him*."

Esme shut her eyes. There was no need to clarify who Diana meant. "*He* would have me stay. Marry him, even."

"You don't want that?" Diana asked.

"I wouldn't belong here anymore," she whispered. "I've seen and done too much to be accepted. I fear I'd drag him down if I stayed."

Diana nodded slowly. "I felt that way once. I wasn't of your world, not ever. But I loved Lucas and he loved me. Enough that I knew the pain of losing each other would far outstrip the pain of facing any problems with acceptance within Society."

"But there were problems," Esme said. "There must have been."

"At first," Diana admitted. "I can't lie and say that the scandal surrounding your disappearance will probably be nothing compared to the one that will stir back up with your return. But there are a tight group of friends who welcomed me with open arms. You'll have that, as well. Me, for example. And I think there are others who genuinely feared for you during your absence. True friends. Family. Like Marianne."

Esme smiled softly. "Marianne is so kind, I don't think she would turn me away even if it would do her better to do so. Doesn't it fall to me to protect her from herself? To protect Finn?"

"They're both grown people with their own minds," Diana said. "They don't need protection. Not from the potential consequences of love or friendship, at least." She looked toward the door. "He loves you. It's evident in every move he makes, every twitch of his mouth and dart of his eyes when he's near you. You've lost so much in your life, it would pain me to see you lose something so precious, as well. This time of your own doing, rather than the machinations of a rotten cousin."

Esme smoothed her skirt. "I-I'll think about it."

"I'm sure you will," Diana said with a kind squeeze of her hand. "Now I'll join Lucas and Delacourt. I'll see you this evening. Perhaps we'll even get to speak of more than these horrible things, start our own path to what I'm sure will be a powerful friendship. Good day, Esme."

"Good day, Your Grace," Esme said, and escorted her to the door that led from the antechamber to the hall.

Once Diana had gone, she crossed back to the settee where she'd been during the ordeal. She sat and placed a hand where Finn had been beside her through every moment, every tear, every terror.

She could hardly think straight at present, and she wondered if that was why she was starting to have a kernel of hope that perhaps her life could work out. Perhaps she could have the future that Finn kept dangling in front of her, promising her the world if she just trusted him.

CHAPTER 25

Finn entered his chamber after the party was over and the guests gone home. He was surprised to find Esme still in the antechamber, standing at the window, her hands clenched before her.

"The party has ended?" she asked.

He heard the anxiety in her tone and moved toward her in the hopes his presence would help calm it. "It has. Sebastian and Marianne wished to stay, but I forced them to go. They deserve a few days of wedded bliss, even if we do decide to involve them in whatever happens with Chilton."

Esme shifted. "Good."

"If it's good then why do you look so nervous?" he asked. "Is it just thoughts of what we discussed with the duke and duchess?"

"Yes, but also no. I'm concerned because I haven't heard from Jane today. I wrote to her last night and expected a response. Even if she was angry with me for putting myself in danger, she would have offered to bring me clothing."

"I understand why you'd be worried. But don't forget, I asked Ripley to look after her. It's possible he's taken her someplace safe."

"I wrote to him, as well. And even if he tried, he couldn't stop

Jane from responding. Or even showing up here to scold me in person for taking off and locking myself in with you. She'd want to make certain I was unharmed."

Finn's frown deepened. "I trust you know her best. And if course your best friend would be a woman with her own mind."

"I'm certain Ripley has decided to guard her. But Jane is capable of slipping a guard if she thinks it's foolish to have one. She's feared for me about all this, but she would likely believe she could take care of herself. She always has, her entire life." She frowned and her worries were apparent. "I hope there's some other explanation than that she got into trouble."

There was a knock at the door at that time and they both turned toward it. "Come," Finn called out, distracted by the number of ways this situation could be wrong. Could be dangerous.

The door opened and Bentley entered. "I'm sorry to disturb, but there's a missive here for a Lady Charlotte. I told the man that no one was here by that name, but he insisted—"

Esme rushed forward. "Charlotte?" she gasped, and grabbed the note.

Bentley looked confused but he exited when Finn nodded. He moved to Esme as she tore the seal and unfolded the pages.

> *Just because I can't get to you doesn't mean I can't get to those you care about. Meet me at my home at ten tonight. Come alone or she'll lose more than her hair. F.*

Esme gasped as she read the words out loud and then held up a crudely cut chunk of blonde hair. "Jane's," she gasped. "He's taken Jane."

Esme's stomach rolled and she gagged as Finn took the note and the long piece of hair and looked at them, himself. "Breathe," he said gently. "Breathe, my love."

He turned and went to the door to ring for Bentley. The butler returned and Finn said, "Send for the Duke and Duchess of Willowby right away. Tell them it's an emergency and to come as soon as they can. When they arrive, have them brought straight to us here."

"Yes, my lord," Bentley said with a quick, concerned glance at Esme, who was bent against the back of a chair, shaking like a leaf.

When the servant left, Finn went to her. "We don't know for certain—"

"It's her hair," she whispered. "I've fixed it a dozen times for her while we giggled about what gentleman she was meeting that night. I *know* her hair. And it would explain exactly what we were just talking about. No matter what we did, he found her thanks to me. He realized who I was because I was foolish enough to turn to you. And now he is going to punish me through her. It's *my* fault."

"It's not your fault," Finn said, and caught her arms. "Look at me." She lifted her chin. "None of any of this is your fault. It's his. His fault for being a cruel bastard. My fault for not taking it seriously enough from the beginning. Your father's fault for not making sure you'd be protected from a man he didn't trust. You were failed, but *you* never failed."

Her mouth fell open at that passionate defense of her, said with certainty in his tone and fire in his eyes. She blinked and rested her head forward on his chest. "I won't survive it if she dies because of her relationship to me."

"We won't let her," Finn said. "Right now she's leverage. I'm guessing he hasn't harmed her if he thinks he can gain something from her."

"He hasn't harmed her because if he can make *me* suffer, he will," she whispered. "He'll harm her in front of me just to hear me scream for her. For you. For my father."

Finn shivered and then pulled her in for a hug. "Well, I won't let that happen either," he said.

"What if Diana and Willowby won't make a move because going for him now could harm their larger case?"

He shrugged. "Then we'll call on Ripley and Sebastian and we'll go on our own. I don't give a damn about what the government wants. I give a damn about *you*."

She wondered at that for a moment, the absolute devotion of this remarkable man. Then she drew in a deep breath and refocused on Jane. "Let's see what they say and then we'll decide our next step." She took his hand. "Together."

"Together," he agreed.

~

Less than an hour later, Willowby was pacing the room, reading and re-reading the missive from Chilton as Diana quietly questioned Esme about her friend. Finn stood to the side, feeling utterly helpless.

He watched Esme for a moment. She was calm now, almost too calm. The only signals of her upset were the occasional flutter of her hands, the slight shifts in her position. Otherwise, she looked solid and serene. She had gifted him her collapse, something that broke his heart, but also gave him hope for the future they could have after they saved her friend.

They had to save her friend.

He crossed to Willowby. "We need to go after her," he said, and folded his arms across his chest. "I don't give a damn about your case."

Willowby's brow wrinkled. "I've no intention of leaving the young woman to the wolves, I assure you." He looked back at Esme. "We're going to rescue her, of course."

Esme buckled a little and then stood. "Thank you, Your Grace. I've some thoughts on that score."

"You do?" Finn asked.

She nodded. "I've been thinking about it since the arrival of the letter. I should go to the meeting at ten."

Finn took a long step toward her. "No. Absolutely not."

"I wasn't asking," she said gently even as she closed the remaining distance and took his hand. "I'm the reason Jane has been taken. I'm the only reason she'll be released. We've no time for more complicated plans. This is the only way."

Behind him, Willowby cleared his throat. "I fear the lady may be correct, Delacourt. I could put together a force, make plans to draw Chilton out, send in a rescue team for Jane…but not on less than two hours' notice." He looked at Esme. "You'd be in danger."

"I know how to protect myself," she said, and lifted her chin, the steel of her bravery on full display once again. How Finn loved her for it. "That was why I started fighting, you know. To protect myself. It isn't for show, or at least not alone. I'm not afraid."

"You are a remarkable woman," Diana said, moving to stand beside her husband. "What do you think, Lucas? A four-square defense might be best, cover each direction. Who could we get on short notice?"

"I'm not sure," he mused.

"Ripley would help if you need someone. I'm sure Jane made it so he doesn't know that she slipped his protection," Esme said. "He…he cares about Jane. Deeply." She smiled at Finn. "You never had anything to worry about when it came to him, ever. And Finn could be the other."

"No," he said. "Because I'm going to be with you."

All three of them pivoted toward him, but it was Esme who spoke. "No! Firstly, my cousin already demanded that I come alone or he'll harm Jane. And secondly, I don't want you in danger."

He shook his head. "If Chilton knows that you're here, he knows that I'm protecting you. He wants my help and if I offer it as part of a bargain, he'll at least listen."

Esme pursed her lips, but he could see she knew he was right. He faced the other two. "You can't stop me. I won't leave her to enter that man's domain alone."

"Of course you won't," Diana said with a gentle smile. "Lucas, this could save the case for the smuggling. If we can determine where in the house Chilton will hold his meeting with Esme and Delacourt, you could position yourself to hear what they say. Not only will you be closer to offer protection if things go wrong, but you could hear the man's treason from his very lips."

Willowby considered it a moment. "I'd want another person on site, then."

"Ramsbury would come if I called for him," Finn said.

"On his wedding night?" Esme gasped. "I already ruined their wedding day *and* wedding gathering!"

"You haven't ruined a thing," he promised. "Marianne and Sebastian know what you mean to me,—they'd do anything to help us secure a future."

Her eyes fluttered shut. "Is there no one else, Your Grace?"

"It would be helpful to call on your friends," Willowby said. "I know Ripley a little, from the few times I boxed at his club. He's solid. I'd say the same about Ramsbury."

"Don't let him hear it," Finn said with a weak chuckle. "Well, then I suppose we have friends to contact."

"Diana and I will go to Chilton's estate and try to determine the situation there, including where he might be holding your friend. And I'll reach out to other contacts, get some more men on our side if we can find them."

"Thank you," Esme said.

"You two stay here," Diana said as she caught one of Esme's hands. "Take your time together, we'll be back by nine-thirty to make final plans."

They departed then and Finn put his arms around Esme. "Let's write our requests and then come to my room," he said. "My bed. Not because I want to make love to you, but because I want to just hold you and look at you for a little while before we do this."

233

He held his breath. He feared this attempt by her cousin had solidified her idea that she was only a danger to him. That she would pull away, but instead she took his hand. "Yes," she said softly.

In the midst of fear and pain, it was the most beautiful word he'd ever heard.

CHAPTER 26

Finn's carriage pulled up in front of her father's estate a few moments before ten. Esme let out a sigh as she looked up at the big, beautiful home. It looked the same, it looked so very different.

"I haven't been here since the night I ran," she whispered. "Not even to drive past. I was too afraid and it hurt too much."

He lifted her hands to his chest. They were bound for the plan to follow, but loosely, with a knot she could easily slip. She felt the solid, comforting beat of his heart even through all the layers which separated them. "You aren't alone. Just focus on the plan."

She nodded as the door opened and a servant she didn't recognize waited for her exit. She did so awkwardly and he glared at Finn as he followed her out.

"Chilton said you was to be alone," the man grunted.

Finn straightened his shoulders and lifted her tied hands so the servant could see them. Suddenly Finn seemed bigger, the lines of him saying danger rather than propriety. "I have something Chilton wants. I'm going with her, so you might as well let me through."

The servant rolled his eyes and waved them toward the stairs.

The butler there wore her father's livery, but again he wasn't someone she recognized.

"Where is Swanson?" she asked as they reached the man.

"Long gone," the new man answered, and gave Finn a similar glare to the one the footman had. "Wait here, I'll tell him you've arrived…with a guest."

"None of these are my father's servants," she said softly as soon as the man was out of earshot. "He replaced all of them, not just the ones Willowby spoke to."

"Perhaps more of the old ones can be found," Finn suggested. "They might know things. Assuming they're well."

"Oh, I hope they weren't harmed," Esme said, hating that fear multiplied in her. "They were always so kind."

He placed a hand on the small of her back and it calmed her a fraction. A good thing because the butler returned and motioned them to follow. As they trailed through the halls, Esme allowed herself to look around. The house had been changed a great deal since she was last here.

"It's garish," she said with a shiver. "My father was so effortlessly stylish, he's probably turning in his grave."

"For a good many reasons," Finn agreed.

They entered a parlor toward the back of the house and Esme breathed a sigh of relief. There were many windows in this room—it had been where she and her father always read together, letting the sunlight and the breeze stream through on fine days. She looked toward where his favorite chair had been as she entered and started. It was still there and Jane was bound to it, her mouth gagged and her eye blackened.

"Jane," Esme burst out, and went to run to her. Finn grasped her shoulder harder to keep her at his side, both for the sake of the game they were trying to play and also because of what she hadn't noticed right away. Her cousin was already in the room, leaning against the mantel. He had a gun trained on them.

"Did you forget how to read while you were out whoring on the street?" Francis said. "I said to come alone."

She straightened her shoulders and forced herself to breathe as she raised her tied hands. "It wasn't my choice. This one intercepted your note. Turns out he's just as much as an arse as you are."

Her cousin's eyes narrowed and he looked at Finn. "Why would you do that? I thought you were fucking my pretty little cousin. Protecting her."

"Of course to the first but the second? Hardly," Finn snorted.

It was what they'd planned, but that word still stung. Rejection, sharp and harsh that she pushed away.

"I don't know if I believe you. After all, you've been having her come and go from your house and then took her in. Is it possible she appealed to your desire to want to save the world, Delacourt?"

Finn shrugged. "It behooves a man to look like he gives a damn about his lessers. I think you would have learned that lesson fairly quickly as marquess. I was shocked when I found Charlotte in dire straits. I used it to my benefit to bed her. But, as you said, she's little more than a common whore, isn't she?"

Jane had been watching the exchange from her position on the chair and her eyes narrowed. She struggled a little against the ropes until they dug into her flesh. Esme wanted to tell her to stop, to relax, but didn't want to reveal the ruse.

"A common whore you couldn't wait to fuck," she muttered, as if she were annoyed. "Goddamn it, *Francis*." She drew out his name the way she knew he'd hated as a child. "It's boiling in here. Open a window."

Francis let out a growl, but he pivoted and opened the window. Esme let out a little sigh of relief. Somewhere out there, Willowby waited and this was the first step in having his full protection.

"And so you dragged Charlotte here as what? Your prisoner? She didn't want to come to save her friend?"

Finn let out an ugly laugh. "No. You think you have leverage with the pretty blonde one? What's her name again? Joan?"

"Jane," Esme said with a shrug. "Why should I care? We share rent, not anything else. One whore is the same as another."

Now she saw Jane's shoulders relax. Her friend understood now, thank goodness, because Jane knew that Esme would never in the world say those things about her. That she did truly care. The ruse was recognized, perhaps she'd even try to play along.

"So you brought her here…" Francis said, his tone laced with confusion.

"As a gift, my lord," Finn said. "When I intercepted the note for her, I realized you might believe I was playing a game with you. You've offered me an opportunity that I want to take, I don't want to miss out on it for a bit of arse. If you want her, you can have her. And let's discuss my investing in your operation."

Francis kept the gun up, but he swung it more fully on Esme now. Terrifying and relieving all at once. This was working. "You wish to invest?"

"Yes. Not the banks. That's too pedestrian. But I think you and I would match very well for the smuggling. My estate in Delacourt is along the sea, you know. The perfect place for boats to come ashore and items of value to be picked up for distribution."

Her cousin's eyes narrowed. "You just decided this? And it happened to coincide with my note demanding my cousin come here alone?"

"I've been thinking about it since our last meeting. I intended to come to you tomorrow, now that my sister's wedding is completed. And then your note arrived and I realized I may have miscalculated by taking Charlotte off the street and enjoying a once-lady ride my cock."

"Pig," Esme spat, aiming it truly toward her cousin rather than Finn.

Francis nodded slowly. "I see. Well, if you truly don't care about her or what happens, I suppose you won't mind if I kill her."

Jane began to rock against her bonds again and Esme tensed as terror struck through her like lightning in a summer storm. To

Finn's great credit, though, he didn't even bat an eye. "I don't care if you kill her. I've finished with her. Seems she might be a thorn in our side, I assume that's why you wanted her here."

"She always suspected me of killing her father," Francis said with a smile for her.

There was the slightest flutter to Finn's fingers, but that was the only way one could see that he was upset by that statement. "And did you? I'd be impressed if you managed it without getting the guard on your tail."

Francis explored his face slowly, looking for any tell, she supposed. Finn showed none. "I thought you loved my uncle. Like your own father, thought him a man above all other men."

"I did," Finn said. "But I can care for him and also understand that his pedantic ways and desire to always do what was right might have gotten in the way of business. He was old, he'd lived a good life. If you took care of him as a problem, I can only respect that. It was harder when I took care of my own father."

Esme pivoted on him. They hadn't discussed him lying about the death of his father, something that she knew pained him after their difficult relationship. But he did it calmly and coolly and without showing an ounce of his emotion on his handsome face.

"Really," Francis mused, and then he nodded. "Well, then you know what it's like to always be waiting. To know you have to claim your place. To claim your future at any cost. I doubt she can prove what I did though, no matter how much she knows it to be true, but I couldn't have her coming back into good Society, could I? When I realized she was the one in your bed, I had to snuff that out. Plus, I've always wished I'd taken care of her the same time I took care of my uncle. It would have been cleaner."

Esme didn't think, she didn't plan, she just let out a primal scream that came from every pain she'd ever felt, every loss that had burned her soul, every horrible moment of sacrifice and surrender she'd been forced to participate in since she ran from this house in terror. She broke her loose bond easily and launched on Francis, swung out her foot and wrapped it around his ankle. As he staggered, she pressed both hands into his chest and shoved.

He was falling when the gun went off. She hardly felt the pain as the bullet hit her across the top of her shoulder, cutting open the skin as it skidded by. She landed on top of him and began to rain down punches, as hard as she could. He was bigger than she was, but she'd had too much practice. She locked her legs around his sides so he couldn't buck her, and hit until he whimpered and squealed, until she felt hands grasping her and pulling her back, her legs wheeling out for kicks until she was out of range.

"Esme!" It was Finn's voice bringing her back as the door to the parlor opened and Ripley, Ramsbury and Diana rushed in. Somehow, Willowby was already there, perhaps he'd climbed in the window as she attacked her cousin. He was binding Francis's hands behind his back none too gently as blood poured from what appeared to be a badly broken nose.

Ripley rushed to untie Jane and knelt before her to look at her eye gently. "You little fool." There was no heat to his tone. "Why didn't you stay where you were?"

Jane didn't answer but looked toward Esme. Ripley moved aside as she pulled from Finn's arms and ran to her friend. They embraced.

"I'm sorry," she sobbed as the full weight of what had happened hit her. "I'm so sorry."

"No, love, no," Jane whispered as she hugged her until she almost couldn't breathe. "You're free now. And I'm fine. Just fine."

She looked over Esme's shoulder toward Finn and Esme moved to do the same. He was watching her, expression wrought with the terror he hadn't allowed himself to show during the whole exchange with her cousin.

"Good work, my lord," Jane said. "I can see why she likes you."

There was a flutter of a smile on his lips even though he was pale. He gave a quick half bow before he turned to Diana to speak quietly, Esme assumed to find out what would happen next with

Francis, who was almost insensible as he was dragged from the room to whatever fate awaited him.

And as she hugged Jane close again, she had to wonder what her own fate would be after this night was over and she was forced to decide her next step.

∼

There hadn't been much to do after Willowby took the Marquess of Chilton away in irons, his bloody face one small consolation for the hell he'd caused. Finn had spoken to Diana, spoken to Sebastian, arranged for one of his carriages to take Jane and Ripley to the boxing instructor's home once it was clear she was uninjured.

Diana had bandaged Esme's injury—a flesh wound, nothing more—then brought in a few more agents. They were interviewing the few servants who hadn't run when they saw their master's games were up. Certainly there would be more to do to clean up the mess, but now Finn sat in his carriage, Esme tucked against his side, her bruised hands on her lap, and they rode silently back to his home.

"What did Diana say about Francis?" she asked at last.

He was actually glad she'd spoken. Her silence had worried him, left him wondering how scarred she was by tonight. He smoothed her hair gently and said, "They'll lock him up in Newgate for now. She thinks the treason will see him hang."

"Good," Esme said softly. "He deserves to suffer and fear and ultimately die for what he did to my father. To me." She let out a shaky sigh and rested a hand on his chest. "You did well."

"It was horrible," he said, and shivered as he was flooded with memories. Perhaps she wasn't the only one scarred. "We knew he might put the gun on you, I tried to prepare myself, but when he did…when you attacked and it fired, I thought I'd die myself. Does your shoulder hurt?"

"It's a mere sting," she promised, and leaned up to kiss him. "I'm sure it will hurt more tomorrow, but it isn't serious."

"I've never before seen a woman I love hit by someone's bullet. I think it was very serious."

"I know. I'm sorry."

They were silent as the carriage turned into the drive. He helped her out, waved off assistance and they went together up to his chamber once again and through the antechamber to his bedroom.

She leaned against the door, watching as he went to the basin of water at his dressing table and wetted a cloth. "Come here," he said. "Let me help you out of that dress and clean up your hands and shoulder."

"I ruined Marianne's gown," she said with a shaky sigh as she did as she was told and turned her back so he could unbutton her. He'd done this so many times now, but this time he was more tender. He'd thought he could lose her. He would never again take this for granted.

"Marianne has plenty of dresses," he reassured her, sucking in a breath as he peeled the bloody gown sleeve away and saw the hastily but expertly stitched wound. "The Duchess of Willowby is a revelation."

"She confessed she's a healer as she was stitching me, while you were talking to Sebastian." Esme smiled. "She's fascinating and also very kind. I'm so glad to know her."

He nodded and gently wiped away the dried blood from around the wound wrapping, then did the same to her bloody and bruised knuckles. "Do your hands hurt?"

"Yes," she admitted. "I've been in over a dozen fights since I became the Hellion and I've never hit someone so hard as I did Francis."

"Well, he deserved it." He glanced up at her. "Did it help?"

"To hit him? To give him a fraction of the pain that he caused me?" She sighed. "Somewhat. But in the end, my father is still dead.

Everything that happened to me still happened. I'm still as lost about my future as I was before."

He set the cloth aside and knelt before her. His dark eyes were filled with emotion. "I'd like to talk about that, if you're up for it."

He held his breath as he waited for her response. He could see her struggling with it. "I know we need to discuss it," she said at last. "I know it weighs heavily on us both."

"I want to repeat that I love you. I want to reiterate that I want my life to be with you."

She nodded. "I know those things are true, not said in haste. And I still can't deny that I feel the same. But…"

The but. He'd known she'd say it, but it still felt like he was the one being shot now, but through the heart, not across the shoulder. "But you don't believe a future is possible. At least not with how things stand now."

"To marry you, to be at your side in an official way, it would mean coming back to the public. There will already be vicious gossip once my cousin's crimes are made public. There won't be any avoiding it. If I return at the same time, on your arm, after all these years? It will put a spotlight on us that could burn us both to the ground. I've survived that before, but I love you too much to let it happen to you."

"Despite the fact that I would burn to the ground for you every day?"

She cupped his cheeks. "Because of that fact, Finn." He bent his head, but she continued before he could. "And I was thinking that I could be your mistress. There would be no shame to me in having a life with you without sharing your name."

"Do you suppose I'd marry someone else eventually?" he said, incredulity dripping from his tone.

"To further your line." She took a shuttering breath. "You must."

"So you would have *our* children be bastards and watch me marry someone else? Not acceptable. I would never do that to you, to us. Nor to any other woman. That would make me my father and I won't do that, even for you."

There was a flutter of a smile on her face. "Then we're at an impasse. Back to the beginning. There is no way. You've saved me, but that doesn't mean we can be together. It would probably be best if I left London, moved to the country. Once Francis hangs and my other cousin takes over the estate, I can petition for a living or a settlement. If he agrees, that plus the money I saved as the Hellion will probably be enough for a simple life. And I won't ever regret you, I could…" Her voice broke. "I could never, ever regret you."

He let her finish, even though every word was like poison. Then he leaned in closer, up higher on his knees so their faces would be even.

"That won't be enough," he whispered. "And you've forgotten one other option."

She shook her head. "What other option?"

"I could abdicate my title. It would take time and a legal process, but eventually it would be resolved. I'd go with you to this simple life in the country. I'd marry you, perhaps take up a trade. Raise our children and be happy with you until the day I take my dying breath."

She let out a little cry and stood. "You would give up everything? I'd never ask you!"

"Well, I'd prefer to have a life with you here, close to my family, to our friends. I'd prefer to live without fear of might have been and should be," he said, and followed her to her feet, even though he didn't pursue her. He wanted to with all his might, but he couldn't. She had to make this decision on her own. To be convinced, not coerced, into giving herself a chance at the future he saw so clearly.

"Oh, Finn," she whispered, almost whimpered.

"I want to face all the dragons that may come with you at my side," he said. "To show you that I don't give a damn what anyone says about you or me. So what if we are shunned either for a short time or forever? We'll have each other."

She pursed her lips and he wasn't certain it was her trying not to waver or becoming annoyed that he was still fighting. "Could you really do without the admiration of those around you? Without the reputation you've created over the years?"

"If I can wake with you beside me? Reputation is nothing." He stepped toward her. "Everything you say could be true. My life *could* become smaller as far as the circle I keep. However, I think you aren't as friendless as you believe. The Duchess of Willowby is very influential and she very obviously thinks the world of your strength. Because she has impeccable taste, I might add."

There was a slight smile that turned up Esme's lips and he clung to that as he continued, "And my sister is the new Countess of Ramsbury. She *will* have weight, as does Sebastian. It might take time, but even the worst scandals are muted after time. Winds change." He touched her hand. "But I'd never force you to do something that would hurt you. I'll walk away if it's what *you* need to be comfortable."

She stared at him. "You would do that for me?"

He nodded. "I would do anything for you, Esme. Anything and everything for the rest of our days."

She ran a hand over her face. The hesitation was beautiful, because he knew he was breaking through. He stepped closer. "What if we agreed to this: we run off and get married first off. Elope to Gretna Green as soon as we can because I cannot wait to call you wife. Then we see how it plays out for a few months. Let the scandal rise and fall the rest of the Season. And if you still don't see a path as the Countess of Delacourt, then we try living in the countryside and…I don't know…clamming for a living."

"Do you know how to clam?" she asked.

He smiled. "I did it once, on a holiday with some friends."

She sighed as a response, her levity gone again. "Do you think you could ever be happy like that?"

He shrugged. "I've never tried it, so I don't know. But I know with all my heart that I could never be happy without *you*. So I choose you. Only you. Forever you. Please, please marry me."

Her eyes were filled with tears and they began to fall as she crossed the room to him and wrapped her arms around his neck. "You've made it impossible to say no to you. Almost from the very start. If you think the risk is worth it, I'd rather spend a lifetime with you than a lifetime without. And I'll marry you, Finn. I'll marry you."

He tugged her closer, his mouth finding hers with only joy and pleasure and hope for a future that seemed to glow out before him like a never-ending beacon. And as that kiss deepened into a physical celebration of the love they had found, he knew the only thing that would definitely happen was that they would live happily ever after. He'd have it no other way.

EPILOGUE

6 months later

Perhaps it was because the disgraced Marquess of Chilton's crimes were so egregious, or maybe it was because there was so much interest in the disappearance and reappearance of Lady Charlotte, or perhaps it was just because she had so many friends old and new…but Esme had to admit that Finn was right. She tried not to mention it too often. He got a terribly swelled head when she did. Her first six months as Countess of Delacourt had not been entirely smooth, but they hadn't been completely shunned either. At least not by those who mattered.

She had swiftly married the man she loved off in Gretna Green like two young lovers from some play. And she had become closer than she ever thought she could with her sister-in-law and brother-in-law. Marianne's goodness was real, it was palpable and it never allowed Esme to fall into questioning herself.

She had even helped Jane exit the life of a lightskirt and enter one as a respectable shopkeep. They saw each other every week and she could tell her friend was becoming more comfortable with her future, even if she refused to talk much about the recent past. About why her gaze grew sad whenever someone talked about Campbell Ripley.

But mostly Esme had reveled in the passion and gentleness and absolute adoration of the man she now stood next to, watching from the balcony above their ballroom as what felt like everyone in the *ton* celebrated the new Marquess of Chilton, a kind man, even if he *was* a bore. The old one, Francis, had been hung after a swift and thorough trial.

She felt Finn's arms come around her and she snuggled back against his chest. "Your sister isn't going to be able to hide her increasing belly for much longer," she said, motioning to Marianne and Sebastian, who were dancing the waltz far too closely.

"She is glowing," Finn said. "I cannot wait to be an uncle."

She turned toward him and looked up into his face, memorizing every line of him. Every curve and angle was so perfect that it made her heart swell with all the love she felt for him.

"And what about a father?" she asked.

He looked confused for a moment and then his eyes widened. "Wait, are you saying…?"

She nodded. "Yes. A baby."

When she said it out loud, there was a thrill that rushed through her. One she welcomed. In the years she'd been forced to fight for every moment of her life, she had put away the dreams she'd had of motherhood. But in the days since she'd realized what was happening to her body, that there was a child growing within her, she had felt nothing but joy. Complete and powerful joy that seemed to erase all over pains.

"And do we need to take the child and run off to the wilderness to raise them outside of Society?" he asked, and she could see he was only half in jest.

"We've seen people treat us with unkindness, of course," she said with a sigh.

"Yes," Finn said with a frown. "There are those who are more concerned with what they view as propriety than anything else."

She nodded. "And yet despite that, my greatest fears about a total shunning haven't been true. There are invitations from those we care about. You haven't been drummed out of your clubs. Do you feel you've lost too much of your life?"

His eyes widened. "Lost? Absolutely not. My life, my happiness, has only become more complete since marrying you."

She smiled. She'd never felt anything different from him, but his absolute certainty in his words was still a relief. "Good. Then I must say I'm perfectly happy just where I am. I won't run if you won't. I'll fight right at your side and at the side of our children for the rest of my days."

His gaze misted a little, as if those words meant the world to him. He caught her hand. "If we fight together, I think we know we're unstoppable. And as for being perfectly happy? So am I. So am I."

EXCERPT OF THE ACCIDENTAL COUNTESS

ABOUT AN EARL BOOK 3 (OUT FEBRUARY 4, 2025)

Clarissa turned toward her parents. "You've found yourself quite the crop of eligible gentlemen for this gathering," she said carefully, trying not to offend even as she pressed her question. "Do we not worry that it will make it too obvious that you are on the hunt for a marriage for me?"

Her father shot her a side look. "Any lady worth her salt is always on the hunt for a marriage, Clarissa."

Her mother nodded. "At any rate, it won't all be gentlemen for you. Your cousin George will be here. And I invited the Earl and Countess of Ramsbury."

Clarissa's smile was more genuine now. "Oh, that's lovely. I saw them at the opera at the beginning of the Season and congratulated them on their marriage. But I do enjoy the countess's company so much."

"And now that she isn't a spinster who could bring you down a peg, you can mine that friendship for the connections it could bring you," her mother insisted with a pat of her hand.

Clarissa pursed her lips and turned her face away. How she hated the mercenary aspects of her parents' husband hunt. It had all grown all the worse in the last year, when Clarissa drew into her third Season out and they seemed to fear that meant she was failing.

Sometimes she felt the same, despite still being invited to every event and asked to dance by many gentlemen. Marriage was the only mark of success that mattered, and it was hard not to feel the sand of her life being pulled away, rushing her toward the next step when she would be bound to some man who would elevate her parents...and herself. Though *she* was an afterthought.

"And I think that is your cousin now," her mother said with a wave at the horses that were coming down the lane. "But who is with him?"

Clarissa lifted on her tiptoes to peer down the curve in the drive. Yes, it was George out front, she recognized her beloved cousin's gait on his mount, but the second man was not known to her. "Perhaps one of the other gentlemen, come from London on a horse rather than in a carriage?" she suggested.

But as they neared, her mother lifted a hand to her chest. "Oh, that is the Earl of Kirkwood, I believe. I didn't think to invite him, myself. It's well-known he isn't looking for a bride."

Clarissa wrinkled her brow. "You didn't invite him and yet he arrives with my cousin?" she repeated and looked toward the rapidly approaching gentlemen again. "That is very rude, to come to a house party uninvited."

Certainly her handbook would have said so. She narrowed her gaze as the men grew ever closer.

"Well, he's rich and powerful," Mr. Lockhart said with a quick glare in her direction. "Imagine if you could land the unlandable! You were certainly raise all fortunes by doing so."

Clarissa pursed her lips as the men pulled their horses to a stop, each swung down and handed over the reins to waiting grooms. She examined the earl, especially. He was well-favored, of course. Tall, of lanky build and with dark hair that looked a little mussed from the road since he didn't wear a hat. His skin was slightly tanned, probably from the travel and when he looked up the stairs with a bored expression, she could not help but notice the finest dark green eyes she'd ever encountered. Ones that slid over her parents and then settled on her for a long moment before he had the audacity to wink at her and then follow her cousin up the stairs.

She huffed out a breath. Rich and powerful or not, this man already had two strikes against him for absolute rudeness. First to arrive without invitation and second to dare to engage himself with a lady he didn't even know.

"My dearest Uncle Gregory and Aunt Violet, I'm pleased to see you both," George said as he shook her father's hand and bussed her mother's cheek. "I hope you do not mind that I have come with a friend."

Clarissa saw Lord Kirkwood glance at George swiftly as her mother stepped forward. "Oh no, not at all! We're so pleased you have increased our party by one so lauded as the Earl of Kirkwood."

Kirkwood bent his head over her mother's hand as he lifted it to his lips. It was a showy act of chivalry, but it didn't ring entirely true. "I see my reputation proceeds me," he drawled. "Thank you for your hospitality, Mr. and Mrs. Lockhart. Your grounds are spectacular, I was admiring them as soon as we entered the estate."

"Couldn't stop waxing poetic about them," George agreed. Then he turned to Clarissa. "And there is the lady of the hour. Clarissa!"

Clarissa didn't have to force her smile for her cousin. He was a rapscallion, but she still adored him. Once upon a time her mother had thought she might be matched with him, after all he, too, would one day be an earl. Happily that notion had passed.

"Dearest George," she said and took his hand with both of hers. "You look a fright."

He laughed as he reached up to smooth his hair. "Do I? Well, that is only because I'm standing to one of the prettiest ladies in all the country."

Clarissa almost rolled her eyes, but then stopped herself. *The Mirror of Graces* would never approve such behavior. Even less so in front of a stranger who was her better.

As if he sensed her thoughts about the earl, George turned toward him. "Have you had the pleasure of meeting my dear cousin, Kirkwood?"

"I haven't," the earl said and stepped away from her mother. He smiled at her and she returned the expression with the smallest one of her own she could manage. She still thought this man abominably rude for inviting himself to a party and she couldn't let it go without some small consequence.

"The Earl of Kirkwood, I present Miss Clarissa Lockhart. My favorite cousin," George said.

Kirkwood reached out to take her hand and for a moment Clarissa thought he might lift it to his lips as he had done with her mother. Instead she shook it briefly and then withdrew. She thought his lips quirked a little in amusement, which she equally ignored.

"A pleasure to make your acquaintance, my lord," she said. "Though unexpected, indeed."

She saw her mother glare at her over the earl's shoulder and so she added a little curtsey to soften her comment. Mrs. Lockhart stepped forward. "George you will be in your usual chamber and my lord, I'll give you the one just down the hall so you two friends may be close. Let me follow you in and tell our butler of the addition."

She motioned toward the door and George took her arm to lead her in. Kirkwood held Clarissa's stare a moment and then smiled. "I look forward to getting to know you better, Miss Lockhart. Good afternoon."

He followed her cousin and mother inside and Clarissa glared after them. When her father touched her arm, she jumped, for she hadn't realized he had moved closer as she focused on the departing party.

"You'll wrinkle if you look so cross," Mr. Lockhart said.

She bit back a little retort. One was to always receive from one's parents with deference, after all. Or so her book stated. She drew a breath. "Thank you, Father. You are likely correct. And I suppose if you and mother aren't upset by the earl's unexpected arrival, then I shouldn't be either."

"No, not when he could be the best potential match here," her father said and rubbed his hands together.

"I've heard he doesn't seek a bride, though," Clarissa mused as she returned her attention to the drive and the next vehicle that was rumbling down the packed sand lane.

"That doesn't mean he cannot be landed. By hook or by crook, every man of his rank must marry."

Clarissa glanced toward her father. His eyes were lit up with plans. Even though the earl was a known rake, even though he would be so bold and uncouth. Even though surely a match between them could be nothing but dreadful. She could already tell they were polar opposites, more likely to be enemies than fall in love. Not that she expected love. Marriages were meant to be meetings of name and fortune, but she also hoped temperament and shared values.

But she didn't say any of that to her father. She couldn't because it would be going against what propriety demanded in a good daughter. And because she was interrupted by the next in a parade of gentlemen meant to be tempted by what she could bring to a union in her comportment and connection.

But the threat of matching with someone like the Earl of Kirkwood made her focus more fully on the matters at hand. She would just have to make herself even more tempting to the men who did align with her values in life. Then her parents couldn't be so foolish as to foist her off on someone frivolous and inappropriate. Handsome or not.

Find The Accidental Countess at retailers everywhere on February 5, 2025!

ALSO BY JESS MICHAELS

About An Earl
The Wallflower List
The Hellion's Secret
The Accidental Countess (February 4, 2025)
The Courtesan's Protector (April 8, 2025)
The Lady Once Known As (July 8, 2025)

Theirs
Their Marchioness
Their Duchess
Their Countess
Their Bride
Their Viscountess

The Kent's Row Duchesses
No Dukes Allowed
Not Another Duke
Not the Duke You Marry

The Three Mrs
The Unexpected Wife
The Defiant Wife
The Duke's Wife

The 1797 Club
The Daring Duke
Her Favorite Duke

The Broken Duke

The Silent Duke

The Duke of Nothing

The Undercover Duke

The Duke of Hearts

The Duke Who Lied

The Duke of Desire

The Last Duke

To see a complete listing of Jess Michaels' titles, please visit:

http://www.authorjessmichaels.com/books

ABOUT THE AUTHOR

USA Today Bestselling author Jess Michaels likes geeky stuff, Cherry Vanilla Coke Zero, anything coconut, cheese and her dog, Elton. She is lucky enough to be married to her favorite person in the world and lives in Oregon settled between the ocean and the mountains.

When she's not trying out new flavors of Greek yogurt or rewatching Bob's Burgers over and over and over (she's a Tina), she writes historical romances with smoking hot characters and emotional stories. She has written for numerous publishers and is now fully indie.

Jess loves to hear from fans! So please feel free to contact her at Jess@AuthorJessMichaels.com.

Jess Michaels offers a free book to members of her newsletter, so sign up on her website:
http://www.AuthorJessMichaels.com/

facebook.com/JessMichaelsBks
instagram.com/JessMichaelsBks
bookbub.com/authors/jess-michaels